WAKING PAN

an *Autumn & Arcadia* novel

WAKING PAN

Nico Silver

WHITE RAVEN PRESS

ISBN: 978-1-998212-35-4

White Raven Press
North Cowichan, British Columbia, Canada

Cover design, digital alterations, and illustration © Nik Sylvan.

No AI was used in any part of the making of this book. We support human creators.

Photo stock (satyr) © Nik Sylvan
Background stock (moon) © Dary423 via Dreamstime.com
Fog brushes © Krist A via brusheezy.com
Title typefaces: Eva Antiqua Heavy by Spiece Graphics, and Snell Roundhand by Linotype

Content warning: This book contains material that is not suitable for all audiences. It is recommended for readers 18+. Some content that may be triggering for readers includes explicit sex, violence, deadnaming, misgendering, and using alcohol as a coping mechanism.

*For all us nonbinary and trans weirdos
just trying to find a place for ourselves.*

Chapter One

A T-SHIRT WITH A LEWD IMAGE of a satyr on it was maybe not the best choice for my first day of grad school. Even with the big "CENSORED" over the satyr's crotch in red letters, it drew the attention of everyone I passed by. Still, it would mean people would get a sense of me without actually having to talk to me.

Of course, it didn't occur to me when I got dressed this morning that my shirt might seem, to some people, like an *invitation* to strike up a conversation. People like the burly guy who stops dead when he passes the bench I'm sitting on, turns, and says, "Great shirt!"

I flush and my fingers clench around the book I have in my lap, but I manage to force out a, "Thanks!" and make my face into something I hope resembles a smile.

He continues to grin at me – his face looks like it was designed for smiling, with wide cheeks, generous lips, and two deep dimples. I just sit there, hoping he'll go away, because I don't think I'll be able to make any more words come out. At least I'm not hyperventilating.

Finally, he realizes I'm not going to say anything else. "Well, have a great day," he says, and carries on walking. And I can't help it, I check out his ass as he walks away. His jeans fit him perfectly and show off the thick, round muscles so well I can imagine what they'd feel like under my hands.

I force myself to breathe normally, to stop thinking about a random guy's perfect butt, and pull out my phone to check the time. I still have half an hour till my first class, which is good, because my stomach has gone iffy and I'm pretty sure I should find a quiet bathroom somewhere to be sick – and I don't mean throwing up.

I somehow managed to finish my undergrad without having to do very many assignments where I'd be noticed. That was the good thing about undergrad; most classes were big, and most profs didn't want the hassle of grading that many presentations.

But grad school will be different. Classes are small and participation counts big. It took me five years of working shit jobs to convince myself that I could manage two years of classes where I'd have to talk, to be visible. Even then, it wasn't until I got drunk with my younger sister and she dared me that I finally sent in my application.

And now I'm here – with a fellowship to pay my tuition and everything – and in less than half an hour I'm probably going to be expected to say things. Out loud. To other people.

I clutch the book to my chest. It's a fancy edition of Edith Hamilton's *Greek Mythology* – not actually a recommended text in Classics departments, by the way. But my sister Alison gave it to me as a congratulations gift for getting into grad studies at Great Valley University, Department of Folklore. In the months since I got my acceptance letter, it's been a reminder of how badly I want this, and therefore a sort of security blanket in book form.

I make myself unclench and put the book carefully in my backpack with my laptop and notebook and zip the bag shut. I check my phone again. There's still time to duck into the bathroom in the library basement and get to class a few minutes early.

It's still too soon in the semester for the library to be anything but dead. I hurry down the broad staircase and discover that they've changed the handicapped washroom sign to one with the wheelchair and "All Gender" in friendly lettering since the last time I was here. I stare at it for too long, hesitating, before finally turning towards the men's room.

By the time I'm done and have washed my hands – stubbornly singing "Happy Birthday" twice over in my head – I only have five minutes to make it to class, but I chose my toilet facilities well and only need to get to the next building over.

A few other students hurry past in the halls, but it's a quiet building. As I approach the room specified on my schedule (I check the uni website on my phone about seven times to make sure it hasn't changed) I can hear the chatter of voices and my stomach clenches.

I'm not sure I can do this. (Yes, Alder, you can do this.)

The door is open, so I duck in and have a quick glance around, not meeting anyone's eyes. It's a small, narrow room with a long table surrounded by chairs and a wall of chalkboard on one side – actual slate with a metal tray for chalk – and a wall of windows overlooking the campus garden on the other. All the other students have taken chairs facing the chalkboard, leaving three spots empty closest to the door. I take the middle one and busy myself with fishing my notebook and a pen out of my backpack, so I don't have to look at anyone.

I breathe slowly, carefully, deliberately, and will my stomach to settle. I'll be fine; it's only the first day. I'm not going to have to get up and give a presentation on the first day.

Right at the instant my phone clock shifts from one fifty-nine to two o'clock, a bearded man in a bright green button-down with a repeating pattern of dark green trees and brown sasquatches on it enters the room and starts to shut the door. There's a scuffle outside and he lets go of the handle so one last student can enter.

I make the mistake of watching it happen, so when he walks through the door, the almost-late student meets my eyes – his are a deep, warm brown – grins, and says, "Hey, guy with the cool t-shirt."

I wince at "guy" but say nothing. I force my lips to smile as he takes the chair next to me, and then I'm saved by the prof clearing his throat and beginning to talk.

"Welcome to Research Methods in Folklore," he says, then starts handing out sheets of paper with the syllabus. "This is all available through the GVU portal," he says, "But if I hand you each a paper copy, you can't pretend you haven't seen it."

Everyone in the class chuckles, including the guy next to me, who has a laugh as deep and rich as his eyes. I try not to stare at the forearm he's resting on the table between us and make myself study the syllabus instead. (Okay, I *do* stare at his hairy, muscular arm first.)

I only realize the prof is taking attendance when the person on the other side of me says, "Here!" really loud and then laughs at herself for it.

When the prof gets to my name, he says, "Alden Lewis," and I don't say anything except to force out a, "Here" that makes me sound like I can't catch my breath. I *want* to say something, to say I don't want to be called "Alden" even though it's my legal name, but I can't. I just stare at the page in front of me and force myself to keep breathing.

"Silas Pan… Panagiotis? Did I say that right?" the prof says, and I accidentally glance up.

"Close enough," says the burly guy next to me, whose ass I did *not* check out less than an hour ago (I totally did), and whose dark hair is *not* falling over his eyes in a way that makes me want to brush it away with my fingers (it totally is). He sees me looking and grins, and I flush, cursing my red-headed complexion that will show it as ugly red splotches up my neck and on my cheeks.

I relax as the prof launches into his introductory spiel and says, with a far-too-pleased grin, that unlike undergrad classes, we don't get to take the first week easy. Which he then – sort of – contradicts by saying we can go once he's explained our first assignment.

I skim down the syllabus to find it while he's handing out another sheet of paper – a bibliography of our required textbooks. When I find the assignment, I swallow hard. It's a project to create a research outline for a suitable topic, to be done in pairs with another student. I try to count how many of us there are in the class without being obvious about it – if there's an odd number, I'll ask to do the project by myself. I survived a lot of group projects in high school that way. Making myself ask will be way easier than having to spend that much time with someone I don't know.

Before I'm done counting, the prof starts pairing up students, starting at the other end of the table. I take a deep breath and say quietly to the guy next to me, or to his sexy forearm, anyway, "If there aren't enough of us, you can work with someone, and I'll work by myself." I want to throw up by the time I get all the words out, but I feel way better about the assignment.

"You sure?" he says, leaning close enough that I feel his breath, warm on my neck.

I nod, and the prof says, "And… Lewis and Panagiotis." Because of course there's an even number of us in the class.

After class, Silas matches his stride with mine as we leave the building. We're close enough in height that we walk easily in step.

I force myself to meet his eyes and his look is friendly, not judging, even though I'm being weird enough I could hardly blame him if he *did* judge me.

"So, you're a Folklore Master's student?" he asks. He folds up the syllabus and bibliography and shoves them in his pocket while I study the concrete path in from of me.

"Yeah," I say, and I know I should say more, to have an actual conversation, but my throat won't cooperate. It's several steps later before I manage, "You?"

Silas doesn't seem to notice my awkwardness. Whether he's oblivious or just doesn't care, I have no idea, and I guess it doesn't matter. I feel my guts unclench, just a little, and it's marginally easier to breathe.

"Cross… uh… cross-posted? Whatever they call it when you're sort of in more than one department."

"Double major?" I say, trying to ignore the feeling of falling into a deep pit that speaking gives me when I actually manage to produce words and don't just freeze up.

"I think double major is only for undergrads," he says, but he says it in a way that doesn't make me feel stupid, the way my ex used to. "Anyway," he adds. "I'm Folklore and Music. PhD, and playing catch-up. I'm not actually sure which department my degree will come from. Both, maybe." He laughs and it's even deeper and richer than his chuckle in class. I can't help looking at his lips. His mouth is wide and never seems to stop moving as his expression shifts. His lips are thick and curvy, and no, I do *not* want to think about kissing them.

(Except I do.)

And what the fuck is wrong with me? I mean yeah, I like kissing and sex, and all, but I'm not usually prone to ogling people I just met beyond maybe a quick assessment of if I find them attractive. (No, I'm just prone to letting people I just met pick me up in bars to take me home and fuck me.)

But Silas makes me want to stare at him, to study him, to wonder if his broad, muscular chest is as covered with dark, curly hair as his arms. I promised myself this year would be different, that I'd find my self-respect. So far, I'm not doing so well with that.

I'm blushing again. "That's cool," I say. Inside, I'm yelling at myself to say something else, preferably something intelligent. Fuck, even something stupid would be better than saying nothing.

Again, he doesn't seem to care, or even notice.

"You want to get started on this assignment right away?" he says. "I know it's not due for a couple of weeks, but anything I get over with now means more time to spend on my thesis."

"You're working on your thesis already?" I surprise myself by getting out a whole sentence without my voice going weird.

"This is my second year," he says. "My advisor thinks I need more research classes because my Master's was an MFA, and I need all the academic credits I can get."

"Oh." Fuck, why can't I say something at least a little smarter? Or at least less monosyllabic?

"My MFA is in music, specializing in archaic wind instruments, but I want to do my PhD on some cool stuff I learned about my family's history with Greek folk music. They weren't even going to let me into the PhD program with so few academic credits, and anyway an MFA is supposed to be the terminal degree for Fine Arts, but I guess I managed to convince them with my research proposal. I still have a lot of ground to make up, but I also need to get my actual thesis research underway if I don't want to take a couple extra years to finish."

"That's cool." I already fucking *said* that. "Sorry." I watch my feet as we walk, glad that I'll soon be able to turn away, to head off-campus to my apartment where I can wallow in mortification and take a long bubble bath.

"Sorry for what?" Silas sounds surprised. "For listening to me babble?"

He laughs. Laughing seems to be his default, like he finds joy in just existing.

"I… I don't talk much," I say, and blush. Why, after all these years of social anxiety, can't I have at least a slightly better explanation to offer?

I catch his shrug out of the corner of my eye and make myself look at his face. I can't quite bring myself to meet his eyes, so I focus on his nose. It's long, with wide nostrils and a slight hook at the end, like you'd see on a statue of a Greek god.

"I talk enough for half a dozen people, at least," he says. "So be as quiet as you like."

I can't think of anything to say to that – the words not only won't come out, they won't even assemble in an order that makes sense.

"Are you shy?" he asks, his lips curving distractingly again. "Or is it social anxiety?"

I bite the inside of my cheek, surprised that he even knows the difference, then look right into his eyes and say, "I'm not shy." The blush burns up my neck and across my belly and I'm sure I must be so red I can be seen from the fucking space station.

His smile curves even wider and his lips part slightly, showing white teeth and the tip of his tongue. I find the expression so sexy I'm having difficulty breathing and my cock twitches in my pants.

Okay, I'll go home and wallow in mortification and a bubble bath, and jerk off, and try not to think about Silas while I do it. (I will definitely think of Silas while I do it.)

"Social anxiety, then," he concludes, and then puts out an arm to steer me around some people coming the other way because I've been looking at his face instead of where I've been going.

"Yeah," I say, turning my eyes back the path and refusing to think about the brief warmth of his hand on my arm. (I want to feel it again.)

"I really do like your shirt, by the way," he says. "Is the image from Greek black-figure pottery?"

"Yeah." I flick my eyes to his face again and then back to the path. "You like ancient Greek pottery?" I make myself ask.

"I like the saucy ones," he says, and laughs. "Do you know what your thesis topic is going to be yet?"

I study the toes of my Docs and notice that one of the rainbow laces has twisted so the order of colors is upside-down. "It's kind of dumb."

"Nah," he says. "Can't be dumber than that persistence of syrinx music in the Greek diaspora of Arcadia County."

"That doesn't sound dumb," I say, and stop walking way too suddenly. He takes a few steps past me, stops, and turns. "I'm heading that way." I point towards town.

"I'm in grad residence," he says and gestures the opposite way. "So, what's *your* dumb topic?"

I meet his eyes and look away. "The worship of Pan in contemporary earth-centered religions."

"That's awesome!"

I check his face to see if he's shitting me, and he looks genuinely enthusiastic.

"Shouldn't you be in religious studies, then?" he asks.

I shrug. "I have to take some religious studies classes, but…" I chew my lip and force myself to continue, and it's a little easier this time. "I'm mostly focusing on the use of mythology as source material, so…" I shrug again. "Anyway, I haven't submitted my proposal yet, so…" Fuck, why did I trail off with "so…" twice? What is wrong with me? (Social anxiety, Alder, remember?)

"Sounds like we should be able to come up with a topic for this project that at least one of us can actually use in our thesis research," he says, and he sounds as pleased with himself as if he chose me deliberately as his partner.

"Sounds like," I say, and I can't help but smile.

"You busy tomorrow night?" he asks, and for a brief, stupid moment I think he's asking me out.

"No," I say, barely managing not to stammer.

"Pizza?" he says. "And we can brainstorm the assignment?"

"Okay," I say. "Where?"

"I'm in res, so not much space, but we could book a study room."

I make myself look into his eyes again, to meet his handsome, wide, high-cheekboned face, his clear olive complexion and curvy lips, his stupid attractive, soft-looking hair, and say, "I've got lots of room at my place."

Chapter Two

THE NEXT DAY I HAVE TWO seminar classes with only a short break between, so by the time I get back to my apartment, I'm wiped. I had intended to go to the campus bookstore so I could get started on my reading, but when I got there, the lines were still stupid long, so I just came home.

As I'm chugging a glass of water and trying to decide if I want a quick shower or a long bath, my phone vibrates.

what kind of pizza?

Oh, fuck. I forgot Silas was going to come over so we can start on our assignment. My breathing speeds up and I lean against the counter, just staring at my phone until the screen goes black.

I'm glad I forgot, because if I'd remembered I'd have been anxious about it all day. Now I only need to get through a few hours until he's been and gone again. I breathe slowly. I can do this.

My phone lights up as I lift it and type, *I'm okay with whatever.*

Is that too pathetic? Should I have just told him my favorite pizza? (I should have just told him.)

what don't u like then? is his response.

Pineapple, I answer. *Anchovies. Fake cheese. Hamburger. Sausage.*

He sends back a laughing emoji. *so not whatever. what else don't you* like?

I flush, glad he can't see me. *Olives*, I type.

you wound me, he replies. *how can u dislike olives?*

I flush again, but this time I smile. He's teasing me, I think, and not in a bad way.

*How can you *like* olives?* I say.

i'm greek. i'm pretty sure i'd be disowned if i didn't like olives.

My smile gets wider.

i teethed on olives instead of animal crackers, he says. *my first baby food was pureed olives.*

I laugh out loud at that. *Fine, your half can have olives*, I send.

so what's your fave toppings? he replies. *pretty sure it's required for every guy to have a fave pizza*

I wince at the word "guy" and my smile fades as I stare at the screen, trying to make myself reply. Texting doesn't give me the same anxiety that talking does, usually, but I really want Silas to like me. And not just because I think he's hot. (Okay, maybe a little because I think he's hot.)

It occurs to me that I could just *tell* him, could just ask him not to call me a guy, not to call me "Alden." I could just tell him I'm nonbinary and maybe he won't come over and I won't have to try to act like a normal, social human being.

Except I *want* him to come over as much as it terrifies me. I want him to like me, to find out who I am slowly enough that I won't scare him away.

Mushrooms, I finally type. *Onions. Red peppers. Bacon.*

extra cheese? he says, as if I haven't just taken way too long to answer.

And extra sauce.

see you at five ish?

I chicken out of typing any more and just send a thumbs up.

A few minutes later, as I'm stripping for a shower, my phone vibrates again.

stupid question, he says. *but where do u live?*

It's way too close to five and I'm still standing in front of my closet in boxers and a sleeveless undershirt, trying to figure out what the fuck to wear. It's September, but the warmth of August is lingering so it's warm enough for a t-shirt, but not so warm I'd be uncomfortable in something with sleeves.

This is not a date, I remind myself sternly. I grab my favorite pair of jeans and pull them on. I have no idea if they look good or not, but they *feel* good, so they'll do. I finally opt for a lightweight long-sleeved t-shirt in deep green, because my sister insists green goes best with red hair. The color looks good on her and we look enough alike that a lot of people assume we're twins, so I guess she's probably right.

A deep breath steadies my nerves a little. I run my hands through my hair, wishing I'd had the guts to start growing it out sooner. It's just long enough to look messy, but there's not much I can do right now.

There's a knock at the door while I'm looking for a pair of socks that match and I abandon the effort. If he's bothered by bare feet, he'll just have to deal with it. I like my feet. I sometimes joke that they're my best feature, except it's not really a joke.

Silas grins when I open the door. He's balancing two pizza boxes and a bottle of wine, and he's got a messenger-style bag slung over his shoulder.

"Hey," I say, feeling stupid again, but his smile widens.

"Hey," he says back.

I take the pizza and let him in. He looks around and whistles and why is even his whistle sexy?

"Your place is huge," he says.

I look around. "I guess." It is pretty big, I suppose. The door opens directly into the living room, which has a giant window along one wall. The kitchen isn't separate, but the bedroom is, and the bathroom is larger than it needs to be.

"You should see my place," he says. "Grad res is bigger than undergrad, but we still share a kitchen and bathroom between four of us, and the bedrooms aren't exactly big."

"I thought grad students got full apartments," I say, quickly, before my throat can decide not to function.

"They have those," he says, "But they cost a lot more." He slings his bag onto the couch and moves into the kitchen area to put the bottle of wine on the counter next to where I put the pizza boxes.

A flush creeps up my neck as I turn away to get plates. Why did I say that? Maybe his family is poor, and he can barely afford school.

"What do I owe you for the pizza?" I say when I turn back, hoping my voice sounds mostly normal. I focus on the top button of his charcoal grey shirt and try not to be too turned on by the little curl of black chest hair that pokes out.

"What?" He looks up from peeling the top off the wine to expose the cork, surprised. "It's on me."

"Oh," I say. "Okay." And there I go saying the wrong thing again. Feeling stupid again. I stare at his hands on the bottle of wine. He has long fingers and thick muscle across his palms. I force myself to look away before I start fantasizing about those hands on my skin.

(This is NOT a date.)

"You okay?" he says, letting go of the bottle and moving around the end of the counter, closer to me.

"I'm fine," I say. "Just…" I wave my hand helplessly.

"Anxiety," he says. "Right."

"Yeah."

He touches my shoulder, just a brief squeeze, and then drops his hand away. "Alden," he says, and I swallow hard. "You don't have to worry that I'll think you're weird or something. I already like you."

When I meet his eyes, I realize how close he's moved. Close enough I'd only have to lean forward a little to kiss him. His eyes, I notice, now that I'm so close, aren't just brown; they have warm flecks of gold in them, and a deep purple ring around the outside. And for just a moment, they seem to flare green, and his pupils look too big and wrongly-shaped. I blink and they look normal again.

"You sure you're okay?" he says, his deep voice soft. His fingers brush my cheekbone, barely touching.

"I'm…" *Breathe, dumbass. Just breathe.* "I'm okay."

He touches my lower lip with his fingertip. "Can I kiss you?" he says, and I think some kind of weird noise comes out of me. His smile this time is lopsided. "You can tell me to fuck off and we'll just work on our assignment."

I can't keep looking into his eyes. I might drown. I let my eyelids drop and manage a tiny nod.

His breath is warm on my face and I'm not sure *I'm* even breathing at all.

"Are you sure?" he asks, his fingers slipping away to my neck. "I don't want to make things awkward."

I nod again, afraid to open my eyes, afraid this is a stupid dream, and I'll wake up alone.

His lips are very warm on mine, and gentle. I sway slightly and put out my hand for something to hold onto. I find his chest, solid and muscular, the curly hair on it feeling crisp under the thin layer of his shirt.

For a long moment, I think he's just going to barely brush my lips with his, but then he tilts his head to the side and presses his mouth more firmly on mine like he's testing the way we fit together. I lean into him, into his kiss and onto his chest, and in response, he puts his hands on my hips and slips his tongue into my mouth.

I shift closer and slide my tongue alongside his, move my hand from his chest to his ribs so I can press against him. We stand there for what feels like forever, tongues tangling, hands slowly moving, and by the time he pulls away, I have both hands up the back of his shirt and his fingers are digging into my waist as he holds me firmly against his body.

He rests his forehead against mine. "Wow," he says softly. "You really aren't shy."

"No," I say, trying to catch my breath. "I'm not."

He shifts away, just a hair, just enough to focus on my eyes. "I like you Alden," he says. "I *really* like you."

It's like a punch to the gut, that name. Not a big one, but enough to knock the wind out of me. Enough to drive out the euphoria I was starting to feel.

"What is it?" he says, his black eyebrows drawing together as he frowns.

I swallow and force myself not to look away. I really like him, too, and I'm not going to make the mistake I made last time. I'm not going to keep my mouth shut and go along with the wrong name, the wrong pronouns, the assumption that I'm gay man, because that's how I appear to the world.

"Alden?" he says.

I move my hands from his back and rest them on his shoulders instead. I'll make it easy for him to get away from me if he wants to. I won't try to hold onto him, even if it means I have to go ask my professor to let me switch project partners tomorrow. Finally, I look away. His eyes are too kind, too concerned.

"My name is Alder," I say. I set my jaw. I can't stop now. "I don't... I don't use my legal name."

"Okay," he says. "Alder." His fingers are gentle on my jaw, and I look up at his face by accident. He's smiling. He's always smiling, but this one is soft, sweet. "Alder suits you better," he says, then his smile gets wider. "*Alnus rubra*," he says.

"What?"

"It's Latin. It means 'red alder.' Some First Nations used the bark for red dye."

"Red alder?" I frown, confused. "I thought you were Greek?"

He laughs. "I like languages. Especially ancient ones. And I like trees." He kisses my forehead. "Alder. You should say something to our prof, so he doesn't call you by the wrong name."

I should say something to *all* my profs. To university admin, even. I *want* to get it changed legally.

"Yeah," is all I can get out.

His fingers brush my jaw again. He traces it to my chin, then touches my lips briefly before settling his hand on the back of my neck, like he plans to kiss me thoroughly again.

"Are you –" I stop, not sure how to finish what I need to say next.

"I'm pan," he says, sliding his fingers into my hair. I have to work hard not to close my eyes and lean into him again. "And I like *you*. I don't care if you're..." He shakes his head. "I just like *you*."

I look away, over his shoulder. "I'm nonbinary," I say, and I know my tone is bordering on belligerent. I can't help it; it's the only way I can get the words out.

"What pronouns do you want me to use for you?"

That makes me meet his eyes again.

"What?"

"Pronouns." He touches the end of my nose with one finger. "Do you use they/them, or neopronouns, or is 'he' okay?"

I blink and stare and realize I really do have to say something. "They/them," I manage.

His lips curve up again, and he slides the hand on my hip around to the small of my back. "Can I kiss you one more time before we eat this pizza and work on our assignment?"

The assignment. Fuck. Of course. I nod.

"I know it's hard," he says, "but can you say it?"

"Say what?"

He bumps my forehead with his. "Say yes, I can kiss you."

"You don't have to ask," I say, and a little bit of astonishment creeps into my voice.

"I want to. I want to make sure you're not just going along with this because I'm a pushy asshole with more muscles than brains."

"You are very… large," I say, and immediately blush again, because I can feel him, pressing against my groin, not hard, but at least halfway there.

He snorts. "Can I kiss you?" he says. "I'm just going to keep asking until you either say 'yes' or 'no'."

"What if I say 'please kiss me' instead?" I feel suddenly giddy, drunk, and bold.

"You'll just have to say it and find out, sweetheart," he says.

For just an instant, I freeze. My ex used to call me "sweetheart" in the worst mocking tone and it sends a jolt of ice to my guts. But the heat of Silas's body against mine melts the ice and the warmth in his voice drives it the rest of the way away. He didn't call me "sweetheart" to mock me; he did it as an actual term of endearment.

I decide that I want to see if I can get him to say it again. Soon.

"Please kiss me," I say.

He looks into my eyes again, the corners of his mouth twitching just a little.

"Do you know your eyes are almost the exact color of your hair?"

I blink. I mean, of course I know. My hair is dark red, on the brown side of fiery, and my eyes are dark brown, with a reddish undertone.

Then I say, "Are you saying my eyes are red?" I raise an eyebrow.

He looks uncertain, but I give it away when my lips curl up involuntarily, and he laughs.

"No," he says, kissing my nose instead of my lips. "They're not red, and your hair *is* red, and yet somehow they're the exact same color." He tilts his head to one side. "Your freckles match, too."

"Are you going to kiss me or not?" My gut clenches and I know I'm not going to be able to get any more words out. I'm not even sure I'll be able to breathe. But his eyes leave mine and he looks at my lips as if studying them. I wonder what he sees.

The corners of his mouth turn up. "You have a freckle right here at the very edge of your lip." His fingertip touches the spot, which I've never much liked. It makes my mouth look misshapen.

"It's adorable," he says. Then he shifts closer, pressing against me, and brushes his lips over mine again, teasing. I give in, and just let him kiss me so softly I almost can't feel it.

And then I bury my hands in his curls – and his hair is just as soft as it looks – and pull him to me, hard, crush my mouth against his, and kiss him as deeply as I can.

Chapter Three

Tʜᴇ ᴋɪss ʟᴀsᴛs ᴀ ʟᴏɴɢ ᴛɪᴍᴇ and ends with us both panting, but as much as I want to keep going, I know it's probably not a good idea. We have an assignment to do and I'm not going to start grad school off by slacking on homework because I'm making out with a cute guy.

So instead, I watch Silas open the wine with strong hands and we take our plates of pizza – his with a lot of olives and feta cheese and some kind of sausage, and mine with all the toppings I asked for – and sit on my couch.

We eat and brainstorm ideas and after tripping over my words a few times, I eventually start to relax, to not even think about how stupid I sound when an idea occurs to me. It helps a lot that Silas doesn't get impatient, like at all. He waits, chewing pizza or sipping wine while I fight to get words out.

Then he talks through my ideas as if they're good. Maybe they *are* good? Anyway, he never makes me feel stupid, and he never acts like I'm taking too long to say things. And I relax. Maybe the wine helps, too, because by the time we've got a couple of good ideas to write up and hand in for the professor to comment on, my anxiety is barely there, just a faint uneasy presence in my belly. I feel good. I feel *happy*.

When he gets up to leave, Silas says, "Can I see you again?"

My heart lurches and I say, "Well, we do have to work on this assignment some more."

He tugs a strand of my hair. "In a week or two, when we have our comments back. But I mean… socially."

I look at him from under my lashes and bite my lip. "I'm not very social," I say, trying to sound teasing.

"A date, then," he says, tugging the strand of hair again, but not hard.

"You don't have to go," I say, lifting my chin to meet his eyes more boldly than I feel.

He moves closer and slips his fingers into the hair behind my ear. "I have an early class," he says, but he takes another step until I can feel his body heat and his breath tickles my nose. He smells like red wine and olives and even though I don't like olives I want to taste his mouth.

"I have an alarm clock," I say.

He laughs softly and then kisses me, lingering, nipping my lower lip gently. "That's a very tempting offer," he says, and kisses behind the point of my jaw. "And any other day I would accept. But this is an important class, and I should be awake for it."

I open my mouth to protest, and he puts a finger on my lips. "If I stay," he says, "I won't sleep. And I won't let *you* sleep." He moves his hand away, kisses me again, and steps back.

"I'm not sure I'll sleep even if you go," I reply, which earns me a smile.

"Movie Friday night?" he says. He touches my face again. "If we're going to do this, I want to do it right."

"What is 'this'?" I ask. "Dating? Fucking?" I bite the inside of my cheek, hoping I didn't sound too weird. Too needy? Too flippant? Can you be both of those at once?

He looks at me very seriously. "I'm a terrible queer man," he says. "I don't sleep around. I don't do one-night stands or fuck random hookups."

I swallow my rapidly returning anxiety. Of course, not all guys who like guys are into random sex, I *know* that. But I want him to want me. "So, you don't want to fuck me?" It just kind of spills out, and why do I have to be so pathetic, anyway?

He frowns and tilts his head. "Is that what you want? Just fuck and go back to being acquaintances in the same research class?" He doesn't sound angry or offended or anything but curious. And fuck, why did I even *say* that?

"No, I…" I blow air out my nose, annoyed with myself. "I'd like to go to a movie with you," I finish, lamely.

He nods and takes a half step back. "I'm not good at flirting or any of that," he says. I can't agree – he seemed damn good at flirting – but I don't interrupt. "So, I'll say it straight out. I like you. You're smart and sexy and funny."

I'm *funny?* I can barely get out three words in a row. But I don't say anything; I just wait.

"And I really do want to fuck you," he says, and I blush. "Very much. I want to take you to bed and spend all night making love to you."

I flush even hotter and focus on the end of his nose because his eyes are overwhelming.

"But I don't want that to be all we do. I want… Fuck, Alder, I want to be your boyfriend."

I do meet his eyes now, and stare at him. "I'm not… My last relationship was… not good," I say, and that's the understatement of the year. My last relationship was a nightmare by the time it ended. I was needy and scared, and I let him walk all over me. He cheated and I forgave him. He cheated again. He refused to call me the name I wanted. He told me I was stupid, and I believed him. He told me that I was imagining that I was anything but a gay man, that I was confused, that I just wanted attention.

Silas's thumb brushing over my cheek brings me back to the present and I realize I'm crying. Only a couple of tears, but fuck, why did I have to start crying?

I turn away. "Sorry," I mumble. "I'm not good at this."

His arms come around me from behind and he holds me, gently, lightly, so I can easily get away if I want to.

(I don't want to.)

"Sweetheart," he says softly in my ear. "It's okay. I'm not going to pressure you into anything."

I swallow, breathe deep, and let my head fall back until it rests on his shoulder. "I'm a fucking mess," I say. "You can walk away, and I won't hold it against you." For some reason, the words come easier. Like he's seen what a freak I am, so it doesn't matter if he finds out I'm even *more* of a weirdo.

"I'm not walking away," he says. "If you don't want a relationship, that's okay. I still want to be your friend."

I let out a huge breath and somethings eases a little. "I could use a friend," I say.

"So, movie Friday, or no?" He squeezes then lets me go, and I slowly turn back around.

"Yeah," I say. "A movie sounds good. My treat."

His eyebrows go up.

"You brought pizza and wine," I say. "And you didn't let me pay. So, movie and snacks on me." I'm not exactly rolling in cash, but my fellowship pays my tuition plus a bit extra, and my uncle owns the building my apartment is in and charges hardly any rent because the building expenses are covered by the restaurant downstairs. I can splurge a little and still be good.

Silas nods. "Okay." I walk with him to the door, where he pauses. "Is it a date, or a friend thing?"

I press my lips together. "I don't know," I say. I *want* it to be a date, but after what I just told him about my past… maybe it's better if we go as friends. Maybe he's right and we should go slow.

"That's okay. We'll just go and see what happens."

"Okay." How did I fuck up so badly? One minute I'm kissing a hot guy who wants me and the next I'm practically shoving him away, saying I just want to be friends. Why am I like this?

"Alder," he says, and warmth fills me. I only needed to ask once, and he's calling me the name I want to be called.

"Yeah?" Once again, I'm reduced to one-word answers and my throat closes when I try to say more.

"I had a great time tonight. Both the studying and the kissing."

"Me, too," I say.

He smiles and turns for the stairs.

"Silas?"

He turns back. In the crappy lighting outside my door, he looks like a figure off a Classical Greek vase, like the satyr on the t-shirt I wore yesterday, or that statue of Pan teaching the shepherd Daphnis to play the flute. For a moment, his hair looks like curling goat horns, and it startles me and turns me on at the same time.

He smiles in amusement and all I see then is a handsome man who for some reason has decided to befriend me.

"Can I kiss you?" I blurt out and he takes a big step towards me, puts his hands on my hips, and stops with his mouth a hairsbreadth from mine.

"I'd like that," he says, and there are no more words for a long time as we stand in the dim hallway and make out.

To my surprise, I sleep really well and wake up refreshed and content. It's been a long time since I slept so soundly, and I just lie in bed enjoying the feeling of being well rested. Anxiety gives me insomnia sometimes, and sensitivity to noise doesn't help. I'd like to sleep with earplugs, but then I stay awake worrying that I won't hear someone trying to break in or something catching fire, or, well, anything.

I reach over my head and twitch aside a curtain. It's a gorgeous day, with an absurdly blue sky and fluffy white clouds. I stretch and run my hands down my body.

Silas likes me. Not only that, but he *wants* me. I look down at myself, not that I can see much under the t-shirt and shorts I wear to bed. But I guess I'm not too repulsive. I'm in good shape, even if my muscle is lean instead of bulky. I'm not exactly well-endowed in the genital department, which worries me a little – will he be disappointed if we do end up sleeping together? I like that my cock is small; it fits better with my version of a nonbinary identity than a big bulge would. I like that it fits in my hand.

I shove those thoughts aside and get up to pee and brush my teeth and put the kettle on. I don't have any classes today, so I think a trip to the climbing wall and the campus bookstore will be a good use of my time. Then I can find a bench somewhere in the shade to get started on my reading.

I have two choices for climbing: I can walk over to the campus gym where it's a only small wall, set up for bouldering, but the routes are switched up frequently and you rarely need to book a time, or I can take the bus across town to the big wall, where I'll probably have to wait unless a slot frees up online. If I catch the bus at the right time, it'll take about the same amount of time to get to either choice.

Not for the first time, I wish I had a car. I know a lot of good bouldering spots and a few decent cliffs I could climb solo not too far away, but none of them are on bus routes.

I glance out the window again as I sip my coffee. It's such a nice day, I think I'll walk across campus. If I take an extra cloth bag in my backpack, I should be able to fit whatever books I buy in it and still have room to carry my climbing gear.

The syllabus for my research class is attached to my fridge with a magnet of a cute anime character my sister thought I would like. I don't even know what show he's from, but he's got big curling horns and bulging muscles, so he definitely fits my type. Instead of getting up, I open the GVU website on my phone so I can look up all my classes and copy the reading lists into one document.

I get dressed, grab a granola bar to eat on the way, and stuff my gear into my backpack.

So many people smile at me as I walk that I wonder if I've somehow put my shirt on backwards or something, but then I realize I'm striding along grinning like a fool. It's sunny and I haven't yet managed to drive away the one person who wants to be my friend by being too quiet.

My ex wasn't the only one who told me I was too much work to be friends with; he was just the one who said it most often. But I refuse to think about that now. Silas didn't seem to think I was too much work.

On such a gorgeous day, the gym is almost deserted and the only person using the climbing wall is getting ready to leave as I walk in. I study the arrangement of hand- and foot-holds for a while, following the color-coded routes with my eyes, deciding where I'll start. And then I place one hand, and the other, and the world fades away as I concentrate on getting myself to the top and back again.

I started climbing when I was a kid because there's a glacial boulder in my parents' backyard in the Bottom Lands. There's an apple orchard all around it, but that rock has always been there, bold in my earliest memories. I spent a lot of time trying to figure out how to climb it.

Two broken wrists, a cracked tailbone and several chipped teeth later, my parents found me a rock-climbing summer camp and I found my second love. My first was ancient mythology, especially Greek, discovered through the children's book my kindergarten teacher read out loud to us one fall.

Where other kids had band and movie posters on their bedroom walls, I had photos of mountains and cliffs, and reproductions of Classical Greek and Roman art. And my own early attempts to draw Pan. I loved – and still love – all myth and folklore, but it was Pan who most caught my imagination.

Maybe it was because he was the odd god out, so to speak. He was important in ancient Greek religious life, but he was not one of the Olympian gods. Some scholars think he was a later addition to the pantheon, while others think he may be one of the most ancient deities, developing out of an earlier pastoral god worshipped in a remote part of Greece.

I liked him because he loved the wild places and protected animals, and because he pursued both beautiful nymphs and handsome shepherds equally. And I guess when I got older, I discovered I have a thing for boys with horns and big cocks unabashedly displayed.

My parents knew I was gay before I had the words for it. My dad wasn't exactly thrilled at the idea, but he didn't reject me, and he was careful not to say homophobic things around me. If he did, my sister would tell him off. My mom was, as she still is, quietly supportive of everything I do. And am.

Even if she doesn't always contradict my dad about it.

Coming out as nonbinary was harder. I told Alison first, and she said, shrugging, "Of course you are." I told my boyfriend at the time, and he said I was just trying to be special. That made me wait two years to tell my parents.

My mom smiled and kissed my cheek and said nothing would change her love for her oldest child. But she's never been able to bring herself to call me "Alder" – substituting "Ald" which could just as easily be short for my given name – or to use gender neutral pronouns for me. Especially around my dad.

As for my dad, he just said, "I'll always see you as my little boy," and refused to talk about it anymore. Not even Alison could get him to understand that I'd never been a little boy at all.

I had hoped, by getting away from a bad relationship and my parents' orchard, that I could start over as the person I knew myself to be. Yet in every one of my classes I had said nothing when my professors called me "Alden" or when people referred to me as "he" or called me a guy. Silas was the only one I'd corrected.

I'm a coward, after all.

I reach the bottom of the wall depressed. Usually climbing lets me leave the world behind. And it had, at first. But maybe I had chosen too easy a route, because on my way back down I started thinking.

So I shake out my arms, choose another starting place, and begin another ascent.

By the time I leave I'm limp as a wet towel, but I feel better, my optimistic mood of the morning returned. And outside, an early-autumn breeze catches at my hair, wet from the quick shower I'd taken in the gym change room, and that cheers me up even more, chasing away the weirdness I feel after having to use the men's change room and showers. There are signs – like the gender-neutral washroom at the library – that GVU is starting to adapt to the twenty-first century, but it isn't there yet, and people like me are still required to make awkward choices.

But whatever. My next errand is book shopping, and book shopping never fails to cheer me up, even when it's books for class and not thick pulpy novels about gods falling hopelessly in love with mere humans.

Nothing is going to stop my relentlessly good mood.

On the way out of the bookstore, arms laden with two heavy bags, because there were more than I realized and I had to buy another bag to carry them all, my bank account seriously depleted, I pause to adjust my burdens next to a bulletin board.

Right in the middle of the board is an illustration of Pan, familiar from my childhood edition of *The Wind in the Willows*. It's a black and white line rendition of the original, but it's really well done. Beneath it, the paper says, "Reawakening the Pan Within." I stare at it, trying to figure out what it's for. I scan the rest of the text. "A workshop presented by the Great Valley University Pagan Alliance," it says, followed by a date, time, and location.

"Hunh." I don't realize I've said it aloud until someone heading into the bookstore looks at me oddly. I flush but ignore them, set my bags down, and carefully unpin the notice.

It sounds like the perfect way to get started on the research I want to do for my thesis. If nothing else, it should be interesting.

Chapter Four

FRIDAY PASSES QUICKLY, to my relief. I climb, go to class, and sit on my couch working my way through the required reading for the week ahead.

I'm too nervous about my upcoming date (or not date?) with Silas to eat dinner, but I'll be having snacks at the movie anyway. Once again, I agonize over what to wear. It's not like I have a huge wardrobe, and most of it is jeans and tees and hoodies anyway, but I want to look *good*.

I settle on army surplus combat pants that are loose and comfortable but not too baggy, and the same white and red on black tee with the lewd satyr that I wore on Tuesday. At least I know Silas likes it. I add a jean jacket because it will be chilly once the sun goes down, and my Doc Martens with rainbow laces. At the last second, I pin a "they/them" button to the lapel of my jacket.

I take so long deciding that I almost miss the bus and have to sprint down the sidewalk. I hang on to the rail and fumble for my bus pass while the driver pulls out into traffic.

"In a hurry?" he says, and I know he's only making small talk while I struggle with the button on my jacket pocket. I finally free my bus pass, show it to him, and put it away.

"Date," I say. "I think."

He chuckles, and I think he glances at my pronoun pin. "Well, good luck."

The bus is crowded because it's Friday night and half the university population is on their way downtown to go drinking, so I end up standing the whole way. I wish I had remembered how many people there were going to be before deciding to proclaim my queerness via a button on my jacket, because I get a few sneers and disgusted looks that don't exactly give me confidence. I'm glad I have to stand, though; it takes my mind off being nervous about seeing Silas again.

He's waiting when I get off the bus, leaning against the wall between two huge movie posters. He doesn't see me at first in the crowd of twenty-somethings that spills out the rear doors of the bus, so I take the opportunity to watch him.

More than one woman turns to look at him as they walk by and a few guys, too, but he doesn't even seem to notice. His eyes are scanning the people passing, looking for someone.

Looking for *me*, I realize, as he sees he and his dimpled smile appears. It's all he does, just smiles, and suddenly I'm breathless.

"Hey," I say, stopping in front of him, then stepping closer to the wall to be out of the way of the passing mob.

"Hey." He turns towards me and reaches for my arm, squeezes gently, then lets go.

We go in, pay, and find seats. The movie's been out a while, so it's not too crowded and we get a good spot, with no one else close. I busy myself with settling my drink and popcorn and taking my jacket off, too nervous to look at him. Again.

When I finally look up, he's watching me. "How are you?" he says, and even though it's the most banal of questions, it feels genuine, like it really matters to him how I'm doing.

"I'm good." I make myself smile, but once I'm doing it, it feels right, and it gets wider. "You?"

"Pretty good," he says. "Even better now." It's such a corny line, and the twist of his lips shows he knows it.

"Really?" I put some mock skepticism in my voice.

He laughs softly. "Yes, really. Yesterday I met with my advisor and found out exactly how much more work I need to do to make up for having a fine arts Master's instead of an academic one."

"Ah," I say.

"Yeah. It's a lot." He settles back in his seat and leans an arm on the armrest between us. "I'm going to be busy."

Is he about to tell me he doesn't have time for… whatever this is building between us? Is this a nice way of getting rid of me?

But he turns his arm over on the arm rest, hand open and fingers spread in invitation. I look from his hand to his face.

"Can I hold your hand?" he says.

I nod and lay my arm atop his, lacing our fingers together. He squeezes and I squeeze back.

"I'm going to have to work my ass off and take at least an extra semester. Maybe two."

I lean back in my seat. "They couldn't tell you this last year?"

He snorts. "Apparently, they did. I was supposed to take summer classes, but I couldn't. One of my cousins died and I went home."

"I'm sorry."

"Yeah, it was pretty sudden, but the family's doing as well as can be expected. Anyway, I can manage the extra work."

"But you won't have a lot of time." I keep my voice neutral, so I won't sound pathetic.

He looks away from the ads playing on the theatre screen and licks his lower lip. "I intend to make sure I still have time for you." He looks back at the screen. "If you want."

Before I can answer, the lights go dim and the sound cranks up, so I settle for tightening my fingers on his again.

As the trailers play, I sneak another look at him. The lights pick out the edges of his face in blue, giving him the profile of a Greek god and reflecting oddly in his eyes. It's an eerie picture, but he's also sexy. (So fucking sexy.) I make myself look away and concentrate on the screen instead, because I could stare at his profile forever.

The movie's okay and at least serves to blunt my nerves for two hours. As the credits roll, he looks at me and smiles and my heart thumps in my chest.

"So, what do you think?" he says, and I prepare to say something noncommittal about the movie. But then he says, "Was it a date?"

I'm so startled I laugh and say, "I don't know, are you going to kiss me goodnight?"

A woman passing by in the row ahead, arms full of empty popcorn and drink cups, glances at me and flicks her gaze over to Silas. I feel dread in my gut, but when she looks back at me, she smiles and continues on her way.

"The thought crossed my mind," Silas says. He shows no inclination to get up, even though employees are slowly filing into the theatre to sweep the aisles and pick up trash.

"What other thoughts have crossed your mind?" I have to say it quickly to get all the words out.

His lips part and he sits up suddenly, leaning towards me. I think he's going to kiss me, but instead he whispers in my ear, "All sorts of naughty things," and leans away again.

All I manage to do in reply is say, "Oh," and tighten my fingers on his in a death grip.

I look around and we're the only ones left besides the employees. The credits come to an end and the lights go up.

"I guess we should go," I say.

"Do you want to go get a drink?" he asks, gathering up his trash and standing. I let go of his hand reluctantly to put my jacket back on. "Maybe some food?"

"Are you hungry?" I say, turning to head down the aisle to the exit.

"Not for food," he replies.

I don't say anything until we're out on the sidewalk. "I think I'd like to go home," I say.

He looks crestfallen, like I've just told him he's a lousy date or something.

"Okay," he says, and heads for the bus stop.

"Silas." I don't usually like calling people by name; I have this irrational fear that it will turn out to be the wrong name once I say it out loud. But I like saying his. I like the feel of it in my mouth.

After our first study session I looked "Silas" up online, because even though I know a bit of ancient Greek, I'm not exactly fluent. I found out it comes from the same Latin root as "sylvan" and means "of the forest." It suits him. He looks like a god of the forest.

Oh fuck. Maybe that's why I'm so into him. Maybe it's not that he's smart and funny and caring and likes some of the same things I do. Maybe it's because he looks like my idealized wet-dream version of Pan: muscular, curly-haired, hairy-chested, stubble edging his jaw. Give him horns and a visible hard-on and he'd be my perfect man.

He stops and turns, then puts a hand on my arm to move me gently to the edge of the sidewalk, out of the way. There aren't as many people out as before the movie, but there are still plenty. He doesn't drop his hand once we're off to the side but rests it on my shoulder instead.

"What is it?" He looks uncertain, like maybe I'm going to tell him I had a crap time and don't want to see him again. But how can he worry about *that*? From *me*?

"Will you…" I make myself breathe out, breathe in again, and shove anxiety aside. "Will you come home with me?" I don't even know why I ask. He's already told me he doesn't want to go too fast, that he likes me, but he doesn't want to fuck me yet.

He looks at my face for what seems like a really long time. When he answers, it comes out in a rush of breath. "Fuck, yes." And then, ignoring the people around us, he steps close and kisses me. It's nothing like our last kiss in the hall outside my apartment, all heavy breathing and tangled tongues.

No, this is a sweet, soft kiss, gentle and… quiet, if that makes sense.

"Take me home, sweetheart," he says into my ear, and I'm not even sure how I make it onto the bus, I'm trembling so hard.

I don't remember the ride home or walking to my building from the bus stop, except we hold hands the whole time and I drop my keys trying to open the outer door and again after climbing the stairs.

Inside, shoes and jackets abandoned by the door, we stand looking at each other as if we suddenly don't know what to do.

Finally, I force out, "Would you like a drink?" I sound stupidly formal and the usual flush creeps up my neck, so I turn away and head for the fridge.

I don't hear him behind me, but his hand on my shoulder stops me and I turn back around. The heat in his eyes has me fumbling for the counter, needing something solid for support.

He shifts his hand as I turn, slipping his fingers into the hair behind my neck. "I don't want a drink," he says, and his voice is breathy. He looks almost predatory, and I shiver, but it's not a bad feeling. I'm not *afraid*. I want him to catch me, to devour me.

I turn my head so my lips brush his wrist. "Tell me what you *do* want," I say, feeling my nervousness drain away, flushed aside by anticipation. Social anxiety makes it hard for me to converse, but sex talk I can do. Sex in general, I'm good at.

He steps closer, leaning his other hand on the counter behind me. "Look at me, sweetheart."

I meet his eyes, feeling bolder now that things have moved from intellectual to physical. Physical I can do.

"I want to kiss you," he says, his voice half growl. We haven't turned on any lights and he's highlighted by the streetlight through the window, a lot like how he looked in the theatre.

Fuck, he's sexy.

"Then kiss me," I say, but before he can, I lean forward and press my lips to his neck, feeling his pulse under my tongue, and he lets out a soft moan. He shifts his hand from the back of my neck to the front, resting his fingers lightly around my throat, and slowly pushes me back, just far enough that he can get his mouth on mine. His teeth scrape mine and then his tongue darts between my lips and I let my neck relax, let him take everything he wants from my mouth.

I want to touch him, to feel his skin under my hands, but all I can manage to do is cling to the counter to keep myself upright. I'm good at sex, but right now I'm so overwhelmed by him that I can only respond to his actions instead of making any of my own.

His hand slides from my neck down my chest to the hem of my shirt, then underneath, his fingers tracing the shapes of the muscles on my belly and back.

When he lifts his mouth from mine my lips feel swollen, and I don't want him to stop. He rests his forehead on mine and says softly, "Do you know how beautiful you are, Alder?"

I don't know how to answer that. I don't think "beautiful" when I look at myself in the mirror. I'm just me. Just Alder Lewis, twenty-seven and older than most of my classmates because I took too long to go back to school.

But I have to say something, and the way he kissed me makes me feel bold.

"Tell me," I say.

He chuckles and the deep rich sound vibrates right to my crotch. I'm so hard it's uncomfortable.

"So fucking beautiful," he says.

I manage to pry one hand from the counter and lay my palm on his face. "Well, you look like a Greek god."

"Oh? Which one?" He presses closer and I can feel his boner, thick and hard, and oh fuck do I ever want to get on my knees and worship it. Worship *him*.

"Pan," I say.

He pulls back a little to look at me. "Don't the myths say he was ugly?"

It's my turn to laugh. "They said he was ugly because he had the legs of a goat. It made him monstrous. But he looks pretty fucking hot in all the art I've seen."

He leans away a little more, enough to trace a finger over the satyr on my shirt. "You're a fan of fauns and satyrs," he says. He sounds amused, but not in a bad way. Not in the way my ex would have been.

"You already knew that."

"I suppose I did." He shifts his hand to my hip. "Can I kiss you again?"

"Kiss me again." I move my hand from his face to his hair. It's so *soft*, especially in comparison to mine, which is coarse and thick.

He brushes his lips over mine but pulls back too soon. His hand moves again, tugging up the hem of my shirt. He traces my belly muscles with one finger and dips it into my belly button. I just manage not to moan.

"Can I kiss you here?" he says, fingers still following the shape of my abs. I'm glad that climbing keeps me really well toned.

"Yes," I say and I'm pretty sure it's more breath than word.

I struggle to *keep* breathing as he slowly kneels and presses his mouth to my belly. His tongue traces the shapes his fingers just followed, and I cling helplessly to the edge of the counter.

Oh fuck oh fuck oh fuck.

His tongue dips below the edge of my waistband and this time I can't keep in the whimper that crawls up my throat.

His palm strokes up my thigh to my crotch, pressing and rubbing over my cock.

"Can I kiss you here?" he says, his voice as ragged as mine would be if I tried to talk.

"I –"

He looks up at me, his eyes hot with desire. "Please?" he says.

"I'm not…"

He moves his hand back to my hip, like he thinks maybe I don't like the way he's touching me. (I like it so much.)

"I'm not very big," I choke out, immediately flushing from my toes to my scalp.

He moves his hand back, as if to confirm my words. I want to sink into the floor.

"Did you know," he says softly, his breath stirring the line of hair on my belly, "the ancient Greeks thought a small penis was a sign of beauty and intelligence?"

"What?"

"I already know you're beautiful and intelligent." He hooks a finger on the first button of my fly and pops it open.

I struggle to keep breathing.

He pops open another button, and another, and traces my muscles with his tongue again. Then he looks back up at me.

"I like small cocks," he says. "I like when I can fit the whole thing in my mouth at once."

He pulls open the rest of the buttons and pushes my jeans and boxers down just enough to get my boner free. Then he just *looks* at me, at my cock, and I wish the fucking earth would swallow me whole.

"Fuck, Alder," he says, and it's not mocking or disgusted or anything else I might have imagined him feeling that I hear in his voice. It's *wonder.* "You have the most perfect cock I've ever seen."

Chapter Five

I'M TORN BETWEEN WANTING to pull away, to hide myself, and wanting to strip naked so he can see all of me and decide if I have too many flaws to be worth wanting.

So I don't move. I just hold tight to the edge of the counter and make myself keep breathing as his fingers brush over my cock gently, exploring, teasing, tormenting me.

His tongue flicks out and strokes my length – not that I have much length – and I can't hold back a soft cry when his mouth, hot and wet, slides over me.

He holds my hips in his muscular hands, and he can indeed fit my whole cock in his mouth, easily. With each bob of his head, I gasp, and when he moves his mouth away to look at me, I whimper.

"You're perfect, sweetheart," he says, and all I can do is stare at him, mouth open. His tongue finds me again and he closes his eyes, looking for all the world like he's enjoying sucking me so much he's lost in it.

My panting gets more desperate as I feel the pleasure he's drawing out of me build and build.

"Silas," I gasp, and pry one hand away from the edge of the counter to touch his hair. "Oh, fuck."

"Mmm?" He answers without taking his mouth off me and it vibrates from my cock to my asshole.

"I'm – oh fuck." I can't get the words out, that I'm going to spurt into his mouth any second now, and if he doesn't want that, he better stop.

He slides his mouth away again and I don't know whether to be relieved or disappointed. Then he says, "Will you fuck my mouth, sweetheart? Can you do that for me?" and I almost come all over his face.

I manage not to, manage to force out some kind of sound that could be taken for assent, and he smiles and takes me in his mouth again.

I clutch his hair, hard, and he makes an approving noise, so I push my hips forward, sliding my cock between his lips and into the hot cavern of his mouth. My head just bumps the entrance of his throat, barely, with his lips pressed to my pelvis, fastened tight around my root. His hands pull at my hips, encouraging me, and I thrust again.

"Oh fuck," I say. "I'm not… I'm going to… oh fuck, Silas." I pry my other hand off the counter and bury it in his hair and fuck his mouth. I manage three more thrusts and then I'm over the edge, moaning out loud and spilling between his lips.

When I stop moving, let go of his hair, and brace myself on the counter again, he slides his mouth off me, slowly, sucking up every drop I produced and swallowing it down.

Then, still on his knees, he tugs my boxers and jeans back up. He looks up at me, his eyes so dark I can't tell what is pupil and what's iris. It's an eerie picture, and beautiful, and I think I'm falling for him, hard and fast.

His smile is soft. "You taste good," he says, and my breath comes out in a rush, not quite a laugh, not quite a groan.

"Stand up," I say. "Please."

"I could kneel for you forever," he says, but he gets up.

"Kiss me," I whisper, and he does, the taste of my spunk salty on his tongue. I let go of the counter and hold onto him instead, sliding my hands up under his shirt to feel the thick muscle of his back, his shoulders. Then I move around to his chest, sliding my hands over his pecs. They're huge slabs of muscle and the tight curls of hair feel fantastic under my palms. I can't say I've ever particularly found hairy men attractive before, but fuck he just *feels* so good. I want his chest against mine, skin to skin. But not yet.

Right now, I've got a favor to return and I want very badly to wrap my lips around the big bulge in his jeans.

I slide my hands down his chest and over his belly, as strong and furry as his chest. When I pop open the button on his fly and start to slide down the zipper he moves his mouth from mine and says, "Wait."

"What is it?" I don't want to wait. I want to unravel him like he just did to me. But I pause and listen.

"Let me wash first," he says. "I've been in these jeans all day."

"I don't care."

His grin is lopsided. "You might. I'm uncut, and shit gets stuck, sometimes. Lint and worse." He strokes my hair back from my face. "Just give me a minute." His smile grows. "I promise I'll be right back."

I drop my hands, and he moves away, finding the bathroom easily even though my apartment is dark. I hear water running and close my eyes, leaning back against the counter.

Quiet footsteps whisper across the hardwood, and I straighten and turn, watching him approach. His shirt is rucked up and drops of water caught in the hair on his belly catch the light.

I have to breathe through my mouth to get enough air.

When he reaches me, I put my hands on his hips inside his jeans and turn him so his back is to the counter in case he needs something solid to lean on. I push his pants down far enough to free his cock and fuck he's big. I mean, not gigantic, but bigger than anyone I've been with before.

I look at him as I kneel. Like he said – warning me maybe – he's uncut, but he's so hard his foreskin is pulling back from his head. His cock is darker than the rest of his skin and his pubic hair is thick and curly, and when I slide my fingers into it, I find it almost as soft as the hair on his head. The curls continue onto his thighs, and I want to strip him naked.

Instead, I curl one hand around his hardness, and he sighs. His fingers comb my hair gently. How can such a muscular man be so fucking gentle?

I slide my hand down to cup his balls and squeeze a little, then trace his underside with my tongue, lingering, feeling every twisted vein along his length and every soft wrinkle of his foreskin. I know I'll never fit all of him in my mouth – even suppressing my gag reflex (I'm good at that) and swallowing him, I'll be lucky to fit half – so I keep my hand curled around him as I take his head in my mouth.

"Oh, sweetheart," he says, barely above a whisper.

I respond by my sliding my lips and tongue over his foreskin, teasing the sensitive skin, then probing his slit with the tip of my tongue. Then I breathe out and suck him in, as far as I can, and bob my head to slide over him, finding a rhythm he seems to like.

His fingers tighten in my hair and his breaths are soft gasps. "I'm not going to last very long," he says. "I've been thinking about this since I saw you on that bench with your perfect obscene t-shirt." He groans and then laughs under his breath. "Oh fuck, I'm so glad you actually like me."

I growl against his cock, let it vibrate through my throat and into him, and his fingers tighten again, until his grip on my hair is almost painful.

"Fuck, Alder."

I use every trick I know to make him feel good, swirling my tongue, sucking, even letting him feel my teeth, just a little.

His gasping breaths become short moans and then one long groan that turns almost into a yell and he floods my mouth with salty bitter spunk. I drink it down like a starving person, suck him hard and swallow.

When I look up at him, his face is soft. He slides his fingers under my jaw as I lick my lips. "How can you be so perfect?" he says, wonder in his voice.

After we've recovered for a few minutes, leaning side-by-side on the counter, we each down a glass of water and fall into my bed, still fully dressed. He tucks my body against his and I curl into him. It's been two years since I let someone sleep in the same bed as me, two years that I let guys fuck me if I thought they liked me but would never let them spend the night.

I don't want him to leave. No, I will *not* think about asking him to move in with me. It's way too soon for that. (I know I *will* think about asking him to move in with me, but I also know I won't do it.) (Not yet.)

I fall asleep more quickly than I ever have. He makes me feel safe.

I wake up spread out on the bed like a starfish. I feel good. Sleepy. Content.

And then I realize I'm alone. I fell asleep with Silas's arms around me, and now I'm alone.

I curl up on my side, suddenly miserable. But what did I expect? Every attempt I've made at a connection for the last two years ended in me asking them to leave my place, or them asking me to leave theirs. It's why I stopped bothering with relationships at all and just settled for getting folded over the back of a couch and thoroughly fucked.

This time, I didn't even get fucked.

Then I hear soft swearing from my kitchen, the kettle whistling, and footsteps. I freeze in my little curled-up ball of misery and listen.

He's still here.

A few minutes later the bedroom door cracks open, and I smell coffee. Silas peers into the room, sees me awake, and comes the rest of the way in. He's got a mug in each hand, steam curling up from both of them.

"I thought you left," I blurt out.

He sets one of the mugs on the nightstand next to me, then skirts the bed to sit against the headboard on the other side. "I'd have woken you up to say goodbye," he says. "Or left a note if you looked too deep in dreams."

I sit up, realizing I'm still in yesterday's clothes, my fly gaping open. I remember *why* my fly is open, and blush, covering it by picking up the mug and sipping.

Silas leans over to kiss my cheek. "I didn't know what you took in your coffee, but you have cream in your fridge and honey in the same cupboard as the coffee, so I guessed."

I close my eyes and let the steam bathe my face. "It's perfect," I say, and it is.

"I didn't mean to fall asleep last night," he says, watching me over the edge of his cup.

"Oh?" I lean back on the headboard and soak in the simple enjoyment of waking up with a lover who's still *there*. Who's made me coffee and kissed me on the cheek.

But wait, is he saying he meant to stay awake so he could *leave*?

He leans his shoulder gently against mine. "I intended to keep you awake all night."

(Ohhhh…)

"Doing what?" I raise an eyebrow and take another sip of coffee.

Somehow, he's put exactly the right amount of honey and cream in it.

"Oh, this and that," he says. Then his dimples appear. "I wanted to see if the rest of your body is as perfect as your mouth," he says. "And your cock."

The heat moving up my neck is familiar by now, so I ignore it. (He thinks my cock is perfect.) I've never been with someone who didn't think I was too small. (He fucking thinks my cock – which *I* like very much – is fucking perfect.)

"I guess you'll just have to take me on another date, then," I say.

He smiles and sips his coffee, and the morning feels so right I can hardly believe I'm not dreaming.

"I hope we can go on a lot more dates," he says.

"That reminds me. There's a thing I want to go to." I hesitate. Maybe he won't be interested. Maybe he's super Christian and will be horrified, even though he seemed okay with my thesis topic.

"Mm?" He's still watching me, as if just seeing me exist is pleasing. I try not to blush again. (I fail.)

"Hang on." I get out of bed and go looking for my bags of books. Except of course I already took them out of the bags and arranged them on a shelf. I emptied a whole row on one of my bookshelves specifically for this semester's reading.

Finally, I find the notice tucked behind the syllabus for our research class on my fridge. I pull it down and take it back to the bedroom, sit against the headboard again, and hand it to Silas.

"Hunh," he says, and I laugh. He looks a question at me.

"That's exactly what I said."

"Well, you have to go," he says. "It's exactly in line with your research." He puts the paper on my lap and sips his coffee.

"I haven't even talked to my thesis advisor yet," I say, but it's more to curb my own enthusiasm than his. "But yeah, I thought so, too."

"Are you pagan?" His tone is curious, not like he thinks it's bad, but I have to wonder if he's Greek Orthodox or something. They're super strict, aren't they?

I shrug and stare into my coffee. "I don't know. I used to study Wicca, but I got turned off by the gender binary emphasis."

He cocks his head to one side. "What do you mean?"

"Divine feminine this, divine masculine that." I turn my coffee cup in my hands. "Even though it's supposed to be metaphorical, you know, everyone has some masculine and feminine in them, it always felt…" I'm not sure how to finish the thought, even though it's something I've pondered extensively.

"Like everything still gets sorted into a binary, even if every person is supposed to be a combination of both?"

"Yeah. Exactly."

"Some traditions keep room for a third gender. Or no gender."

I meet his eyes, my own curiosity piqued now. "Are *you* pagan?"

He considers the thought like it's not a simple answer. "My people… My family… We came here a very long time ago, and even before we left Greece, we were… isolated, I guess."

I watch him. He stares into his coffee, like he's reading the answers there. "I know it sounds completely unlikely, but we – my ancestors, I mean – were never converted to Christianity."

So may questions are building up in my head that I can't separate any of them out to ask.

He looks at me, then back into his coffee cup. "I *know* how it sounds. So many pagan 'traditions' –" and he makes air quotes with his fingers "– say they descended unbroken from a pre-Christian religion, but turn out to be basically Wicca with the names of different gods substituted in…" He laughs. "I would totally understand if you didn't believe me."

It *does* seem unlikely. Impossible, almost. Definitely improbable. But I *want* to believe him.

"What gods do you worship?"

His smile this time is a bit wry. "Worship isn't really the right word," he says. "'Honor', maybe."

"Work with?" I say, letting a smile curl up the corner of my mouth, and he snorts.

"Those neo-pagans do like to 'work with' their gods." Air quotes again. I wonder if I should feel offended. Not that long ago, I was almost happy following a neo-pagan path.

"I think I'm really more of an animist," I blurt out, then snap my mouth shut. But he looks at me and his smile is warm.

"Me, too, really," he says. "We – my family, I mean – we honor mostly what would be considered minor deities. Like spirits of place and that."

"Not the Olympians, then?" I ask.

He laughs again. "Not so much." He looks into my eyes, hesitating, and I wonder why.

"We do have one god we honor above the others." He drains his coffee cup and stares into the dregs.

"Which one?" I ask, suddenly curious, *intensely* curious, about this new facet of the man who said he wants to be my boyfriend.

Does he *still* want to be my boyfriend? (I want him to be my boyfriend.)

He shifts on the bed so he's sitting sideways, facing me, and he takes one of my hands. His fingers are warm from the coffee, and I want them on my skin. I lift his hand to my lips and kiss his fingertips.

"Alder," he says, softly.

"Mm?"

"You might get mad at me."

"For what? For which god you honor?"

"Maybe."

"You said you're not Christian so… I'm pretty sure you're not about to tell me your family is Satanists."

"Would you care if I was?"

I consider that. "I guess that depends on how you define Satanism."

His lips curl up. "Some evangelical sects would probably say I worship the devil."

"They'd say that about all non-Christians. Probably a lot of other Christians, too."

"True, but my god has goat horns and very hairy legs."

I lower his hand from my mouth, but don't let go. "What?"

"You're studying the modern worship of Pan," he says. "I should have told you that you could use me and my family as research subjects."

Chapter Six

MY EXCITEMENT VANISHES almost as quickly as it appears. (It doesn't even occur to me to be mad that he didn't tell me.)

"I'm planning to study *neo*-paganism, though," I say. "And, you know, earth-centered traditions, New Age stuff, that kind of thing. If your family never converted in the first place, if they really *do* follow a religion directly descended from ancient Greece, then they're outside the scope of my research."

He smiles and squeezes my hand. "Either your advisor is going to assume we're bullshitting and actually follow a reconstructed faith and not an ancient one, and therefore fit within your scope, or you could just add to your study parameters." He lets his dimples and a few of his teeth show. "I'd be happy for you to study *me*."

I shove his shoulder, lightly, but feel my smile growing. "I don't think I'd share *those* results with my advisor," I say. Then, thoughtfully, "I'll have to revise my proposal." It really is too good an opportunity to pass up. A comparison between the practices of a religion that's genuinely derived from ancient worship with neo-pagan worship of the same deity would be perfect, and would not only make the subject more interesting, it would provide the structure for my arguments. Even if my advisor doesn't accept Silas's family practices as genuine, I could frame them as being derived from extensive scholarship and compare them to more Wiccan-derived practices.

"You've already written your proposal?" Silas asks. "I thought you hadn't even met your advisor yet."

"It's not due till the end of the year," I say, distracted by the possibilities he's just offered me. "But I had a draft written before I even applied for grad school."

He laughs, but like most of his amusement, it's not directed at me, and it grows out of delight, not an urge to make fun. It's the same reason I laugh most of the time, if it isn't my nerves.

He taps the paper on my lap. "Do you want me to come with you to this thing?"

I bite my lip and study the drawing on the page. "You don't have to," I say.

He touches my chin with one finger, asking me to look at him but not actually trying to make me. I turn my head and meet his eyes.

"Not what I asked," he says and moves his hand to rest against the side of my face, warm and comforting. "If I don't want to do something, I'll tell you." His thumb brushes my lower lip. "What do *you* want?"

"I wouldn't mind if you came with me," I say. "Two observers are always better than one." I have to work to get the words out; I'm not used to being asked what I want as if it's just as important as what the person asking wants.

"What if they want people to participate?" His voice is careful, like he doesn't want to imply I'm incapable, but he knows I hate being observed, and participating usually means being seen.

"I think I'll be okay," I say. "I have to participate in things sometimes, and I really want to go to this thing, to start gathering stuff for my thesis." I flick my tongue out to touch his thumb and he draws in a sharp breath. "It will be easier with someone I trust with me."

"You trust me?" His smile grows until he's beaming. "So, you *do* want me to go with you, then?" His thumb strokes my lip harder, and I open my mouth.

"Yes," I say, just as he slips his thumb between my lips and the words turn to a quiet sound of want.

"Sweetheart," he says, leaning closer. "Right now, I will do anything you want me to."

I stare into his eyes, wondering how bold I can be, wondering if I should laugh and ask him to make me breakfast instead of what I really want to ask for. *He* could ask *me* to do anything right now, and I would do it.

I wait too long to decide, and the moment passes. He moves his hand away, leans over, and kisses me, then gets up and collects our coffee mugs.

I slump onto the bed as he walks away, wishing I had asked him to kiss me again, to undress me, to do any of the whole list of things to me that I've been thinking about since the day we met.

"What's your plan for today?" I ask when I come out of the bathroom after brushing my teeth. He's drying a mug with my ratty dishcloth and the sink drains noisily behind him.

"Just getting some reading done. Maybe work on an outline for an essay that's not due until the end of the semester."

I laugh, glad I'm not the only one who likes to get a head start on class work. "Me too," I say. "More or less."

"I should probably let my dorm mates know I'm not dead." He puts the mug in the cupboard and picks up the other one, rubbing it vigorously with the dishcloth.

It's nice to have a hot guy in my apartment, doing dishes. (I will *not* suggest he move in with me. I haven't even known him a week.)

(I totally want to ask anyway.)

"And I should call my parents. They worry if I don't check in occasionally." He leans on the counter. "I haven't lived at home for a decade, and they still treat me like a kid."

"Yeah, mine, too." I want to ask him on another date. I don't want him to have to always be the one asking. (*Always*, as if we've been on more than one actual date.) (Two, if you count studying while eating pizza.)

Oh come on, Alder, say something.

"Do you –" I start to say, just as he says, "Maybe –"

We both laugh.

"You first," he says.

"No, it's okay."

"I said it first," he says, pretending to scowl. "You first."

"Fine." Except the words get stuck again.

He puts the mug away and hangs up the dishcloth, moving around my kitchen like he's not waiting for me to say something.

I sit on one of the stools that are pulled up to where the end of the counter sticks out like a table. The part of the counter I was clinging desperately to last night while he went down on me.

"Do you want to do something?" I manage, finally, looking at the colorful paper napkin that's somehow ended up on the counter, though I have no idea where it came from, so I don't have to look at him.

He slides onto the stool across from me. "Something like what?"

I shrug. "Um…" I fiddle with the napkin and refuse to look up. I don't want to see the impatience in his eyes. But there's nothing in his posture – what I can see of it without looking up – that suggests he's tired of waiting. He just… waits.

"Go for a walk, maybe?" I say to the napkin. "I could make dinner?" Why did that come out as a question?

"You cook?"

I glance up then, but it's not surprise I see; it's curiosity.

"A little. I like noodles." Oh God, Alder, do you have to sound so thick? (Though I do really like noodles.)

"Noodles are good," he says. "Especially the spicy Thai ones. Growing up we never ate anything that wasn't somehow Greek. Or Italian. My mother figured Italian was close enough, which is kind of weird when you think about it." He takes a breath and laughs.

I blink at him.

"I told you I babble," he says.

"I make something resembling Asian food, usually," I say.

He chuckles again. "Something resembling?"

"I learned from old episodes of *Wok with Yan* and a couple cookbooks I found in a thrift store. Japanese and Thai." I point to shelf near the sink where the two battered books lean, along with a few others I got since, mostly as birthday gifts from my sister.

"Why'd you decide to learn to cook?"

"My family's English," I say.

It takes a minute for that to make it in, but when it does, he erupts in laughter. "So, the stereotype is true? English cooking is bland?"

My anxiety eases off. I made him laugh. I just wish I didn't have to wait for the anxiety to go away again every time we have a conversation.

"I suspect there's a good reason curry's popular in England," I say. "Aside from the large population of people of Indian descent."

He laughs again. "So, if I ever get invited to have dinner with your parents, I should be prepared for tasteless?"

I feel warm at the thought that he's thinking about meeting my parents. "Consider yourself warned," I say. "And don't expect much texture, either."

"Well, in the spirit of fairness, then, you'll need to be prepared for olives. My dad fucking loves olives, so Mum puts them in everything."

"I don't *hate* olives," I say. "I just don't generally choose to eat them."

He reaches across the counter to take my hands. "You realize we're talking about meeting each other's parents," he says, tone very serious. But the corners of his eyes crinkle.

"Does that mean you have a crush on me?" I ask, and my anxiety slips away like it was never there. (It will be back.)

"*Such* a crush," he answers. His fingers encircle my wrists lightly and his thumbs stroke my palms.

"So, dinner tonight?" I say, before I get lost in his touch.

"When was your pagan thing again?"

"Tomorrow afternoon."

"How about dinner after that?"

I try not to be disappointed that he isn't as eager to see me again as I am to see him. Tightness creeps back into my belly. (Told you it would be back.)

"Okay," I say.

His thumbs don't stop and my skin tingles where they touch. "I'm going to go home and do all the shit I was going to do tomorrow night, so I won't even have to think about school."

"I don't have class until Monday afternoon," I say.

"Oh?"

I lick my lips. "So, you can keep me awake all night Sunday." I cock my head to one side the way he does. "If you want."

His lips curl up and the heaviness in my gut eases again. "I also do not have class until Monday afternoon," he says.

"Oh?"

"So, you can keep *me* awake all night Sunday." He leans a little closer. "And if they're going to be invoking Pan…"

"Re-awakening, I think the flyer said." Oh, shut *up*, Alder.

"Right. If they're going to be re-awakening Pan, you might want to stock up on condoms and lube."

I flush hot from the roots of my hair to the ends of all my digits, but if he notices, he doesn't say.

"Already prepared," I say, refusing to be embarrassed now.

"Good." That word he rumbles into my ear, then he kisses my cheek and gets up. "I better get to work, then. I've got a couple of things I need to hand in on Monday."

He comes around the counter and when I start to turn, he holds me in place and embraces me from behind, kissing my neck. "See you soon, sweetheart."

Then he's gone and I sit where I am until the door closes and his footsteps fade away down the stairs.

I'm flushed, and hard, and I wish I'd asked him to stay, but the promise of Sunday – *tomorrow* – makes me giddy.

I get up to take a shower – a very cold shower – so I can get the rest of my weekend's worth of reading done.

The thing about Great Valley is, it's not very accepting. I mean, like all cities it's got its good people and its bad, but unlike Riverbend, where I've seen same sex couples walking hand-in-hand in public, you have to be more careful in Great Valley.

Not that I've ever had issues, but I've heard of people getting beat up for looking like they might be queer, and it's the areas around GVU that are supposed to be the worst. So maybe Silas and I got lucky when he kissed me outside the movie theater.

Anyway, I guess I've always assumed that pagans would be more welcoming than most people when it comes to non-hetero sexualities and non-cisgender presentations. Which is dumb, really, since pagans are just people like everyone else.

But that's why I don't think anything of it when Silas holds my hand as we go into the coffee house where the "Re-Awakening the Pan Within" thing is to take place. It's not until we're sitting at a table, mochas in front of us, that I realize we're getting an unfriendly stare from two guys at the front of the room, right near the little stage where I assume the speakers will stand. One guy in particular looks at us with open animosity. The other glances between us, narrows his eyes, and then looks away.

No one else in the place seems to notice or care that we – a guy and someone who probably looks like a guy – are holding hands while we sip our coffees. Everyone sits facing the stage like we are, mostly hetero-appearing couples, but a few small mixed groups. But that one guy at the front glares, says something to his buddy, and glares some more.

"Silas," I say, under my breath.

"Yeah, I see him," he answers.

"Maybe…" I don't want to finish the sentence, to say, "Maybe we shouldn't hold hands," but I don't have to.

"Maybe," he says, and lets go, holding his coffee cup with both hands instead. I do the same. "I don't fucking like it, and most days I'd say if he wants to start something, let him." He looks at me. "But I know you want to see what this is all about, not get us kicked out before it even starts."

"Sorry," I say. "I don't like it, either."

"I'll try to be invisible," he says. "Just this once."

I laugh, a little, even though I feel more unhappy than anything else.

Just then a tiny woman in a long swirling skirt stops at our table. "Is it okay if I sit here?" she asks. "Only all the other tables are full."

"Yeah," I say.

"Of course," says Silas.

She smiles and puts her cup on the table and takes the chair next to me. "I thought this would be cool, but the way that guy glared at you, I don't know," she says. She pushes her hair, long and intricately braided, back over her shoulder.

"I guess I'm used to it," I say. It sounds stupid out loud.

"But you shouldn't have to be." She flashes a bright smile at Silas. "I'd want to hold his hand, too."

He snorts and holds one out to shake. "I'm Silas."

She reaches over and shakes, taking his huge olive-skinned hand in her tiny dark brown one. I watch her look at Silas and feel a momentary stab of envy. She's beautiful and curvy and if I were at all inclined towards women, I'd probably be tempted to flirt. And Silas is, at least a little, attracted to women.

She holds a hand out to me and I shake, my pale skin pasty next to hers. I can't even tan to save my life.

"I'm not after your man," she says with a grin, then looks at Silas. "Or yours."

"Alder is nonbinary," Silas says, his voice sounding flat.

"Oh, shit. Sorry," she says. "They/them?"

I nod.

"Cool. I'm Celeste." And that's all she says on the matter, which feels good for some reason.

Then there's a tapping at the mic from on stage and I look up to see the glaring guy there. Of course. It would have to be him running the show. I hope I was wrong about the glare; maybe he just had a bad day, and I just happened to be in line with his scowl.

"Welcome to Re-Awakening the Pan Within," he says. I try to push aside the fact that I already dislike him because of the look he gave me and just listen. He's a decent speaker, and most of his spiel about the history of the Cult of Pan is pretty accurate, or at least speculative in a way that mostly fits current research.

I have a little notebook and pen in my jacket pocket, but I don't get them out; there's nothing exactly new to me in what he's said. And anyway, my plan was to ask the presenters if I could meet with them at a later date if they're open to being interviewed for my research.

He speaks for a good half hour before finally saying, "Let's take a short break now, and then my colleague will get to the main event," and he steps off the stage.

"Well, that wasn't terrible," says Silas. He looks at me. "He seemed to know what he was talking about, more or less."

"More or less," I say.

Celeste looks back and forth between us. "You guys like scholars of Pan or something?"

Silas laughs. "Not me," he says. "Them." He points at me. "And they're not a guy."

Before Celeste can start apologizing, I say, breathing carefully, "My MA research is on the modern worship of Pan." I get it all out in a rush, so I can make sure the whole sentence makes it past my lips.

"I'm just a myth enthusiast and a syrinx player," says Silas.

"Seriously?" says Celeste. Her voice has a faint accent. English received pronunciation, I think, just like my cousins who used to visit in the summers when I was a kid. She points at Silas. "You play the Pan pipes?"

Chapter Seven

"YOU TOLD ME YOU PLAY wind instruments," I say. I'm not angry, of course, but it is a little irritating that it's another thing he left out, just like he didn't tell me his family had a direct connection to ancient Pan worship – even knowing the focus of my research.

"I *do* play wind instruments," he says. "Pretty much anything that isn't brass, and the more ancient the better. I never could get sound out of a tuba."

The mental image of Silas blowing into a giant brass instrument, cheeks puffing up and no sound coming out, makes me laugh.

"What's your favorite?" Celeste says, leaning on the table with both elbows. "I couldn't play an instrument to save my life."

"Obviously, the very manly syrinx is my favorite," he says. "But I've got a Japanese flute that had the loveliest tone."

And now I'm picturing a delicate silver-trimmed wooden instrument in his big, muscular hands and a sudden flush rushes up my neck when I think about what other delicately-sized things he likes to put his mouth on.

"Will you play for me?" I say, hoping I don't sound too childish, too needy.

"I would do anything for you, sweetheart," he says, and out of the corner of my eye I see Celeste roll her eyes, lean back in her chair, and shake her head slightly. She looks away towards the stage.

The glaring guy taps the mike again before I can say anything, and the look he shoots me makes me uneasy.

"Okay, folks, welcome back to Re-Awakening the Pan Within," he says. "For the next hour, we're going to be led on an inner journey by our special guest Ego Arcadia."

Silas chokes on a sip of his coffee and snorts some of it out his nose. I dig in my pocket for a clean tissue, but something about the name is tugging at my mind, aside from its obvious absurdity. A lot of students of Wicca and other neo-paganisms like to choose their own "craft names," and fuck, I get it. I chose a new name for myself, too, when I came out. But "Ego Arcadia"? And then I remember why it's familiar – I have one of his books. It was one of the first ones I read specific to Pan worship, and it made me want to find out more.

"What?" whispers Celeste. "What's funny?"

"Later," Silas says, and she scowls but turns back to the stage.

The other white guy who shot us a slightly less nasty look takes his place behind the mic, and I recognize him now. He's quite a bit older than in the author photo on the back of his book, but now that I'm looking for it, I can see he's the same guy. (And fuck, why does the person whose writings I wanted to follow have to turn out to be one who looks at me with disgust when I hold my boyfriend's hand?) (Oh my God, is Silas my boyfriend?)

The guy has changed out of his ordinary clothes and is now dressed in a toga and sandals – a little more Roman-looking than Greek, if you ask me. I guess it fits the Classical-revival aspect of the evening, but it hardly seems practical for Great Valley in fall, even if it *has* been warmer than usual.

He's got hair that was probably dark blond once, but is now mostly grey, cut in short curls, and he wears a gold laurel wreath on his head. Around his neck is a thick leather cord with a small and probably non-functional set of pan pipes hanging off it.

"Welcome, seekers," he says. His voice is smooth and soothing, the sort of voice you could imagine hypnotizing small children and old ladies. Something about it pricks at the anxiety in my gut, but that's true about almost everything, so I push the feeling aside. It's probably just that the look he shot me earlier gave me a bad impression.

He asks us to close our eyes and imagine ourselves in a green forest, the smell of pine trees all around us. I hear the flare of a match and soft footsteps as someone moves around the room, lighting candles that fill the space with the scent of fir needles. It's not quite pine – a childhood spent in the coniferous forests of Autumn County has made me sensitive to its smells – but it's close enough to add realism to the mental picture.

There's a crackle and then a sound system starts playing soft, whispering music. I recognize the Zamfir album my mother was so taken with when I was a cranky little kid who didn't like to take naps. She'd play that music to get me to fall asleep.

I find myself getting drowsy.

"Imagine the sun is bright and warm, but it's sunset, and soon it will be dark."

I've never been good at these visualization exercises, but something about the guy's voice, the fir scent, and the music draws me in, and I really do picture myself standing in a forest clearing at sunset, warmth quickly fading as the sun drops and stars come out and a big, bright moon rises.

"All around you, there are quiet noises of animals stirring, small creatures in the underbrush. Far away, a wolf howls. And then, a sudden overwhelming fear that is gone almost as soon as you feel it."

Several people in the audience gasp as panic-like anxiety stabs through me and I almost open my eyes. But Silas's hand calms me, warm on the back of my neck, and I relax and the fear is gone. (How did he know I needed him?)

"You don't run," says the man. "Because you know the panic only means *he* is drawing near."

I feel anticipation now, making my breath quicken, and some detached part of my mind is surprised to be so affected. I'm the weirdo who couldn't even be hypnotized by their therapist when they were a kid insisting they were going to grow up to have breasts like Mommy and a penis like Daddy.

"But you know, also, that he is as much a part of *you* as a part of nature. He is inside you. He *is* you, just as much as the wild goat, the pine tree, the wolf that hunts, and the owl that flies on silent wings."

A warm feeling fills me, a feeling of strength and wildness, of oneness with the world.

"He is you and you are him, because he is Pan and Pan means All."

The soothing voice goes on and on, taking us deeper into the forest, where we meet animals and spirits and mythical beings, and finally approach another clearing, lit by the moon and surrounded by twisted pine trees.

Women dance around the clearing, forming a chain, hands caressing and lips meeting, and in the middle, reclining on a bed of pine boughs, a man – goat legs and large curling horns, and huge erect phallus.

Several people in the audience chuckle or giggle or snort and the scene I've been picturing wavers and fades.

The voice goes on, detailing the scene, the feast, the unabashed sensuality – *sexuality* – but the spell has broken for me, and I slowly open my eyes.

The audience sits, transfixed, eyes closed and listening. A few of them shift in their seats as if they're not quite as absorbed as the rest. And Ego Arcadia speaks, mouth close to the mic, eyes slitted open, observing his audience. I don't look away quickly enough, and he sees me watching, smirks, and keeps speaking.

At our table, Celeste listens with her head tipped to one side, resting on one hand, her eyebrows pulled together like she's concentrating on picturing the scene as Ego describes it.

And Silas… Silas watches with his eyes open, no expression on his face. The overhead lights are out, and the candles light his face the way the screen did at the movies, flickering and uncertain, but somehow sharpening his features, turning him from a handsome man to a forest god. His beard – but I thought he had shaved – is picked out in glints of light, and his eyes seem to glow. Curling up from his forehead, the curls of his hair look like horns; no, they *are* horns, so dark they seem to absorb all light until they look like a spiral void on each side of his head.

I must make a noise, because he turns and looks at me, and his eyes flare green, his wide pupils horizontal and almost rectangular like a goat's and even though he still looks like Silas he is *not* Silas. He's…

"Oh fuck," I say and the grey that's been hovering around the edges of my vision creeps in and turns black and the linoleum of the floor is getting closer awfully fast.

Silas's eyes don't have horizontal pupils, and he doesn't have horns, and I'm so mortified at passing out that I want to sink into the floor.

Tears burn behind my eyes, but I hold them back.

The room is still dark, and the soothing voice is still talking about forests and dancing and wild gods.

"Do you want me to take you home?" Silas says quietly. And then Celeste slips back into her chair and I realize I didn't even know she was gone. She hands Silas a cloth and he folds it neatly and presses it to my forehead. Somehow, I'm not sprawled on the cafe floor; I'm sitting in the same chair, only Silas has moved closer so I'm leaning against him.

No one else seems to notice anything is wrong, except Ego, who shoots us an unreadable look, but continues murmuring into the mic.

I take the cloth, cool and damp, and press it to my face, letting the heat of my embarrassment soak into it.

"I'm okay," I say. "I must've just… got to into the visualizing or something." I frown and try to remember what was happening when everything went grey. I remember opening my eyes, but that's all.

"It was pretty intense," says Celeste.

"Sorry," I say. "I also haven't eaten much today."

She shrugs, an impossibly elegant motion. "I thought the whole thing was a bit corny, honestly," she says.

I breathe slowly, in and out, letting Silas's strength hold me up, hoping Ego and his buddy don't glare at us again.

"I'm okay," I say again. "I still want to talk to them after." I look at Silas. "To see if I can interview them for my thesis."

"You want to get some air while we wait?"

I shake my head.

"Okay," he says. "Just tell me if you feel off again."

I nod and we stop talking and wait, and before too long the man in the toga wraps up his visualization, thanks everyone for coming, and mentions he has a book that can be purchased from the coffee shop.

Before I can get up and approach him, he's gone, off to change out of his toga, I suppose. I look around, and the other scowly white guy, the one who gave the preliminary talk, is gone too.

"Maybe his contact info is in his book," Silas says.

"Maybe." I stretch out my neck and sit up straighter, carefully in case I get dizzy. "I have a book of his already, but if this one is different, I want to buy it."

"Hey, it was nice to meet you two," Celeste says. "You ever need any more spiritual advice, I work at the Spiral Gate."

"Oh," I say, still feeling dopey. "Thanks."

"What's the Spiral Gate?" asks Silas.

"Metaphysical bookstore," Celeste answers. "I'm a herbalist there, among other things."

"Cool," says Silas, and there's something in his voice that says he's ready to end the conversation.

She smiles and leaves and I push myself to my feet.

Silas stays close and even though the overhead lights are back on, there's something like a shadow over him, making his hair look longer and curlier. It pricks at my memory.

"Just before I passed out," I say, taking a tentative step and finding that I'm steady enough. "I opened my eyes." I look at him and he's just watching my face, waiting. "Or… I guess I *imagined* opening my eyes."

He tilts his head to look at me and follows close beside me when I head for the counter to see how much Ego Arcadia's book is, like he wants to be sure to catch me if I lose consciousness again.

"You're not sure?" he says.

I shrug. "I *thought* I opened my eyes, but when I looked at you, you had horns, so obviously I was still visualizing, or whatever you'd call it."

"You sure it wasn't real?" He grins. "I *am* pretty horny."

I laugh and something I didn't realize was tight relaxes in my chest. "You also had a beard and horizontal pupils, so I'm pretty sure it wasn't real."

His face is unreadable, despite the grin, but he says, "I don't know, I'd make a pretty good satyr."

"You should get resin horns for Halloween," I say, suddenly feeling playful. "They make some pretty realistic ones."

"Mm," he says. "I'll go as Pan, and you'll be the nymph I'm courting. We can dress you all in leaves and branches, like you're mid-transformation into a tree."

"Probably best not to be too openly queer," I say, glancing back towards the stage to see if Ego or his assistant have reappeared.

"I have cousins in Riverbend. We can spend Halloween there, where there is a significantly lower percentage of homophobes."

I stop because we've reached the counter and the start of the line of people waiting to buy toga guy's book. Ego Arcadia's book. I can at least call him what he wants to be called, even if I think it's kind of a dumb name.

"We never told Celeste why we laughed," I say, not elaborating on what we laughed at in case it offends anyone around us. Because "Ego" is just Latin for "I" and Arcadia is the region of Greece where Pan originated. Basically, it makes it sound like the guy is claiming to *be* Arcadia, or at least to be from there. And okay, maybe it isn't *that* dumb of name, unless you consider the other meaning of "ego."

"Maybe we can go to that store she works at. You might find more books for your thesis, and you could even put up a poster looking for Pan worshippers to interview."

"That might not be a bad idea," I say, and then it's my turn to buy the book. It's called *Pan is All: The New Ancient Faith*, which is not the same title as the other book of his I have. I just hope the contents are different enough to make it worth the money I drop on it.

As we're leaving, the early evening air refreshingly cool on my face, I hear someone call out, "Hey, wait." I ignore it, because why would anyone be looking for me?

Then someone pushes past me to tap Silas on the shoulder. He turns and looks, and so do I, and it's Ego Arcadia – no longer dressed in a toga – and the scowling guy, who never did introduce himself to the audience.

"What can I do for you?" Silas says, sounding like a shopkeeper annoyed when a customer comes in right at the end of the day.

"I saw you in the audience," Ego says. "You seemed to be getting a lot out of the visualization, and I just wanted to let you know I offer one-on-one workshops." I can't help the slight twinge of envy I feel that Ego noticed Silas and not me, when I'm the one who's been studying Pan my whole life. But then I guess Silas has, too.

"Thanks, but I was mostly here to keep Alder company." Silas half-turns towards me. "They're studying the worship of Pan and were hoping to interview you, actually." He looks at me and lets the corner of his mouth curl up. I want to kiss him. "And sign their book."

Ego turns to look at me, and I feel like a bug under a microscope. He's got that same weird look on his face that he had when he noticed I had my eyes open – except that wasn't real, was it? "Oh," he says. "Yes, perhaps we could arrange something." He turns to scowly guy and holds out a hand. "Have you got a pen, Steve? And one of those business cards I told you to bring?"

Steve scowls an even deeper scowl than the one he aimed at me. "I told you, it's Stefan. You make me call you Ego, so you can fucking call me Stefan."

I wonder what that's all about, but keep my mouth shut and just hold out my book for Ego to sign when Stefan hands him a pen, almost stabbing it into the other man's hand.

"Alden, was it?" Ego says, pen poised over the book's title page. I can't read the way he's looking at me, but there's something challenging in it.

"Alder," I reply, too annoyed to get the word stuck in my throat, because I'm pretty sure he got it wrong on purpose. "Like the tree."

"Of course." He signs and then tucks a business card between the pages before handing the book back. "Send me an email. We can do the interview electronically, if you like, or we can meet in person. Just let me know." He turns back to Silas, his look shifting to something more intense, cunning maybe, or calculating, like he's sizing up a valuable antique he just found underpriced at a thrift store. Or, no, not really like that. I don't know. (I just know I don't like it.)

"Please, consider my offer," Ego says. "I think you would make an excellent addition to our group." Again, I feel that stab of envy that Ego wants Silas and not me. I push it aside, because it's stupid.

Silas looks like he wants to tell Ego where to shove it, but he glances at me and then says, "Sure, I'll think about it," and takes the business card Ego's holding out and tucks it into his jacket pocket.

"Excellent," says Ego. "You have strong Pan energy. I felt it resonating in you." He looks sidelong at me and then back at Silas. "I believe I can teach you to use it to gain everything you desire in life." He smiles beatifically and squeezes Silas's shoulder, then disappears back into the crowd. Stefan follows, after staring a heartbeat longer, first at Silas, then at me.

"Well, that was fucking weird," Silas says, something uneasy in his voice.

"Don't you want to learn how to gain everything you desire in life?" I tease, and even though he smiles, there's something troubled in his eyes.

He says, "Do you need me to pretend to be interested in whatever he's selling to get you more material for your thesis?"

"I don't think so." I hold up the book. "Between his books and an interview, I think I'll have enough. I'm not writing my whole thesis on one person."

"The name 'Ego' really suits him," Silas says, which makes me laugh.

"It really does."

The walk to the bus stop clears what fog remains in my head and I feel good by the time we're settled in our seats. I don't feel like I just passed out at all.

"Anyway," says Silas, picking up the threads of the conversation as if we hadn't just spent several quiet minutes walking and waiting. "I'm pretty sure I already have the one thing in life I most desire."

He glances around the bus, which is nearly empty, then puts a hand on my knee and squeezes. I work hard to keep breathing normally. He doesn't need to know how strongly he affects me. Not yet. Not until I can give back as good as I get, and that's not going to happen on public transportation.

I look at him out of the corners of my eyes. "You looked good in a beard," I say. "In my… whatever that was. Visualization weirdness."

"Yeah?"

"It was a little unkempt," I say. "But then again, so is your stubble." I dare to reach out and rub my fingers over his jaw.

"Unkempt!" he says in mock indignation. "I'll have you know I shaved."

"When?" I rub the dark hairs sprouting on his chin.

"This morning." He touches his jaw. "I think. I *meant* to shave this morning." He looks at me. "I might have forgotten."

"Oh well. I guess I'll just have to put up with stubble burn."

He cocks his eyebrows and then, as we're getting up to exit the bus, he says, "Why do you think you'll get stubble burn?"

I wait until we're both on the sidewalk, and then I say, "Because you're going to kiss me until I swoon, and then you're going to take me to bed." And I turn and walk down the block towards my apartment.

"Am I that predictable?" he calls after me, and hurries to catch up.

"You said you'd do anything I want," I say, letting a cheeky tone creep into my voice. "And I want you to kiss me until I swoon."

Chapter Eight

WHEN WE GET INSIDE, I'm suddenly nervous again, so I hang up my jacket, plop my Docs onto the boot tray, and head for the kitchen without looking to see if Silas is still behind me.

I put the book on the counter, next to where I've already set two places for dinner, and open the fridge. Behind me, I hear the soft click of the door latch and then the sound of a jacket being removed.

I was too anxious this morning to enjoy the day off, so I spent the hours before meeting Silas cleaning my apartment and prepping the food I'm about to make. The bowls of cut vegetables make an impressive array next to the stove, and even the pots and pans I'll be using are oiled and ready to go. I flick on the fan over the stove and light the burners.

And then I almost jump out of my skin when Silas comes up behind me and puts a hand on the small of my back.

"How can I help?" he says.

"I'm good," I answer. "Everything's prepped, so…" I wave my hand vaguely at the stove.

"I see that," he says, and leans over to kiss my neck. "If you hadn't just almost passed out from not eating, I'd suggest we skip dinner." His hands slide around my waist and his chest presses against my back. I let myself lean into him for a moment, enjoying the unfamiliar sensation of someone touching me in a way that's intimate when we aren't even fucking.

I can't keep in the sigh that escapes me, and Silas tightens his arms around my waist.

"Are you okay?" he says, his voice gentle in my ear.

I nod. "I'm just… not used to this." I have to pull away to reach the bowl of chicken that's been marinating all day, to get it into the wok before the oil starts smoking.

"Not used to what? Cooking for someone?" His voice is teasing, but kind. "Not used to being hugged?" He hugs me again as I stir the meat.

"Pretty much," I say.

"You might want to *get* used to it, then," he says. "Except maybe the cooking part – I can take turns." He kisses my neck again, right behind my ear, and I can't help but shiver. "Because unless you ask me to leave you alone, I intend to hug you frequently. And kiss you. And hold your hand at the movies."

I twist around to face him. If he's thinking about taking turns cooking, does that mean… (No, Alder, don't think about that. Not yet.) "It's nice," I say, and how lame is that? *Nice*. It's so much more than nice. But if I tell him exactly how good it feels to be wanted as much for myself as for the tightness of my ass, it'll get pathetic real fast. And I want him to *like* me, not feel sorry for me.

"It *is* nice," he agrees. "And, by the way, I'm nervous, too."

I look at him again, and he steps back to give me room at the stove. The water's boiling and I need to add the noodles.

"*You're* nervous?" I say. "You're so… outgoing."

He laughs. "I mostly don't give a shit what people think of me, which helps. But when I'm trying to impress someone, yeah, I get nervous."

I turn back to the stove to stir the chicken and hide my smile. "Are you trying to impress me?"

"Definitely." He puts a hand on my back again, then lets it drop.

"I'm pretty impressed so far," I say, adding one of the bowls of vegetables to the wok and stirring. Silas takes the empty bowl to the sink and washes it.

I gather my courage and say, "For example, you're doing dishes. In my apartment."

He glances at me and one of his dimples appears.

"Do you know how sexy it is when a man helps with dishes?" I ask.

He dries the bowl and sets it aside. "Do you know how sexy it is when someone cooks for you?" he replies.

My betraying flush creeps up my neck, so I concentrate on the food I'm making, adding another bowl of vegetables to the wok and stirring the noodles.

Silas takes the bowl and washes it, like he did for the last one. "This whole room is just packed full of sexiness," he says, and I laugh. Fuck, it feels good. Sure, I'm still nervous, but I'm relaxing because he's not *expecting* anything from me, he's just letting things unfold, and if I don't talk much, he just lets the silence be. It's comfortable in a way I've only ever felt at home, with my immediate family.

And for the last couple of years, not so much even with them.

When the food is ready, I serve up two plates and turn back to the fridge. Silas slides a dish into the sink of soapy water, then asks, "Which side do you want me to sit on?"

"Whichever." I bring the bottle of cider I've taken from the fridge over and struggle with the cap. It's a swing-top, the stopper held in place by heavy wire, and for some reason I've never been able to get the hang of opening them, even though my parents have used them on their bottles since before I can remember.

"Can I?" says Silas, and when I glance up, he's holding out a hand.

"Thanks." I hand the bottle over, slide onto my stool, and point at the food. "Have seconds if you want; I made lots."

He nods but doesn't look up from examining the bottle. "This is Rock Bottom cider," he says. Now he does look up. "You didn't have to splurge on me."

I can't help the grin that comes over my face. Rock Bottom Cidery is one of those artisanal places, and they're won all kinds of awards, especially for their pear cider, which is what happens to be in the bottle he's holding. It's expensive, and it sells out fast.

"Read the back," I say, leaning my chin on my fist to watch him.

He turns the bottle around. "Rock Bottom Cider has been brewed in Autumn County by the Lewis family since nineteen seventy-two," he reads. There's more about the variety of pears and the natural spring water, but that first bit is what I want him to see.

He looks up, eyebrows raised, so I tap my finger on the label.

"Lewis family," he says, reading the bit I'm pointing to again. My grin gets wider as I watch understanding come over his face. "Fuck, I'm slow," he says. "Lewis. Your family owns Rock Bottom Cidery."

"That's us," I say.

He flips the top open and pours into the glasses I've set out – stemless wineglasses because I like the way they fit in my hands.

"Well, now I don't feel so special." He pretends to pout.

"Believe it or not," I say. "I don't have an endless supply. My parents don't make me pay for it, but I only get a few bottles each season. That's my last one until this year's batch is done." I sip mine, and it really does taste award-winning. "Most of it has to be sold to keep the orchards profitable."

"I get that," he says. "My family are sheep farmers, mostly. We eat plenty of mutton, but hardly any lamb."

After that, we talk more about our families and our childhoods, and I even manage to keep up my side of the conversation pretty well. Maybe being nervous about what might happen later helps me be less self-conscious about what's happening now.

(Or maybe it's the alcohol.)

Then, once we've eaten and the leftovers are put away, Silas herds me out of the kitchen.

"You relax while I wash up," he says. I start to protest, and he puts his fingers on my lips. "No arguments. You cooked; I do dishes." Then he kisses me, slow and soft, pulls back, and steers me towards the couch, a second glass of cider in my hand. Once I drink it, I'll have had just enough booze to make me thoroughly buzzed – my parents' cider is not for lightweights – which should make whatever comes next less stressful.

(It will still be stressful.)

And yeah, I know, I shouldn't rely on alcohol to get me through normal human interactions. But social anxiety doesn't let *any* interaction be normal, and until I can get the coping mechanisms my therapist taught me to actually work, I get by however I can.

Because it turns out there's no real cure for social anxiety. It's possible to improve, but it takes time and forcing interaction to "get used to it" can backfire. It can make it worse instead of better. Or at least, that's how it's been for me.

I sit on the couch and relax into the cushions, glass cupped in both hands. The therapist my parents sent me to as a kid told them that me believing I was both boy and girl wasn't something I needed counselling for, that I'd either grow out if it or I wouldn't, but I'd be who'd I be.

Years later my parents sent me to her again, when I hit puberty and suddenly became, in their words, "painfully shy." It's thanks to her – and to my sister Alison, my biggest supporter and best friend – that I eventually came out.

Whereupon my dad said therapy had been a waste of time and money because it had obviously made me worse instead of better.

"You look lost in thought," Silas says, sliding onto the couch next to me.

"Yeah," I say. I look into the clear pale yellow of my drink. "If you ever meet my parents, well… My dad…"

He settles next to me, leaning his shoulder against mine. "Is he…"

I look up and meet his warm brown eyes and the look of compassion he gives me – but not pity – helps me go on.

"He's not a bad guy," I say. "I know he loves me, but…"

"He doesn't get you?"

"He doesn't get me. He doesn't get what nonbinary is and doesn't care to. He just figures I've lived as a guy this long, and I'm not a trans woman, so why not just keep being a guy."

"I'm sorry."

"I think if I was non-gender-conforming but still male-identified, he'd be fine. He didn't like it when I told him I was gay, but he got used to it."

"Is he shitty to you? About being nonbinary?"

I shake my head. "He just refuses to call me anything but…" I don't want to say my legal name, even if it's only one letter different from the name I chose. "But the name he gave me. And he won't use anything but male pronouns for me. When I try to explain, he just keeps saying 'you'll always be my little boy'." I lean my head on Silas's shoulder, and he shifts so I can get more comfortable. "I tried telling him I'd never actually been a boy, but he doesn't listen."

"What about your mom?" He puts an arm around me, and I snuggle closer. He smells like the forest and the peanut sauce we just ate.

"She's better. Except she never uses my pronouns at all if she can avoid it. And she shortens my name to 'Ald' instead of choosing a version."

He kisses the top of my head. "If I ever make a mistake," he says, his breath warm on my scalp, "Please remind me."

"You've been great," I say. "You've been perfect. My sister's been perfect. I guess I'm lucky that way."

"I want you to be happy, Alder," he says, and he puts a hand under my chin so I look at him. "I know we've only known each other for what, a week?"

"Not even." But I smile.

"Not even a week. But I feel…" He looks away and shrugs. "I just really like you. You feel… You feel like we fit together, you know?" He sighs. "Sorry, I know I can be too much sometimes. My oldest brother says I fall in and out of love too easily. That I meet someone, fall for them, then realize they weren't who I thought they were, and that's that."

My stomach clenches. Is that what's happening? He thinks I'm the perfect match, and that's why he's being so amazing, but when he finds out who I really am, he'll stop liking me? I look back at my drink, then take a long sip. If this is going to be over soon, I intend to get everything I can out of it. If I'm going to end up in tears, I want some amazing sex first.

When I set the glass on the table and turn back to him, he's watching me and something in his face stops me from leaning over and kissing him, from suggesting we get naked and head for the bedroom.

"What?" I say.

He shakes his head. "This doesn't feel like that."

"What?" Oh, yeah, I'm eloquent. You'd think the two glasses of cider I've had would've loosened my tongue at least a little bit.

"Being with you. It doesn't feel like falling for someone just because they pay attention to me," he says. "And I don't think you can be anyone other than exactly yourself."

I frown and he smiles in response.

"I'm saying I don't think I'm idealizing you, that I'm not falling for you because I think you're someone you're not," he says.

Only one part of that sinks in. "You're falling for me?"

He tilts his head. "Is that so surprising?"

I want to look back into my drink, but I finished it and put the glass on the table. It takes too long to find words, but he waits, playing with a bit of hair near my neck.

"I guess," I finally say. (Really? "I guess"? Fuck.) "I told you my last relationship wasn't great."

"You don't have to talk about anything you don't want to."

"Two years ago, I finally got the guts to break up with him." I stare at my hands, clenching and unclenching them in my lap. "That last day, when I was trying to get all my stuff out of his place, he said…" I can't force the words out.

"Hey. Sweetheart," Silas says. "It's okay. You don't have to say anything."

"I want to." I keep staring at my hands. They're thin, my fingers long and skinny, but they're strong. *I'm* strong. Or I can be. "I want you to know what kind of person I am, so you can go ahead and stop falling for me now and save us both a lot of grief." I snap my mouth shut, realizing I've said things out loud I didn't mean to say, things I didn't really mean at all.

"Okay," he says softly. "But I don't think you're going to reveal anything that'll make me stop liking you."

I bark out a strangled laugh. "He told me nobody likes a freak, and I was lucky he put up with me as long as he had." I wait for his reply.

For a while, he just strokes my hair. Then he says, "That's it?"

That makes me look at him and once I meet his eyes I can't look away.

"You're not a freak," he says. "And I think you know that. I think you're actually very happy with who you are, but you're afraid of being judged."

I open my mouth to answer, but he corrects himself. "No, not of being judged, of being *noticed*." He touches my face, tracing my jaw with careful fingers. "You want to be invisible, and it's hard to be invisible when you're different." He smiles, just a gentle curve of his lips.

"You're a redhead," he says, and tugs my hair. "Which is remarkable in itself. But you're also nonbinary, which is just unusual enough that people do notice. So, you wear nondescript clothes and try to look enough like a guy no one will comment, but not so much like a guy that you can't face yourself in the mirror."

It's hard to breathe. I want to be angry, but I can't. He's right. He's read me so well he's telling me things about myself I didn't even realize.

His fingers touch my lips and brush softly over them. "I'm surprised you wore that satyr t-shirt in public," he says. "Unless you were trying to keep people's attention off your body by distracting them with the lewd ancient Greek imagery."

"I was trying to be bold," I say. "It backfired."

"It got *my* attention." He grins, but then it fades. "Unless you don't *want* my attention." He straightens up, just a little, but it's enough to feel like he's pulling away from me.

"See," I say. "I'm all kinds of fucked up. I want you; I want to *be* with you, but I'm afraid to do anything… emotionally attaching. If you'd just fucked me and then ghosted me, I'd know how to act."

His black eyebrows pull together. "So, you're saying you don't know what to do when someone values you for more than sex?"

I shrug. "I'm a weirdo who sometimes wears a bra so I can pretend I have tits. I *like* having a small cock, when I'm supposed to want it to be huge."

He cocks his head. "You're nonbinary, Alder," he says. "Right? So, neither of those things makes you weird. I mean, they wouldn't even if you were a cis man or a trans woman or anything else." Then he leans closer and presses a kiss to my cheek.

"Besides," he says, his voice low and rumbly. "I think you'd look spectacular with perfect little tits."

Chapter Nine

I STARE AT HIM, BREATHING HARD. "You what?" I choke out.

He turns so he's facing me directly, one knee bent so his leg is tucked next to mine on the couch.

"I think you're perfect exactly as you are," he says. "And I'm very much looking forward to seeing you naked." His hand squeezes my knee. "But I like *you*." He pokes me lightly on the chest. "Whatever bits and pieces you have. And if you want breasts, I'm all for it."

The entire surface of my skin is burning and my heart's beating too fast. "I thought about HRT," I finally say. I put both hands flat on my chest. Flat on my *flat* chest. My pecs are toned, but I'm wiry, not big. "But there are too many effects I *don't* want."

He puts a hand over mine, still pressed to my chest.

"Like what?" he says.

"Mostly that there's a good chance I could stop getting erections, and even if I didn't, the way they feel could change."

"I can see that might be a problem."

"I like my dick exactly as is it."

His lips curve distractingly, and he moves his hand up to my collarbone, then back down, pushing my hand aside so he's pressing directly on my chest. "I like your dick exactly as it is, too," he says. "What about implants?"

I shrug. "Maybe." I bite my lip and put my hand on top of his, moving it so he's cupping my pec as if I had really, *really* small breasts. "I think that what I want most is…" I look at his eyes, and away.

"What?" His thumb grazes my nipple, and it feels… like not enough.

"I want *that* –" and I nod at his hand, "– to feel… arousing."

"You want sensitive nipples?"

I nod. "I mean, I'd like little tits, too, but mostly it's the nipples."

"I know I'm not qualified to give advice, but what about a really small dose of HRT?"

"Maybe. I don't know."

"Whatever you decide," he says, his face going serious. "I'm not going anywhere." His thumb brushes my nipple again and there's just a tiny bit of response, a slight hardening and a little zap of sensation. Like maybe I can feel more, if it's him touching me. Which is stupid, sure, but let me have my fantasies. (I have so many fantasies.)

Then he leans closer, and I lift my face to meet him, open my lips under his, and I'm the one who slips my tongue into his mouth.

We sit on the couch a long time, just kissing, tilting our heads slowly one way, then the other, until we fit as closely together as possible. He doesn't move his hands anywhere below my waist but where he does touch me his skin on mine gives me goosebumps and I want to press myself as close to him as I can.

I dare to slip my hands under his shirt, first yanking it out of the waistband of his jeans. His hair is crisp under my palms, the curls tickling me as I touch him, and I want to feel that under *my* chest, to feel the tickle of his hair on every part of me. His muscles are much bulkier than mine, even though we're the same height, and I want to see if he has supermodel shrink-wrapped abs or a normal strong belly. I wasn't paying that much attention to his belly last time I had occasion to pull his pants down and his shirt up. My hands find definition overlaid by bulk – not fat, but also not dehydrated lean.

"I want to see you naked," I say, and immediately blush.

He chuckles and rests his forehead on mine. "The feeling is very mutual," he says.

"So?" I say.

"Come here." He stands up and holds out his hands. I let him pull me to my feet, pull me into his arms until there's no space between us. Then he turns and backs slowly across the kitchen and into the hall.

"The bedroom's that way," I say, pointing left when he steers us right.

"But the bathroom's this way," he replies, "And I noticed that you have a very large bathtub."

I don't say anything else, a little confused and a lot aroused. Does he think I need a shower? Has my deodorant stopped working? I try to smell my pits without being obvious about it and all I can smell is his forest scent.

"You want me to take a bath?" I finally say. Then I remember how he made me wait for him to wash before I went down on him. Maybe it's *himself* he wants to bathe first. Or maybe… if he wants to fuck me, maybe he wants to flush me out.

"I want to try out your huge bathtub," he says. "Together." He kisses my nose. "I want to relax and digest that delicious meal and soak in the tub, and very slowly explore every part of your pretty pink freckled skin." I flush again. "Just like that." His fingers trace my cheekbone, which I know must be bright pink.

He kisses my forehead. "I want to take my time with you, Alder," he says. "And when we finally do…" He pauses.

"Fuck," I say. "When we finally fuck."

His mouth twitches up on one side. "When we finally fuck, I want it to be perfect. But also…"

We're in the bathroom now and he leans away to put the stopper in the bath, a huge old clawfoot that's probably big enough for a foursome.

"I want you to understand that I want more than your body." He turns on one tap, then the other. "I want *you*."

I toy with the top button of his shirt. It's deep blue and somehow makes his eyes look darker brown.

"You meant it, then, when you said you want to be my boyfriend?"

"I meant it." His hands slip under the hem of my hoodie and my t-shirt and find my skin. "I want to be your *friend* friend, too," he says. "Your companion. Your partner."

I don't know what to say to that. I want those things, too, but I'm also afraid they'll be temporary, that once he's been inside me at last, he'll lose interest. But, like I already decided, if that's what happens, at least I'll get laid once or twice. (Such an optimist, me.)

"Can I take your shirt off?" he asks, and I pull my thoughts away from their pathetic turn and concentrate on the sexy man in my bathroom.

"Yeah," I say, and it comes out breathy.

He pulls my hoodie and tee off in one go and tucks them over a towel rack – this bathroom is overstocked with towel racks, like whoever built it couldn't decide what to do with the extra wall space and just filled it with things to hang stuff off of. Like they wanted to be able to hang a whole linen closet of towels at once.

My skin instantly gets goosebumps, but they subside as he runs his hands over my back.

"Can I take *your* shirt off?" I say, hooking my finger over a button and popping it free of the buttonhole.

"Please do," he says and when I've got enough buttons open, he reaches behind his neck and pulls it off, tucking it with mine on the closest towel rack.

I lean back far enough to look at his chest, to run both hands over it. He's very hairy, but it's surprisingly soft under my hands, curly and black, carpeting his pecs and making a line down his abs that disappears under the waistband of his jeans.

"Where does this go?" I say, tracing a finger down the furry path, over his belly button, and stopping at the button of his jeans.

"Mmm…" he says, and mimics my movement, running a finger over my chest and abs, over the much sparser hair there, and stopping just above my waistband.

Suddenly bold, I step away from him and tug open my own fly. I hold his eyes with my own as I pop open one button after another until a triangle of purple boxer shorts shows at my crotch.

"Oh, sweetheart," he says, his voice mostly breath.

I take another step back and ease my jeans over my hips and let them fall to my ankles, leaving me wearing only my boxers.

"Your turn," I say.

He grins and pops his fly button, slides down the zipper, and tugs the denim slowly down. He's wearing black boxers with little green aliens printed on them and he's already got a distinct bulge. Do I really excite him that much? (He excites me that much, but my bulge is much less noticeable.)

When he steps out of his jeans, I let my gaze drop down to his legs. They're like pillars, muscular and sturdy, olive-skinned and dark-haired. I want to touch them. But not yet.

He watches me look at him, and then he hooks his thumbs into the waistband of his boxers and pulls them slowly down. His pubic hair is dense and dark and curly, and I want to bury my face in it. His cock stands proud, thick and hard, and I remember the feel of it in my mouth, the way his foreskin slipped over his head, and the way he moaned when I sucked.

"Your turn," he says, deep and throaty.

I remember to breathe. For a moment all those times come back when I was made fun of in the showers after gym class until I just skipped showering and went stinking and sweaty back to class. But then I remember Silas looking at me, at my cock, and telling me I'm perfect, and then taking me in his mouth and seeming to get as much enjoyment out of pleasuring me as I did.

I lick my lips, slowly, and pull off my boxer briefs, let them fall to the floor, and kick them to one side.

"Fuck, Alder," he says, taking a half-step towards me. Then, "Shit!" as he turns and grabs for the taps on the bathtub, and I laugh, because it's full and the bathroom fills with the sound of water in the overflow drain.

"We'll just have to get in one at a time," I say.

"And very slowly," he replies. Then he looks at me and holds out his hand. I take it and he tugs me closer and closer until we're almost touching. I can feel the heat of his skin and the tickle of his chest hair. He puts a hand on the side of my face, sliding his fingers into my hair, and shakes his head.

"You're so beautiful, Alder," he says. "So fucking perfect." Then he grins. "I feel like a monster next to you, all bestial and hairy."

I close the last bit of space between us, so his chest presses on mine and his cock bumps mine before pressing into my belly.

"I have a thing for monsters," I say, and point to a framed painting of a satyr by a local artist that hangs across from the bathtub.

He chuckles and kisses me, and the water is no longer running down the overflow by the time we pull apart.

"You first," he says, so I step slowly into the tub, easing myself down to let the excess water escape without sloshing over the side. I stretch out and lean back.

He steps in and eases himself down to sit at the other end. The taps are in the middle, so it's comfortable for both of us. He runs his hands over my legs under the water.

"Why Pan?" he says, tucking my calves over his thighs and leaning back to watch me.

"What?" When will I stop answering everything with a surprised one-word question?

"Why study Pan? Neo-pagans worship lots of gods."

I consider how to answer. "In fourth grade we did a unit on mythology, and we had to make a poster about a Greek or Roman god. It had to have a drawing and a little write up about them and one or two of their myths. I didn't even have to think about it." I move so my foot is resting on his belly and dig my toes into his hair.

"When I got older, I… I guess it's because in the myths he's… he's both strong and gentle, aggressive and sweet. And he pursues men as well as women."

"Are you bi? Or pan? I mean, I am…"

"Not really. I think women are beautiful, but I've never wanted to fuck any." I let myself blurt out, "I think I just really like cock," and he laughs.

"I'm glad for that," he says.

"Anyway, I don't really know why, but Pan's kind of become a sort of patron deity for queer people of all kinds."

"What about Hermaphroditus?" he says, his fingers feeling out the shape of my knee. I push my foot up from his belly to his chest and he catches my ankle in his other hand and kisses the pad of my foot.

"Was he… they… actually worshipped?" I ask. "I've read the myths. How the gods combined him and the nymph he was courting because she loved him so completely."

"Small cults, probably," he says. "But you're right about Pan. My family knows him as literally the god of all – all shapes and sizes and sexes and genders. We even have legends about him changing sex that you won't find in any of the standard books on Greek myth." He chuckles and I love the sound. I close my eyes to absorb it better. "It doesn't even matter that the name Pan and the word that means 'all' derived from different roots, originally."

"Do you have, like, priests, or is it just individual people honoring your gods?"

He kisses my foot again and rubs his thumb over my toes. That should not feel so sexy.

"We have priests. Anyone who feels called to serve that way can do an apprenticeship, but..." He hesitates and I almost open my eyes. "People who are... not... not cis-het, I guess, queer people, and especially trans people, are very strongly encouraged to become priests."

Then I do open my eyes, but I don't know how to frame the next question.

"If you were part of my family, you'd be asked to serve," he says. "You'd be... honored, I guess. Considered semi-divine, almost."

I feel drowsy and content and let my eyes fall closed again. "Is that why you like me?" I ask. "Because I'm sacred to your people?"

He strokes the top of my foot and down my leg. "I liked you before I knew you were nonbinary." I want to press, to ask more, but for now, it's enough.

"Can I interview you?" I ask instead. "For my thesis?" I open my eyes when I feel the water move and his thighs slide under my legs.

He kneels in front of me, my legs hooked over his, and leans on the edge of the tub, an arm on each side of my head. "Of course," he says. "You can do anything you want to me."

"Silas," I say. I don't have a reason; I just want to feel the sound of his name in my mouth.

"Mm?" He leans closer and kisses me, but just barely. The end of his cock bumps my stomach, and I wonder if he's been hard this whole time, or if he just got hard again, just now. I know I've been hard this whole time.

"Kiss me?" I say and reach up to lace my hands behind his neck, to pull his head down to mine. His mouth is hot and hungry, but I match him for heat and hunger, stroking my tongue alongside his and making a complaining noise when he lifts his head away.

"Can I ask you something?" he says, shifting closer so I'm almost in his lap.

I nod.

"Something sexual?" He sounds uncertain.

"Of course." I shove anxiety down, hoping he's not going to suggest a kink I'm not into.

"Do you prefer to top or bottom?" he asks, avoiding my eyes. "Or are you versatile?"

I lick my lips. It's an easy answer but I want it to be the *right* answer. Would I lie just so he'd still like me? (Yeah, I might.) "Bottom," I finally say, opting for honesty. "I have topped, and I will if you really want, but I don't really like to."

"Oh," he says, breathing out with a sigh. "That's good, because I prefer to top."

I crack a grin. "I like cock, and I like getting fucked. Does that make me a twink?"

He laughs and pulls me closer. "You're too smart to be a twink." He pulls me up so I'm straddling his lap and slides a hand down to my ass. I rock my hips so my cock slides next to his and nip his earlobe when I feel his hand tighten on my butt cheek.

"Can I touch you?" he murmurs into my neck.

"You *are* touching me."

"I mean *here*," he says, and his hand moves lower so the tip of one finger brushes my asshole. I have to work hard to hold back a moan.

"Fuck yes," I say. "You don't have to ask."

"I *want* to ask." His finger presses harder and fuck I want him inside me. I know I'm ready for him, for his fingers at least. "I want to hear that you want me," he says. "That you want me to touch you." His voice is almost pleading. "Alder, I want to fucking worship you."

I lean away to look into his face. "I want you Silas," I say.

His finger presses harder, and I feel my asshole start to open for it.

"I want you," I repeat, and grab his hair, pulling his mouth to mine.

His finger slides inside me, slowly, carefully, because there's no lube and he doesn't want to hurt me. He massages me, gently, inside, circling me.

"Gods, you're so…" He doesn't finish whatever he was about to say. "Alder."

"More," I say.

He pushes farther in, still slow and careful, and I open for him, and moan because it feels too good to be silent.

"Alder…"

"More."

He's as deep as he can get without changing our positions, so he pulls out, grabs the bar of soap and lathers his hand. When he reaches for my ass again, he presses two fingers into me and I cry out, torn between pushing my hips forward to rub my cock on his and pushing my ass backwards to meet his fingers.

With the help of the soap, he buries two fingers up my ass until I feel him bump my prostate, rub against it, then probe deeper.

He's breathing hard, as excited as I am, as turned on as I am.

"Silas," I say, again, just to say it.

"Alder." His free hand cradles the back of my neck. "Can I take you to bed, sweetheart?"

"Fuck yes. Take me to bed. Now. Please, Silas."

Chapter Ten

WE LEAVE A TRAIL OF WET footprints down the hall to my bedroom, barely taking the time to dry off before falling into bed.

I can't get close enough to him, can't get my mouth, my hands, my skin everywhere I want at once. My breath is ragged, and I keep making needy sounds, but I don't care. Let him think I'm desperate. I *am* desperate.

"I want you," I tell him, again and again, and every time I say it, he touches me somewhere else, sliding his hands over me like he wants to memorize the shape of me.

His mouth is hot on my skin, leaving burning kisses down my neck to my collarbone and across my chest. He pauses to touch the tip of his tongue to my nipple, and I swear I feel it more than I did before, that it hardens for him when he sucks gently on the tiny nub.

Then he follows my abs to my belly button, and lower, until his tongue slides over my cock and then he sucks one of my balls into his mouth, holds it for a moment, and lets it slide out again.

"Fuck, you taste good," he says into my thigh.

I grab his hair in both hands, not wanting him to stop, but also wanting other things.

"Silas," I say. I can't seem to stop gasping out his name, but it feels right on my tongue. "Come back here so I can touch you."

He kisses his way back up my belly and my chest and takes my other nipple between his teeth and I feel it like a zap of electricity to my crotch.

"Oh fuck," I say.

"Okay?" he murmurs as he lets go and works his way up to my neck.

"Oh, yes," I say. "Very okay."

He moves a hand down my thigh, and I wrap my leg around him.

"You have lube?" He watches my face, as if looking for a reaction, like maybe I'll have changed my mind.

"On the floor between the bed and the nightstand," I say.

He raises his eyebrows but reaches down and finds the bottle. He laughs when he lifts it up to the table.

"That's a lot of lube," he says. And it is; the bottle is huge, which is why I keep it on the floor.

"It was on sale," I say. "And it has a pump top."

"Good for one-handed use," he says, and grins.

"Condoms are in the top drawer."

"Mm." He kisses my neck, then my mouth, taking it like he's proclaiming me his property, and I'm completely willing. I open my lips, draw his tongue in, and grab the big muscles of his ass with both hands.

He shifts his weight so I have to let go with one hand, but that's okay; I curl my fingers around his cock instead and it's his turn to let out a needy sound.

When he reaches for the lube, I let my knee fall to one side so when he slides his hand between my legs, he has lots of room.

The cold of the lube on my ass startles me and he breaks our kiss to touch my face.

"Okay, sweetheart?"

"Just cold." I trace his lips with one finger and close my eyes as he rubs circles around my asshole.

"Tell me if you want me to stop," he says, swirling fingers pressing against me. One fingertip slips inside, and I gasp and rock my pelvis, wanting more, wanting everything he'll give me.

"I don't want you to stop," I say, and reach behind me for the lube so I can slide my hand over his erection, so I can tease him until he can't resist fucking me.

He moves as slowly as he did in the bath, slipping first one finger and then two into me, pushing gradually deeper until his thick fingers are as far into me as they'll go.

"You feel so good, sweetheart," he says, pushing himself up on his free arm to look at me. "Fuck, look at you." He sounds almost reverent, like I'm a holy relic or a piece of art, and he pushes himself up farther until he's kneeling between my legs, one hand gently fucking me with his fingers and the other stroking my belly, my thigh, my hip. He leans awkwardly to reach the lube, and his fingers slide most of the way out.

I make a complaining sound, and he moves back into place, pushing his fingers deep to massage my prostate, to rub me from the inside. And then he slides his other hand, slippery with lube now, over my cock and I try to hold in the desperate sound that works to escape my throat.

"Let it out, sweetheart," he says. "Make as much noise as you want and let me know I'm doing a good job."

I open my eyes, not realizing I've squeezed them shut, and look up at him, muscular, hairy, and hot as fuck, kneeling over me, fucking me, concerned to be making me feel good. "Can you do that for me, sweetheart?" he says. "Can you stop trying to hold back?"

I nod, feeling drunk. Sex drunk. "Just don't stop," I say.

"I won't." His hand slides over me and I remember I'm supposed to be reciprocating, that I wanted to tease him until *he* loses his inhibitions. I can hardly think with the way he's making me feel.

I slip my fingers loosely over his cock until I find his foreskin, pulled back from his head with how swollen and hard he is. I play with the soft skin, tease the head of his cock, press my fingertip to his slit until he's gasping.

"I'm not going to last long if you keep doing that," he says.

"Then you better fuck me quick," I say. "Because I'm not going to last long, either."

He doesn't say anything to that, he just keeps working his fingers in my ass, and whatever he's doing feels incredible. I know I'm going to come any second now, and realize he has no intention of fucking me. Not yet. Like he's already told me more than once, he wants to go slow.

I look up at him with the new realization that he really *is* serious. He wants everything to be perfect, and he doesn't just want to fuck me. He wants… I think he wants to *love* me.

And then I can't think at all, because his hands on me, his fingers fucking me faster now, and his fingers sliding over my cock, are pushing me over the edge until I have to yell out, loud, and spurt all over my belly, just managing enough presence of mind to keep stroking him, squeezing and tugging and teasing, and seconds after I come, he does, too, with a deep groan and the patter of spunk hitting my skin.

For a moment neither of us moves; we just breathe. I listen to his breaths grow deeper and slower, and then I open my eyes. (When did I close them again?)

His smile now is soft as he looks at me, his eyes roving over me, but always returning to my face.

"Sweetheart," he says.

I make myself uncurl my fist from his cock. "Silas."

"I love how you say my name." His fingers slide out of my ass, and reaches for the box of tissues on the table next to the lube. He cleans his fingers and wipes his cock, then pulls out more tissues to wipe away the puddle of spunk on my belly and chest. His touch is gentle, caring, and it feels so nice I don't even protest when he wipes lube off my ass.

Then he settles next to me and tucks me against his chest. "Was that okay?" he says.

Surely he can tell by the noises I was making, by the fact that I came all over myself, that what we just did was not merely *okay*.

Maybe he thinks I was faking. Except I don't think I *could* fake with him. I mean, it's possible to come and not enjoy it, I guess. (Don't ask me how I know.)

I nestle closer to him, wanting this sweetness to last forever. God (whichever one is listening), please tell me this really is real. (Let me have this.) (Please.)

"That was very okay," I say. "It was very much better than okay." And then it occurs to me that he might be asking because it wasn't okay for him. I can't look at his face, but I manage to ask, "Was it okay? For you?"

He kisses my forehead. "Like you said, very much better than okay."

"Will you stay?" I still can't look at him.

"I'm not going anywhere." He tucks the covers carefully over me. "Except the can. I *am* going to have to piss soon."

I laugh at that and roll over so he's spooning me. "Just make sure you come back," I say, stifling a yawn.

"I will always come back," he murmurs into my ear. "Always."

He's gone when a ray of sun slips through the curtains to poke me in the eye. Just like last time. But when I push the covers back and sit up, I listen. And just like last time, I smile when I hear the whistle of the kettle and the sound of water pouring into my French press.

I stretch, feeling decadent to be waking up to a lover making me coffee on a Monday morning. But I don't have class until afternoon, so there's no rush. I can enjoy the happy butterflies in my stomach and the relaxed, open feeling in my asshole that tells me clearly I was fucked skillfully recently, even if it was only his fingers.

(*Only* his fingers; his fingers are very very good at fucking.)

It feels strange to be cared for after. And I know it's fucking pathetic that it feels strange, but there it is. I've had exactly one other real relationship in my life (oh, fuck, am I in a *relationship?*), and it started great and ended badly, and I realized afterwards that he never actually wanted me, he just wanted his ideal version of me, which bore less and less resemblance to who I actually was the longer we were together.

I can look back now and realize the crumbling of that relationship wasn't my fault, that I should have left long before I did. The two years since, I've spent putting myself back together, rediscovering the things I loved before I let him convince me I didn't.

And I spent those years letting random men fuck me because it was the only way I felt like I was worth anything.

So even if this turns out not to be real, if Silas turns out not to be who he seems to be, or if he realizes I'm not who he thinks I am, it hasn't all been for nothing. I've had good sex, and not just *good* sex, but sex where the other person cared about me. Cared about *me*. Even if it's only for a little while, at least I know what it feels like to be valued for myself, to be the object of tenderness.

I don't dare think about being loved. (I *want* to think that maybe I'm loved.)

Finally, I get out of bed, find some clothes, and go to the bathroom to brush my teeth. I rub a hand along my jaw and decide I can go another day without shaving.

The tub is still full of water from last night, and I flush thinking about how Silas touched me, how he said he wanted to worship me. I reach into the cold water and pull out the plug.

When I walk into the kitchen and see him sitting at the counter, two mugs, a jar of honey, a bottle of cream, and the French press in front of him, flipping through the book on Pan worship, it hits me. I'm falling for him. I'm falling very fast and very hard, and I have no desire to even try to stop myself.

He looks up, and smiles, and I'm filled with warmth. I smile back and we grin like idiots at each other.

"Good morning," he says, and I slide onto the stool across from him.

"You're still here," I say, and fuck, Alder, why did you say something so stupid?

"So I am," he says, and reaches out to push the plunger down on the French press and pour us each a big mug of coffee.

He taps the cover of the book with his finger. "This guy has some interesting points in here," he says.

"Oh yeah?" I add honey to my mug, then cream, and stir. The first sip tastes like heaven.

"Mm." He sips his own coffee, black. "He's got some stuff dead wrong, too, but there's lots of good material." He sips again. "If you wanted to start a religious practice," he says. "And I should say that my idea of 'wrong' might just be 'different' according to what I learned from my family."

"Who have an unbroken line to the original worship of Pan." I take another sip of coffee and let the steam soak into my eyelids, wondering when I decided to just believe Silas regarding his family, and not dwell on the improbability of it.

"So our traditions say," he says. "But there's also the possibility that there were different beliefs and practices, even in ancient times."

"Well, I'll be interested to compare." And I smile, because we're talking like classmates, like fellow scholars with research to conduct. Which we are, of course, but we were also just naked and moaning only last night.

"I was thinking," he says, and I raise my eyebrows to let him know I'm listening.

"I might take that guy up on his offer," he says.

"Mr Ego?"

He snorts and touches my hand, stroking one finger from my wrist to my knuckles. Such a simple touch has no business feeling so good.

"Now, now," he says, pretending to chide. "He certainly *has* an ego."

"I know," I say. "I, of all people, should know to just call people what they want to be called. It's just…"

"A stupid name."

"I guess Alder is a stupid name too, for some people. I named myself after a tree."

He shrugs. "I like trees. Anyway, I admit I'm curious about his practice, even though there's something a bit off about him."

"Off how? I liked him, dumb name and all. It was the other guy, Stefan, who felt off to me." (Wait, did I like him?)

"That's because he glared at us like he thought queer people shouldn't exist in public. Or at all, probably."

"That's part of it, sure. But you don't have to do this on my account. I plan to email him an interview once I talk to my advisor about what questions would be best. Assuming my proposal is okay." I turn the book towards me to look at the cover. The illustration is a stunning watercolor of Pan playing his pipes and I wonder if it says anywhere who the artist is.

"I might just send an interview now, anyway," I say. "I can always send a follow up later."

"You're cute when you're scholarly," he says.

I stick my tongue out at him. "So you're going to join his group?" I feel I little left out, I guess, that I don't have that option.

He shrugs. "I don't know that I'll go that far. But I'll meet with them." He pauses, staring out the window, or at least in the general direction *of* the window. "I should probably let my family know he and his group exist. It could just be a coincidence that a group of Pan worshippers has formed in

Arcadia County where… well, where my family is." He focusses back on my face. "They'll want to know what he's up to."

"Is his group in Arcadia? I thought they were here in Autumn County."

He flips the book over to where there's a bio of the author and a photograph of him, complete with toga and gold laurel wreath and syrinx on a leather strap. And the bio says he's raising money to buy the farm he's renting in Arcadia County, to form the world's first pagan commune.

Except I'm pretty sure it's *not* the first, though I couldn't name any off the top of my head. Give me a few minutes online and I could have a list, though, I'm pretty sure.

"Do you think his group could be… what, a threat to your family? Should I interview your people if they're supposed to be secret? Should you even have told me about them?" (I'm glad he told me.)

He's contemplating his half-empty coffee mug when I look up from the book.

"It's not the safety of my family I'm worried about, and our existence might not be *known*, but it's not really a secret."

"There's a difference?"

One of his shoulders lifts and falls. "Maybe. I did plan to make sure it was okay before I tell you too much." He flashes me a quick smile. "And before I invited you to a feast."

I return his smile. "I'd very much like to go to a feast," I say. "Maybe I'll even let you convert me."

"How can you make a religious conversion sound like a forbidden sex rite?" He leers, joking.

"I'd be more likely to convert if it *was* a sex rite," I say. "And we *are* talking about Pan." I point at a framed poster from the Great Valley Museum of the same ceramic vessel depicted on my lewd t-shirt, only it's a photograph of the artifact and not a line drawing. The satyr with his massive hard-on is still clearly visible, though. Apparently, the poster was the Museum gift shop's biggest seller that year.

Silas laughs. "This is true." He finishes his coffee in one long draft and sets the mug down. "But, Alder, there are things I can't tell you, things I can't show you. Not without permission from the elders. Things that *could* be threatened by the world finding out about them."

Chapter Eleven

Okay, I admit I feel a little resentful that there are things Silas believes he can't tell me, and that he'd admit that fact but then won't tell me what they are. My curiosity overwhelms my annoyance, but no matter how I badger him, how I lick his neck or slide my hand teasingly down the front of his pants, he won't reveal any more.

He moves away from me, laughing, and says, "I will tell you everything I *can* tell you, sweetheart, I promise." He catches my hands when I try to grope him again, when I try to make myself look seductive. And sure, it's a game, but I do really want to know what he's keeping from me.

He pulls me close to trap me against his chest, and I pretend to pout.

"I thought you wanted to be my boyfriend," I say. "Boyfriends aren't supposed to keep secrets."

He takes my lower lip, stuck out in a mock sulk, between his teeth, gently, then turns the motion into a scorching kiss. When he leans back to look at me, I've forgotten what we were talking about.

"When I get permission, I'll tell you," he says, his palms warm on my back. "I meant what I said. I'm serious about you, Alder. About us."

"I want to believe that," I say, all the teasing suddenly gone out of me.

"Believe it." He kisses my nose. "I know you've been hurt." His hand cups the back of my head like he's holding a baby bird, soft and careful. "And I'm going to do everything I can to make sure you're not hurt again."

"What about you? Have you been hurt?"

"Only by my own expectations," he says, his lips twisting into a self-deprecating smile.

"What does that mean?"

"It means… I fall in love too easily, because I always think people are better than they are. I've never had a relationship last more than a few months, no matter how hard I work at it." He pauses, considering. "Or maybe it's just that I'm too much. When I meet someone I want to get to know, I tend to go all-in right away."

The ache of anxiety settles in my belly again. If his words were meant to be reassuring, they're having the opposite effect. But maybe he's just trying to be honest.

"Are you sure you're not doing the same thing now?" I don't want to say it, to make him realize he's making another mistake, that he's expecting too much of me, because I want to believe what's building between us is real.

Why the fuck can't I just stop doubting and accept that maybe someone really does want to be with me? (Because it will hurt when he doesn't, that's why. Better to get the disappointment over with.)

His smile turns gentle, directed at me now, not at himself. "I'm sure," he says. "I'm trying very hard to go slow, to not overwhelm you, to let you show me who you are instead of deciding I already know."

I can accept that he believes that to be true, at least, even if it's hard to think that I might be an exception to his usual pattern.

"And now," he says, "As much as I'd like to spread you out on that couch," he nods towards the living area, "And make you say my name in that breathy, sex-drunk way you do…" He pauses to kiss my neck. "I really do have to get to class." He studies my face, and I try not to look too needy.

"I suppose I do, too," I say. "My thesis advisor is the prof."

He keeps studying me for a moment, then says, "I promise I'm not making a mistake with you, Alder. I promise this is real."

I make myself smile and try to believe him. (I want to believe him.)

"See you in class tomorrow?" I say, even though I really want to ask him to come over again tonight. He's probably right; it's better not to rush things, no matter how perfect this feels.

"Yes, you will." He kisses my forehead, then my lips. "And just so you know, I'm not going to be shy about holding your hand."

This time, the smile on my face is all real and anxiety fades to a background buzz. "What?" I say. "You're not going to ask first?"

He snorts. "Can I hold your hand in class tomorrow, sweet Alder?"

Something about that word, *sweet*, sends a pleasant thrill through me. "I'll think about it," I say, and he laughs.

When he's gone, I sit at the counter, flipping through Ego Arcadia's book, just scanning the chapter titles to get an idea of the contents, and compare it to what I remember about his other book. I'll start reading it more in depth tonight. For now, I get out my pen and notebook and jot down a few ideas for questions for a preliminary email interview.

I get so absorbed I'm almost late leaving for class and have to walk fast to get there in time.

I'm especially anxious about this class, both because the topic is Belief, which means I'll either find lots of useful approaches for my thesis or I'll discover I need to come up with a whole new topic, and because my thesis advisor is teaching it, which means he'll have plenty of opportunities to decide if I'm worth his time.

It's in the same seminar room as my Tuesday Research Methods class, so I take the same chair near the end and settle in. Instead of calling roll, the prof hands around a sheet for us to initial and watches us as the page is passed down the row, as if he can tell what sort of student we'll be by how we examine the paper.

He's short, white but tanned dark gold from a summer probably spent outdoors, and has brown hair pulled back in a ponytail. He's got a friendly look that never quite becomes a smile.

When it's my turn with the attendance sheet, I find my name and pretend he's not watching as I cross out "Alden" and write in "Alder," then sign my initials. I'm last in the row, so I hand the sheet back and flush hot as he examines it closely, then looks up at me.

"Is this an official name change?" he asks, and I bristle, even though his tone is polite curiosity and not at all confrontational.

"Not yet," I force out.

He nods. "Make sure to let Student Services know when it is." He sets the sheet down next to his notes. "And you'll have to notify the library separately, because apparently they don't actually share information." His tone is a little wry and some of the tension leaves my shoulders.

"I will." I study the notebook in front of me.

"Pronouns?" he says suddenly, and I look up, but he's pointing to a student at the other end of the table, and I realize he's going to ask everyone in the class so I won't be singled out.

"He/him," says the student, and one by one everyone at the table answers. No one seems offended by the experience, either, which I take as a good sign.

Not unexpectedly, everyone else in class uses pronouns that match how they look, but I make a point of paying attention anyway, because these are mostly students who have been in my other classes, other MA students who I'll be studying with for the next two years.

I'm the only one why answers with "they/them" and I know I turn red when I say it, but I survive and no one comments.

"I'm Jason McKay," the prof says. "He/him, and you can call me either Jason or Professor McKay, whichever you're comfortable with." Then he turns to me, "And Alder, if you have time, see me after class to talk about your ideas for your thesis."

"Yes, sir," I say.

"And don't call me sir." Then he actually smiles, brief and fleeting, but genuine, and I find myself smiling back. I kind of want to cry, but in a good way.

He starts directly into a lecture after that and I'm too busy taking notes to think about anything else. By the time he wraps up, I'm confident that I'm going to learn a lot that will be useful for my thesis, and that my topic will be suitable. I'm also sure I'm going to have to work my ass off to do well, but that I'll love every second of it.

After class, I follow him to his office and take the chair he indicates. The room is lined with bookshelves, and I'm able to ignore that fact that he sits there looking at me for a few long minutes by studying the titles. Then he says, "How are you finding life as an MA student so far?"

I'm surprised into meeting his eyes – pale blue and bright with curiosity – and stammer out, "It's fine."

"You're quiet," he says, and I blush (of course). "It's going to make things difficult in classes where you're expected to participate." He taps his fingers on his desk. "You're going to have to learn to speak up, to share your thoughts with others."

How he can tell how quiet I am from one class where he lectured almost the whole time, I don't know, but he's not wrong.

"I'll manage," I say.

"I'm sure you will, but I'd like to see you do better than just manage." He considers me again. "You'll do well if you want it badly enough, but make sure to go easy on yourself when you need it."

I blink, surprised again.

"Take breaks, and don't feel you have to participate in every single discussion. Choose topics you're knowledgeable about or passionate about." He pauses again. "And let me know if it gets to be too much. It's my job to get you through this program successfully."

"Okay," I say.

"Now, I've read your entrance essay." He reaches for some pages on one side of his desk, and I realize it's a copy of my application. "Your ideas are sound, but I'd like to see them resolved a little better by the end of the semester."

I nod, then make myself say, "I have a new draft. And I've found some potential interview subjects."

It's his turn to look surprised. "Already? You know you don't need to hand your final proposal in until the end of the year?"

That makes me smile, just a twitch at the corner of my mouth. "I know."

"Let's see it, then."

I hand over a copy of the latest version of my thesis ideas and try not to fidget as he reads it.

"You *have* done a lot of work," he finally says. "Can I keep this? I'll make some suggestions for reading and possible changes to your theoretical direction. But this is an excellent beginning."

This time, the warmth I feel is not mortification, but happiness.

"Yeah," I say, shifting in my seat. "You can keep it. I also have this." I hand him another page, this one hand-written. "It's just some ideas for interview questions for a guy I met recently. He's written a couple of books on his tradition of Pan worship."

His eyebrows go up. "I must say, I don't think I've ever had an MA student so prepared this early in the semester." He scans my notes, then hands the page back. "This is a good start. If your interview subject is open to it, go ahead with a preliminary interview. His answers will give you ideas for further questions."

He contemplates me again, and I take too long putting the page back in my bag so I don't have to look back at him.

"You're older than most of your classmates, aren't you?"

I manage not to bite my lip and just nod. "I took a few years off to work." I hesitate, then say, "I'm twenty-seven."

"And most of your fellow MAs are twenty-two." He gestures at my proposal draft, in front of him on the desk. "That's going to give you an advantage, I think. You're serious about this. That will go a long way towards making up for your social anxiety."

That he knows immediately that I'm not just *quiet* or *shy* when it took me years to find the terminology, even with the help of a therapist, is oddly comforting. I know I won't be able to hide anything from him, to fudge my answers, and it's a bit terrifying, but it also makes me want to live up to the challenge.

"I read your book," I blurt out.

"I assume you mean the one on religious rituals, and not the one on the moral panic about heavy metal music." That makes me smile again.

"Yeah." I make myself ignore the tightness in my gut and go on. "Though the moral panic one sounds interesting."

"It was not widely read," he says, a frown twisting into the expression that seems to be as close as he usually gets to smiling. "But I think the library has a copy." Then he stands up and I do, too, realizing I'm being dismissed.

"I think you're going to be the easiest graduate student I've ever worked with," he says. "Or possibly the hardest. I'll read your draft again and make some notes for you. Make sure I have your up-to-date email." He walks me to the door. "I'm old-fashioned and don't text, but I check my email far more than is healthy."

"Okay," I say, one more time, then escape down the hall. Fuck, how many times did I answer him with, "Okay"? (Too fucking many.) But despite that awful thought, I feel good. He thinks my topic is worthwhile and he thinks I'm already doing good work. It's a relief and a bit of an ego boost. I let the thought buoy me all the way to the gym and I don't even mind when I have to wait an hour for a turn at the climbing wall.

I get home tired and happy and ready to launch into writing my email questions for Ego Arcadia. If I send them tonight, maybe I'll even have something new to show my advisor next week.

Unless that's pushing it. Like he said, I don't even have to have my proposal done until the end of the year, to start the real research next year. Shit. What if he thinks I'm an overachiever, or worse, sucking up? (I am totally an overachiever, though.)

I sit down to a dinner of leftover noodles and chicken in peanut sauce, thinking pleasant thoughts of the evening they're leftover *from*, and just as I'm about to take the first bite, my phone vibrates in my pocket.

I let the book I was holding propped up in front of me fall shut (*not* a school textbook, but a smutty gay romance) and fish out my phone.

how wuz class? Silas, of course. I mean, the only other person who texts regularly is Alison, but she prefers to phone even though she knows I hate talking on the phone.

Good, I type. *My advisor's cool.*

He sends back a thumbs up. *did u use ur right name?*

I feel a flash of annoyance that he's asking, like I can't be trusted to do things for myself, but it fades quickly, because I know he's just concerned. He just wants to make sure people aren't walking all over me, and that I'm not letting them.

Yes, I type back, omitting the rest of what I'm tempted to say. I stare at the screen for a bit, then add, *He went around the class and asked pronouns.*

good, he says. *as long as he didnt make u go 1st*

He did not, I answer. Then, *It felt good.*

u deserve to feel good, he says, and I turn hot, just as if he had whispered it in my ear.

I hesitate, wondering how bold I should be. I let my thumbs hover over the on-screen keyboard, then say, "Fuck it," out loud, and type, *You make me feel good.*

He immediately answers, *u make *me* feel good*, and I wonder how he can type so fast with his big, muscular thumbs.

im looking forward to holding ur hand in class 2morrow, he says.

I type, *You can come over and do it now if you want*, but I don't send it. Finally, I backspace and just write, *Me, too.*

I probably stay up too late after that, typing out and editing my interview questions for Ego Arcadia, but my meeting with my advisor has me full of excitement about my research. Finally, around one in the morning, I hit "send" on the email, and crawl into bed with my smutty novel. I only make it through a few pages before I doze off, and wake in the morning with my thumb still stuck between pages to keep my place.

I take a shower, make coffee, then sit at my laptop to send an email to my advisor so he'll have *my* email to send me his comments on my proposal.

There's way too much spam in my inbox, and I almost delete the message from Satyr Rising LLC before I realize it's from Ego Arcadia. Then I make myself scan through the rest of my messages, including a long, rambling family update from my mom, before opening the mail from Ego. If it's a "fuck off," I'd rather wait.

Instead, it's an invitation to join his group for a small ritual next weekend, in honor of the fall equinox. It's a form letter, so I guess I've ended up on his mailing list, but at the bottom there's a postscript.

Thank you for your email and the intriguing interview questions. I will reply with answers soon, as I wish to make sure to give your inquiry my full attention. In the meantime, I do hope you'll join us for the Equinox. It will be a small group, hopefully to include your friend Silas, and I believe you will find it most useful for your research. It is my hope you will also wish to join us as spiritual equals and not only as research subjects.

Yours in Pan, Ego.

It's an oddly friendly message, if also oddly formal, especially compared to how he focused on Silas after his presentation at the coffeehouse. Then, I was merely someone who wanted something from him.

I type a quick reply after checking my schedule – pretty much wide open, but even this early in the semester I need to be mindful of assignment due dates – letting him know I'll be happy to attend, and that I believe Silas will be there, too, barring any schedule conflicts.

Then I type out a dutiful reply to my mother, attaching some snapshots from my phone, showing the campus and my apartment. And then it's time to head to class.

I try not to think too much about holding Silas's hand, but my steps feel lighter as I head towards the Humanities building.

Chapter Twelve

I ARRIVE EARLY FOR CLASS and wait in the hall for the professor to show up. I lean against the wall by the door, glancing up as each student passes, and I'm surprised when several of them smile and say "hi" and one woman who sits near the far end of the table in two of my classes even calls me by name. My chosen name.

Silas hurries up just as I spot the prof approaching down the hall.

"Hey," he says, taking my hand and kissing my cheek.

"Hey." I squeeze his fingers. "I'm just waiting to talk to Dr Arbreau."

"Do you want me to stay?" He moves slightly closer, like he wants to protect me.

"I'm okay," I say, and when he hesitates, I add, "I have to be able to do this shit myself." Which is, of course, right when the prof arrives.

He looks at us, eyebrows raised, and Silas flashes a grin, lets go of my hand, and goes into the classroom.

"Um, sir," I say, and he looks at me. Like most of my profs so far, his look is friendly.

"What can I do for you?" Today he's wearing a shirt completely covered in a repeating pattern of multi-colored fish. For some reason, it makes me feel more at ease.

"It's just…" I take a breath and try to relax. Attempting to force words

out never works, but sometimes breathing does. "My name," I say. "I um…
I need to change it. On the attendance list."

"Ah," he says, turning towards the door. "Take a seat, and I'll find the
right piece of paper." He holds up a battered folder labelled Research
Methods in Folklore that is stuffed full of papers.

I head in and he shuts the door behind us. "You're Jason McKay's new
MA student." I look up from pulling out my notebook, startled. (Who
knew I could startle so easily, but it's happening a lot this month.)

"Yes," I say.

"He told the rest of the faculty about you."

I get a heavy feeling in my gut, but he smiles.

"He seems to think he's got the best graduate student this year.
Possibly any year ever. He's very pleased with you."

I blush and feel Silas's hand on my back. "Oh," I say.

He finds the attendance sheet and scans it. "Last name?"

"Lewis."

"Mm… Right, there you are. Alder, was it?"

"Yes, that's right."

I blush even hotter at that, but it feels so stupidly good that I don't
even have to tell him that I feel a grin spreading across my face.

He nods and makes a note. I sit and stare at my notebook until I
realize it's completely quiet, save for the squeak of chalk on the chalkboard.
I glance up to see the prof writing on the board, so I peer down the table
and more than half of the other students are watching me. A few smile and
look away when they see me notice. One frowns like he can't figure me out.

Then Silas puts his hand over mine on the table, and the rest of them
turn away, pretending they weren't staring at all. And I realize that the
people who didn't even look at me were all students from Belief class
yesterday – the ones who would have already heard about my name and
pronouns.

I know I'm beet red and breathing too fast, but Silas's hand on mine
steadies me and I manage to focus when Dr Arbreau starts his lecture.

The rest of the week is much the same. I talk to my profs, get them to
change my name on their files and try not to pay attention when anyone
else notices. It helps that so many of the students are the same from class

to class, and with each class more people already know. By the end of the week, everyone calls me Alder, and most of them remember to refer to me with gender-neutral pronouns. And I wonder why I was so afraid to say anything.

Silas and I are both busy with early-semester stuff – getting organized, finding a rhythm in each class, starting assignments, and figuring out our work duties to fulfil the terms of our fellowships – so we only see each other in passing. I've got hours working in the archive every week, and he has to TA for one of his profs. We manage lunch together a couple of times, quick kisses in the library basement, and not much else.

I try not to think about him too much (I totally think about him too much) and just concentrate on school. I came to GVU to get a degree, not to fall in love.

On Friday at dinner time, my sister Alison calls. She's the only one besides doctor's offices and my parents that I answer for. Everyone else can leave a message.

"Hey Monkey," she says. "How's school?"

"Monkey" has been my family nickname since I can remember, because I tried to climb everything, but Alison's really the only one who still uses it. Mum still does occasionally, but Dad stopped when I was twelve and told him I thought I'd like to marry a boy.

"Good. You decided to apply yet?" It's a joke between us. We're only eighteen months apart and she always wanted to do everything I did, insisting we were twins. As we got older, we realized that she'd be the one to take over the orchard and cidery from my parents, while I was better suited to being a scholar. Except for the social anxiety.

I listen as she talks about all the people I know at home, who's hooked up with whom and whose kid got arrested for drunk driving, and all that. The usual rural gossip.

Finally, I guess I've been quiet long enough, because she says, "Meet any hot guys yet?"

I must not answer quickly enough, because before I can even speak, she says, "Oh my God! You have! Spill!"

I sigh. "I might tell you if you'd stop talking long enough."

"Like you'd voluntarily say anything to fill the silence."

I snort. We have shared a lot of silences in our time.

"I did meet someone," I say, and then listen to her congratulate herself on guessing correctly.

"Is he hot?" she asks.

"You are too focused on hotness," I tell her. "He's very nice, and funny. And smart."

"Oh God, he's a nerd, isn't he? Does he have glasses and a squint? Is he skinny? Fat? Ugly? I mean not that any of those things are bad. But you deserve cute, at least."

I laugh. "It's nice to know you care." I contemplate what to tell her, as if I haven't thought it over a million times already. We never had secrets growing up, and she's still my best friend, but I've always been a private person.

"He is hot," I finally say. "Or at least *I* think so."

"Tall?"

"My height."

"So middling height."

"I'm considered tall." Okay, maybe calling five nine and a half "tall" is a bit of a stretch. (No pun intended. Probably.)

"Muscles?"

"A lot. You'd probably think too many."

"You always did like bulk. Is he a bodybuilder or something?"

"Wrestling team." Which is not something he told me, and I'm not even sure it's current, but I saw his photo in the trophy case at the campus gym.

"Hmm. Not sure about that."

"Good thing you're not seeing him then."

"Wait," she says. "Are you *seeing* him?"

I ignore the question. "He's got dark curly hair and brown eyes."

"And he's nice?"

"He's nice."

"He's… He's an ally?"

That's her way of being tactful and not outright asking if he's okay with me being nonbinary.

"Yeah, and he's pan."

"Polyam?"

"Not that he mentioned."

"I mean that's fine if you're cool with it, but I think my little sibling deserves someone who wants only them."

"I'm your *older* sibling, Allie." She just laughs. Ever since our parents measured us one time and she was half an inch taller, she's called me her "little sibling" and I retort that I'm older. It's dumb and pointless, but it's *our* joke and I'd be sad if we ever stopped sharing it.

After she wrings a few more details out of me I hang up and wash my dinner dishes. I'm filled with warmth, thinking about Silas. Should I text him? It's been a few hours since we checked in, but I don't want to seem too needy.

Instead, I open my laptop and sit with it on the couch. There's just spam in my email, so I spend a little time poking around online to see if there are any good websites or blogs I can use for my thesis research. I'm about to get up and get Ego Arcadia's newest book so I can finally dig into reading it when my phone vibrates.

u home? can i come in? And I smile. Silas.

"Get your coat," he says, when I open the door.

"Why?" I don't say it, but I never liked when my ex just decided we were going out without asking me first if I even wanted to.

I guess Silas hears the edge in my voice because he says, "Or can I come up?"

I move out of the way so he can get up the stairs, then close and lock the street door behind me. When we get into my apartment he says, "I said the wrong thing, didn't I?"

I look at the floor. "No, it's okay."

"No." He moves close enough to put a hand on my shoulder, tentatively, like he's not sure if he's welcome to touch me. (He's always welcome to touch me.) "Sweetheart, if I say something stupid, I want you to tell me. Please? I don't ever want to say the wrong thing."

I keep looking at the floor. "I don't want you to feel like you have to be careful about what you say. Not ever."

He puts his other hand on my other shoulder and steps closer to kiss my forehead. "Oh, sweetheart, I don't feel like I have to watch what I say.

I feel like I can just be myself around you. But I also know you have some shit in your past you probably don't want to be reminded of."

"Yeah, I guess." I force myself to look at him. His eyes are dark and deep and fuck, why can't he just kiss me instead of talking?

But I know it's because he *likes* me, because he *cares*, and he wants to build something together. Something more than sex. So I know he has to talk, to ask questions, and I have to answer honestly, if I want this to mean anything. (And I do, I want it to mean something so badly I feel sick.)

"I just... My ex always decided when we'd go out and where, and if I didn't want to, he'd start a fight."

"Oh," he says. "Oh, shit, I didn't even think of it that way." His fingers brush my cheek. "I'm sorry, Alder. I should have thought."

I shake my head. "It doesn't matter. You didn't know."

"It *does* matter. From now on, I'll ask. I'll tell you what I'm thinking, and you decide what you want to do." Then he smiles. "Or even better, we'll think up things to do together."

Something loosens in my chest. "I don't want my past shitty relationship to get in the way of... whatever we have." (But it will, won't it? Because that's the way with shitty pasts; they screw things up when you least expect it.)

He kisses my forehead again. "Let it stand in the way," he says. "I'll go around. Or help you banish it. Whatever you want, sweetheart."

And fuck, I admit I melt when he calls me "sweetheart." (Which means I'm a fucking puddle several times a day at least.)

"So why did you want me to get my coat?" I ask.

"Oh, right!" I got a call from a certain Ego Arcadia wanting to meet for coffee this evening, to fill me in on the upcoming equinox thing. You got the invite, right?"

"He emailed," I say. "But he didn't say anything about coffee tonight."

"Ah, no, he wouldn't have."

I frown at him.

"He wants to meet with me. Just me and him. I told him you and I come as a set." He pauses and his eyebrows crowd together. "I probably shouldn't have said that without checking with you, but he annoyed me. I mean, you obviously don't need my permission or my presence to interview him, or whatever. I only meant that I don't want to be involved if you're not welcome. I –"

I shake my head and kiss him, just a quick gentle peck to get him to stop talking.

"I was babbling, wasn't I?"

"I don't mind," I say. "Then there's less silence for me to fill."

"Anyway, you don't have to come. Obviously. And I won't go if you think it would be weird. But yeah. Coffee tonight with Ego at the same place he had his re-awakening deal."

"You don't need my permission to go."

"I know. But… I'd like you to come. I want… This whole Pan worship is something we can do together, you know? I mean, it's your research, but my actual spiritual path. My religion, I guess, though my parents would be the first to tell you I'm not very religious."

"Can I ask you a totally irrelevant question?"

"Anything."

"How old are you?" Yeah, don't ask me where that came from. The workings of my brain are a mystery even to me sometimes.

He stares at me for a moment. "That really is irrelevant, but I'm thirty-two."

I smile hesitantly. "It's just, when you talk, sometimes you sound like a teenager, and sometimes you sound like an old man. And you look like you could be anywhere from twenty-five to forty." I blush and snap my mouth shut. He doesn't really look forty.

He looks confused and then laughs. "Yeah, that sounds about right." He taps the end of my nose with his finger. "Though I could say pretty much the same thing about you."

"Twenty-seven," I say.

"Ah, just a baby," he teases.

"Sure, compared to you, old man." That gets me a glare, then a kiss.

"I'll be your silver fox, then," he says, with his mouth still so close to mine I feel his lips move.

"You do not have one single silver hair."

"Pretty sure I found a white pube last week."

"Do you want me to check?" I reach for his fly, and he catches my hand.

"Very much, yes, but how about coffee first?"

I sigh. "Okay. I admit, I'm curious, too." Then I gather my courage and say, "I think I'm a bit jealous that he wants you to join his group because of your 'strong Pan energy,' but when he invited me it felt like he was just being polite."

"Is that what envy looks like on you? Damn, Alder, do you have to look sexy in absolutely every mood?"

"Fuck off," I say, but stick my tongue out so he knows I'm not serious. As I'm getting my coat, I add, "I guarantee I'm not remotely sexy when I ugly cry." Then we walk to the coffee shop.

Ego is already there and it's almost disconcerting to see him looking like a normal everyday person. He's older than us, though not quite as old as my parents, and dresses like maybe he has an office job, though as far as I know he just writes his books and runs his commune. He waves us over when he sees us. Or he waves Silas over. Me he nods at absently and then only glances at me once in a while, so he won't seem to be completely ignoring me. Which is such a switch from the tone of his email that it leaves me confused.

Silas insists on getting me coffee – Ego already has a mug in front of him – so I sit awkwardly across the table and try to think of something to say.

"Alder, was it?" he finally says, just when I'm thinking I should excuse myself and go to the bathroom to avoid any more awkward silence.

"Yes."

"Why did you choose a tree?"

For some reason, that pricks me. "Why do you assume I chose it?"

He smiles suddenly at that and lightly touches the back of my hand. The warmth in his expression wins me over a little, makes me relax. "I chose my name; I suppose I assume many people choose theirs."

I return the smile, and it feels good. "I did choose it," I admit. "It's similar to my... to my legal name, and I like trees."

"Oh, I like trees, too," he says, and laughs, a light, almost tinkling sound that doesn't fit his businesslike clothes. It would sound better coming from the man in the toga and laurel crown. "I could hardly be a follower of He Who Brings Fear in Quiet Places if I didn't."

I know he means Pan, who was known as "the god who brings fear in quiet places" because he can cause panic, which is named for him, but it seems odd that Ego chose to say that instead of just naming him.

"Why 'Ego'?" I ask. "If you don't mind saying."

"You know its meaning?"

"I," I say. "In Latin. Or part of the psyche in psychoanalysis."

"Indeed. And I can be no one but myself. It's a pun, I suppose, and it amuses me. Most people assume it means I'm full of myself."

"I can see that," I say, then blush when I realize I've made an unflattering statement by accident.

He doesn't seem offended. "You're clever one," he says. "I must admit, I didn't notice anything special about you during the visualization. It's how I find new people to join my inner circle, you see. Your friend had very strong energy that I noticed straight away, but sometimes the strongest energies are not Pan himself, but only the bestial satyr. But you…"

I should be offended on Silas's behalf, but it seems like too much effort. Ego looks at me solemnly, considering me with disconcertingly pale eyes. Then he puts his hand over mine where it rests on the table, just where he touched it earlier. I almost pull away, but the urge passes, and his touch feels friendly, comforting.

"What about them?" Silas sets our coffees on the table and sits next to me, pointedly looking at Ego's hand over mine. Is he jealous?

Ego moves his hand away, but casually, as if he was doing nothing wrong. (And he was doing nothing wrong. Right?)

"I think our Alder here has unexplored depths, a most subtle energy I find intriguing. I think he –"

"They," says Silas, voice flat. The "he" stings but I wouldn't have bothered to correct it, even if I should. I don't understand why Silas is being so protective it's almost hostile. I pick up my coffee and sip. It's just exactly the right sweetness.

"My apologies," says Ego, completely unruffled. "I think *they* will make a good addition to my group. As will you, dear Silas, if for very different reasons."

Didn't he say Silas was bestial? Or did I imagine that? (I totally imagined that.) (Didn't I?)

"I haven't decided if I want to join yet," Silas says. Some of the hostility is gone, but he still looks at Ego from narrowed eyes.

"Of course, of course. That's why we're here this evening."

What he proceeds to describe sounds like a pretty standard neo-pagan group, though maybe less Wicca-like than many. It *does* sound like it's based on actual ancient Greek sources, which should make a more interesting addition to my thesis.

And, I must admit, I'm starting to warm to the idea of a spiritual practice again, after many years of feeling left out because I didn't fit the sacred binary. My childhood didn't involve church, though we owned a Bible, and my parents always listed us as generic protestant on the census. Until my dabbling in Wicca as an older teenager, my more spiritual tendencies were fulfilled by reading fairytales and fantasy fiction and by just being outside, climbing a rock or watching a stream flow by.

I realize I've lost track of the conversation when Silas gets up to use the washroom and I can't remember what anyone just said. As I get up to follow him, Ego puts a hand on my arm and hands me a small booklet.

"Some reading for you," he says. "Let us keep this between us, yes?" and his smile is so warm and friendly that I nod and tuck the booklet into my jacket pocket.

Chapter Thirteen

OUT IN THE COLD AIR of the evening I suck in a deep breath to try to shake off the weird feeling being in the cafe has left me with. It doesn't make any sense – even if the mocha was decaf, coffee tends to wake me up, not make me sleepy.

"Do you feel dopey?" I ask.

"Not really," says Silas. "When was the last time you ate?"

"I had dinner," I say, more sharply than I meant to. Something has made me irritable, but I don't know what. I try to shake it off and just enjoy walking in the autumn evening with my… is he my boyfriend? Oh God, I think I have a boyfriend. (I want him to be my boyfriend.) I scratch the back of my hand absently.

"So, Ego… he seemed a little… touchy, didn't he?" Silas says. He's got his hands in his pockets, and I know why he's not holding my hand. I might have had good experiences in class so far, but Great Valley isn't known for being tolerant, and Friday night brings out the frat boys and other unsavory types. Even though most of the bars are farther downtown, there are too many rowdy pubs and houses to pass on the way home. Neither of us fancies spending our evening getting beaten up.

"He seemed fine to me," I say.

"I don't mean touchy as in sensitive," he says. "I mean touchy as in he kept touching you."

Did he? I remember him putting his hand on mine once.

"I didn't really notice," I say, after thinking about it for too long.

"You *like* him," Silas says, and though his tone is teasing, I think there might be an accusation in it, too.

"Jealous?" I say, and then regret saying it. Why am I like this? Am I trying to provoke him into a fight? Was my ex right and I'm the cause of all the bad things that happened between us?

Silas stops suddenly and I've taken several steps past him before I realize. I turn to look at him, and I expect him to be angry, or annoyed, to be ready to snark back at me until everything is a shouting match.

But he doesn't look angry, he looks concerned. "Are you okay, Alder? You seem… off."

"How do you know how I seem?" I say, and what the fuck am I doing? Usually, I can't get words to come out; right now I can't seem to keep them in. And they aren't even words I *mean*. "You don't even know me." I turn away and keep walking, hands in fists inside my jacket pockets.

"Sweetheart." He's suddenly right beside me, arm over my shoulder, steering me into a doorway. My apartment doorway, I realize. I almost stomped right past my own fucking door. I fumble for my keys, and I realize everything is blurry. I'm crying. Why am I crying? (Seriously, why the fuck am I crying?)

"Hey," he says, taking my keys, unlocking the door, and pulling me inside, where he wraps his arms around me.

"What's wrong with me?" I say, clinging to his jacket like it will keep me afloat.

"It's okay, sweetheart. You're okay. Let's go inside." He keeps me tucked under his arm as we climb the stairs, then lets us into my apartment.

"I don't know why I said any of those things, Si. I'm sorry. I'm… such a shit person." Now I'm just feeling sorry for myself and it's almost worse than trying to pick a fight. But at least I'm not attacking him anymore.

"Shh… It's okay. You're tired and stressed. And you're not a shit person." His hand rubs up and down my back.

"I'm not though. I'm not tired, or at least I wasn't until we went into the coffee shop. And I'm not any more stressed than usual." I sniff and wipe my face with one hand.

"Am I right that you're not yourself, at least?" His smile is tentative, and I realize it was a similar comment that set me off in the first place. But no, it wasn't; it was him saying that Ego kept touching me. I don't like being touched by people I don't know. I don't even like being touched by most people I *do* know.

I pull away a little and look at his eyes. "Did he really keep touching me?"

"You don't remember?"

"He put his hand on mine when you were getting coffee. I thought he was just being friendly, trying to put me at ease."

"Did it? Put you at ease?"

I study his face carefully, but there's no anger, no accusation, only concern. For me.

"I..." I frown, trying to remember. "At first... no. I felt really awkward. But then, he just seemed... nice. Like he wanted to be my friend, and I wanted that, too."

Silas takes a deep, slow breath.

"Maybe we shouldn't go to his equinox thing." He says it carefully, like he's afraid I'll get mad.

"I'd still like to go," I say. "But you don't have to if you don't want." For a moment I feel confrontational again, but I lean my head on his shoulder and breathe in the smell of him, and it goes away.

"I think... I think I want to go not just for my thesis, but for myself. To... I don't know, to explore the path he's offering."

"Okay." He says it softly. "But remember I can give you that, too, if it's a spiritual practice you're looking for."

"I know." I look up at him again and for a moment I'm lost in his eyes. "I just... I want to find my own way. To try different things, I guess." I don't know why I want to explore Ego's tradition and not the one Silas can give me; it only seems important that I investigate both before choosing a direction. "I thought I might go to that shop Celeste works at, too, to see what else I can... you know... try out."

"Celeste?"

"From the Re-Awakening thing. She sat at our table."

"Oh, right, The Spiral Gate."

"Silas?"

"Mm hmm?"

"I'm not *interested* in him. In Ego. I just want to see what his group is all about, if maybe there's a place for someone like me."

"I wouldn't be mad if you were interested in him." He strokes my hair back from my face. "Though I might question your sanity. And I'd much rather you were interested in me."

I summon up a smile. "I *am* interested in you. *Very* interested."

That gets me a smile in response.

"Will you stay tonight?" I say it hesitantly, knowing I don't deserve the comfort after I just tried to pick a fight with him for no reason.

He strokes my hair again. "I'll stay," he says. "But… I don't want to start any bad habits with you."

"Bad habits?"

"Like fucking because we almost had a fight."

"Make up sex is a bad habit?" I know I sound incredulous, but I can't keep it out of my voice.

"No… I just mean… You seem fragile right now."

"But you'll stay?"

"I'll stay, and I'll hold you, and I'll tell you how wonderful you are." He kisses me lightly. "And I'll wake up before you do so I can make you coffee in the morning and see you smile when you realize I'm still here."

"Okay."

So we go to bed and he tucks me close to him and holds me while I try to fall asleep. I know I must be disturbing him, so finally I just lie still and try not to toss and turn, and when I hear his breathing change and know he's asleep I get carefully out of bed and go into the living room.

My jacket is draped over the end of the couch, so I pick it up to hang it on its hook by the door. There's something stiff in the pocket. I pull it out and find the booklet Ego pressed into my hand in the coffee shop.

"Let's keep this between us," he'd said. What could it be that he didn't want Silas to see? Especially since he seemed to favor Silas as a better fit for his group – at least to Silas's face.

I sit on the couch and pull a blanket over my lap then study the cover of the booklet. Like Ego's book, there's a satyr on the cover, but unlike the book, this one is crudely drawn and leering.

A True Account of Satyrs in Arcadia County it's titled, and the author is George L. Small. I flip it over and the author photo is Ego Arcadia, only younger – about my age – and the bio says nothing about a farm or a pagan commune. Instead, it talks about his certificate in cryptozoology and his passion for searching for Bigfoot.

"That's weird," I say softly, then open the booklet and start to read and once I've begun, I can't seem to put it down, even though with each page I feel more and more uneasy.

I wake up to the smell of coffee and Silas's hand on my shoulder.

"Hey, sleepyhead," he says. "Trouble sleeping last night?"

I sit up slowly and feel something slide into my lap under the blanket. The booklet. I open my mouth to tell him about it, but no words come out.

"I didn't want to disturb you," I say instead and take the coffee he's holding out.

"I was going to ask you if you wanted to do something today," he says, sitting next to me. "But I think maybe you should get some rest." He licks his lips. "If you want, I mean."

"You don't have to tiptoe around things, Si," I say. "I'm not going to go off on you again. I don't know why I said those things last night, but I feel better this morning." I take a long sip of coffee. "You might be right about needing more sleep, though. I feel like crap."

"If that's an example of you going off, I don't think I've got much to worry about." He smiles as he says it. "That's the mildest 'going off' I've ever seen. And that's the second time you've called me 'Si'."

"Oh," I say. "Sorry."

"No, I like it." He watches me as he sips his coffee then seems to realize he's doing it and looks away. "Last night," he says, hesitantly.

"Mm?" The coffee is so good; way better than when I make it myself.

"You really weren't your usual self." He hesitates again. "Are you sure you're okay?"

"I think so." I stare into my coffee and then look at him sharply. "Are you implying something?"

"No, I –" He cuts himself off and I realize he thinks I'm trying to start a fight again.

I shake my head. "I'm fine. And I don't have… a mental condition, if that's what you're thinking. I'm not off my meds. I'm not *on* any meds to be off of."

"I don't think that," he says. "You were just… You were acting like Ego was your best friend at the cafe, and then you tried to start an argument. I'm not accusing you of anything, Alder. I'm just concerned. I know I don't know you that well yet, but everything I *do* know about you says you were…"

"Not myself." I say it carefully. I *don't* want to provoke him, and he's right; I was not myself. "Was I really acting like he was my best friend? Because I don't remember being all that friendly with him, and those things I said… I was trying to stop myself from saying them, even as the words came out. Because you're right, that *wasn't* me."

"So, what happened?"

He's not really asking me for an answer, he's just raising the question we're both thinking.

"I felt really slow," I say. "Like I couldn't think straight. Like nothing really made sense."

"You asked me if I also felt dopey," he says. "After we left."

"I felt…" I don't know how to describe something I only partly remember. And why can't I remember?

"Drugged?"

"You think someone drugged me?" I sit up straighter and scratch an itchy spot on the back of my hand. "All I had was the mocha, and you got it for me."

"Well, *I* didn't drug you," he says. "And I watched the barista make it."

"Ego didn't do it," I say, not even sure why I defend him.

"Are you sure?"

I shake my head. "I don't remember him being anywhere near my drink. But then, I guess I don't remember a lot of things." I scratch my hand again. "Anyway, why would he drug me?"

He shrugs. "I don't know. I feel weird even thinking about it. Maybe you were just tired."

"Yeah, maybe."

We sit a while longer, just sipping and leaning slightly against each other. Finally, he says, "Alder, I don't want to fight with you."

"We're not fighting. Are we?"

He smiles. "No, but we almost were, and it felt bad. Really bad."

"Don't all couples fight?" That sounds like something people say, but it doesn't feel entirely true.

"My parents don't fight," he says. "I mean, they get annoyed at each other sometimes, and they disagree, but they talk about stuff. They work things out without getting angry."

"Yeah," I say. "My parents, too." And I guess that's why that saying never felt true.

"I want us to communicate," he says. "To discuss things like rational people."

"And I wasn't rational last night."

"That's not what I meant," he says, and I lean my head on his shoulder. It's strong and warm.

"No, but *I* did. I wasn't rational, and I really don't like it. Silas, what if something's really wrong with me?"

"Like what?"

"I don't know. Mental illness. A brain tumor. What else makes people act like… like not themselves?"

He puts an arm around me. "This happened once. Let's not worry unless it becomes a pattern, okay, sweetheart?"

"Okay."

"Get some sleep if you can. I've got a paper I should probably work on."

I nod, even though I don't really want him to go.

Once he leaves, I try to sleep, but something's picking at my thoughts. I roll over, trying to get comfortable, then decide to move to my bedroom. My couch isn't awful, but the bed is better.

When I stand, something falls to the floor. Ego's booklet. I meant to show it to Silas, but somehow it escaped me. Last night it seemed urgent to tell him what I'd read, but this morning… I hadn't even thought about it.

I take it with me to bed, where Ego's new book sits on the nightstand, still only partly read. I get into bed and absently flip through the booklet. Ego, before he changed his name, was convinced that satyrs were real, like some kind of cryptid, and that they moved to Arcadia County from Greece long before any white people – or white *human* people – had even thought of crossing the ocean.

There are supposed eyewitness accounts, carefully retold in Ego's flowery prose – his writing style has improved since then, at least – and a blurry photo of a cave opening high in a cliff face where the satyrs supposedly worshipped their god. Pan, of course.

It was the photo I wanted Silas to see, because I thought maybe it was one of his family's secrets, and they should know that someone knew it existed. And then I remembered what *else* had seemed so urgent.

I had concluded, in my sleep-deprived state, that what Ego thought were satyrs running around in the woods of Arcadia County must actually be Silas's family. And in the darkest part of the night, I had even woken suddenly from strange dreams, wondering if maybe they really *were* satyrs.

I laugh and shake my head at the absurdity and toss the booklet onto the nightstand and settle under the covers. But something else picks at my memory and I still can't sleep. Finally, I roll over and reach for Ego's new book, flipping pages impatiently to the table of contents.

There, the final chapter is titled "Waking the Satyr." I turn to the chapter and begin to read. I'm uneasy, but not as weirded out as last night. I pause for a minute to get up and fetch Ego's previous book from my bookshelf, but it doesn't have a similar chapter. It reads more like someone trying to build a Pan-centered spiritual path from a foundation of Wicca. I set it aside and go back to "Waking the Satyr."

In it, Ego outlines a ritual, to be conducted at the full moon, or on a solstice or equinox night, in a cave if one is available, or a forest clearing if not. The purpose of the ritual is to "Wake the Pan Within" by conducting a sort of magic that is supposed to turn an ordinary human – or at least a human considered worthy of it – into an avatar for the god Pan. Less worthy acolytes could become little pans, or priests of Pan, and work their way towards a sort of enlightenment to become more worthy.

He doesn't specify if he thinks this transformation will involve growing horns and goat legs, but it's supposed to awaken a person's innate but deeply buried connection to the natural world.

Once awakened, Ego says, the person can attain – or obtain – anything they want, just by asking, just as the Pan of myth could convince any nymph to sleep with him.

I shake my head at that part. I don't think he read all the same myths I did. And then I feel disappointment. I had thought Ego's purpose was a spiritual connection to the earth, to the wild places, that the awakening of that connection was the *point*. But all along, it turns out to be selfish, a path to wealth and meaningless sex.

But despite that, I still want to find out what his group does at their rituals. Maybe it's stubbornness, or maybe stupidity, but the rest of his book – the parts I've read so far – seemed lovely, a step beyond what his first book outlined into something profoundly spiritual. Maybe it's possible to follow his path and not go so far as trying to fulfill selfish desires.

Or maybe I should step back and just use him as a source for my thesis like I originally meant to. After all, I still have Silas, and he's promised to tell me all he can about his family's traditions, to invite me to a feast, even.

I wonder if he's hurt by my insistence on exploring Ego's group, despite his offering something much more genuine.

And I hardly dare hope that maybe someday I'll be *part* of his family. (But, yeah, I do hope.) I hold that thought in my heart while I read the last part of the chapter where Ego lays out the awakening rite and the sort of things that would be acceptable as offerings to Pan. Only the word he uses is "sacrifice."

Chapter Fourteen

I SLEEP OFF AND ON for most of the day, then spend the evening and Sunday reading and working on outlines for upcoming assignments. I manage an hour at the climbing wall Sunday afternoon to clear my head between a paper on the definition of "folklore" (more complicated than you might think) and a very dense book on the iconography of saints in South American folk religion.

Silas checks in with frequent texts, mostly silly emojis, and every time my phone vibrates, I smile.

Early Monday morning, before class, I get in another climbing session and realize I'm starting to recognize some of the other regulars, who nod at me in passing. After class, my advisor tells me to expect notes and suggested readings for my thesis proposal. A few of the other students overhear as they're packing up to leave, and one guy mutters, "Suck up much?"

I feel my chest tighten and I try to think of something to say that won't make me sound pathetic. But then a woman speaks from behind him. "Oh, shut up, Quentin. Some of us actually know what we want to study." She leans closer to him. "*Some* of us didn't have Daddy buy their way into school."

Quentin looks like he's going to say something back, something snarky, but he scowls and abruptly pushes past me into the hall.

"Thanks," I say. It's the woman who said "hi" to me last week and called me by name. She's got black hair pulled back into a loose ponytail and grey eyes.

"I'm Kristy," she says.

"Alder."

She falls into step beside me as we leave the room, and I scour my brain for the sort of thing one might say to a classmate you've just met.

"So, what's your thesis?" I manage to get the words out without sounding too awkward. (I hope I don't sound too awkward.)

She laughs. "I only said that to piss off Quentin. He's kind of an ass. But it will be something to do with First Nations traditional knowledge, like maybe something on how colonization damaged craft production."

"That sounds cool." I want to ask if she's First Nations, but I don't know if it would be rude. She looks like she *could* be, but maybe I just have a white person's idea of what First Nations people look like.

"I kind of have to do an Indigenous topic, actually," she says. "So it's a good thing I like the idea."

"Why do you have to?" I glance at her as we walk down the hall. She has a nice face, pretty, and made even more appealing because she's smiling.

"Because my band is paying my tuition." She laughs again and it eases the ache in my belly. "Anyway, I've got another class. See you tomorrow?"

I almost blurt out, "What?" but then I remember she's in the research class, too. "Yeah," I say. "See you."

I find a bench to sit on and pull my backpack into my lap. I had hoped to get through my two years without having to interact too much with people. It's not that I dislike friends; friends are great. It's just that friends take a lot of time and energy, and I always feel like I'm not contributing enough, like they end up doing all the talking and the planning activities and eventually they'll think I'm not worth the effort.

And anyway, I like having a lot of time to myself. A boyfriend is enough. (Isn't it?)

But exchanging a few sentences with a classmate isn't starting a friendship. It doesn't mean anything except that some people are kind. And it was nice. Maybe interacting with other people won't be so bad.

And on that note, I think of Celeste from the coffee shop. I get out my phone and look up the shop she works at, then check my bank balance to make sure I have enough money in case I find any books I can use for my thesis. I laugh when I see the total. My mom has sent me money again. I wonder if Dad knows how often she drops a few hundred dollars in my account.

Thanks, Mum, I text.

And my phone vibrates with an incoming call. Usually my mom just texts back, because she knows I hate talking, but sometimes she forgets. I almost don't pick up, but then I do.

"I was wondering when you'd notice," she says, without even a greeting.

"You don't have to send me money," I say. "I *am* an adult."

"You're still my child, and I worry," she says. "And speaking of worry, I've been having one of my dreadful feelings."

"Dreadful feelings" are what my mom calls what other people might refer to as "premonitions." She's had them ever since I can remember, and even though I don't really buy into supernatural stuff, she's right often enough that Alison and I – and even Dad – have learned not to discount them.

"I'm fine, Mum. Better than fine," I say.

"Alison says you met someone. Maybe it's not them the feelings are about, but something bad is going to happen."

"I'll be careful, I promise."

"I know you will." She pauses and I can hear her breathing. "Is this person nice?" she asks, and I glance around to make sure no one has noticed me grinning into the phone. People pass by and a few glance my way, but I'm glad to say that I might as well be invisible.

"I really like him," I say. "And yes, he's nice. He's… he's pretty amazing, Mum. I think you'd like him."

"Okay, Ald, just be careful. My feelings say you've met someone who means you harm."

"I'm sure it's not him, Mum. I've met a lot of people this month. Kind of goes with starting school."

"Promise me you'll pay attention and not let anyone hurt you."

"I promise."

When I hang up, my phone vibrates again, and I see she's sent me a string of rainbow-colored hearts. It's her way of showing support for my queerness, I guess.

Since I have my phone out, I decide to text Silas. *Want to go book shopping?*

yes! he sends back, then, *wait do u mean now? im trapped in a training thing for tas*

I can wait, I say, though I don't really want to. I'm in the mood to browse books, and there's just enough time left before the shops all close.

no u go, he says. *just tell me ur not going to hawthorne books*

The Spiral Gate, I reply.

say hi to celeste, he sends back. *ill take u to hawthorne soon, ull love it*

On impulse, I text him the same string of rainbow hearts my mom sent me, and he replies with a kissy face emoji. So I'm in good spirits when I get on the bus heading downtown and blend in with the rest of the university students out running Monday afternoon errands.

The Spiral Gate is right on the other side of town, so it's a long bus ride, but at least I don't have to transfer to a different route. I manage a window seat and pull Ego's book out of my backpack for something to do while I wait, even though I'm too nervy around so many people to get really absorbed.

I skim over the section on "Waking the Satyr" again, trying to figure out exactly what Ego is trying to accomplish with the ritual and if it's something he's done before.

And then a paragraph I don't remember reading catches my attention. This must be where I drifted off the other night.

If an existing satyr can be located, Ego writes, *it is a simple procedure to modify the ritual to borrow their satyr nature, their Pan energy, and add it to your own and thus make the path towards waking your internal Pan much swifter. This can be done multiple times, each time increasing your own energy.*

I read it over twice, and then finish the chapter, but he never says what the "simple procedure" is to modify the ritual. In fact, the rest of the book is techniques for increasing your own Pan energy without reference to anyone else, to eventually wake your inner "little pan" completely.

The last couple of chapters I just flip through quickly; I'll go back to them later. They're mostly a collection of rituals and spells, including a "ritual year" calendar – on which the fall equinox seems the most prominent – for gaining a deeper connection to Pan as a patron deity. A lot of the text is borrowed from actual surviving ancient and Classical texts like the Homeric Hymns to Pan and Dionysus, and the ritual seems to be extrapolated from what is known of ancient Greek religious practice.

It gets a shade too close to a generic neo-pagan practice in sections for my taste (nothing wrong with that, but I have my reasons for not wanting to follow it). Still, I could see myself making use of some of this material to build a personal spiritual path. I'll have to show it to Silas and see what he thinks.

And I wonder again why I don't just let Silas teach me his family's traditions. Like, am I afraid it will be too much, too soon? Or that when he inevitably gets tired of me, I'll lose both him and my newfound spiritual practice all at once? Or is it just what I told him, that I'm curious and want to try to find my own way?

I shove the book back into my backpack and get off the bus at the stop that the Spiral Gate's website says is the closest. Shops won't be open for much longer, not here in town, anyway, so I hurry on my way, find the store – it has a brilliantly lit display of crystal specimens and cauldrons in the window – and check the open hours on the sign on my way in. I've got an hour and a half to browse, and money in my bank account.

I'm still smiling when I look up and meet a pair of bright curious eyes.

"Hey, stranger," Celeste says, returning my smile.

"Hi," I say, giving an awkward half-wave.

"Welcome to the Spiral Gate. Did you get tired of what Ego Arcadia was peddling?" She comes out from behind the counter to greet me, surprising me by taking one of my hands and shaking it. My pale, freckled skin looks anemic against her rich dark brown and for a moment I think that if I was into women, I'd be into women like her – outgoing, kind, and beautiful.

"It was an okay book," I say.

"No, you're right," she says. "It was okay." She waves around the store. "And I've got much worse on these shelves. But a lot of crap sells, and selling stuff keeps me open so I have a chance to convince people to read the good stuff."

"Do you have any good stuff on satyrs or Pan worship?"

"I have some so-so stuff on Pan." She leads me to a shelf deep in the store and I breathe in the smell of the jasmine incense she's got burning.

"Did you know that some cryptozoologists think there are actual satyrs running around out there?" she says, and points in passing to a shelf labelled "Cryptids & Aliens."

"That reminds me, I was going to ask if you have anything by George Small."

She gives me a funny look but keeps walking. "That's a name I haven't heard in a while."

"He wrote a booklet on satyrs," I say. "I was just curious if he wrote anything else. You know, before he changed his name and started writing about the cult of Pan."

She stops next to a shelf labelled "Greece & Rome," and looks at me sharply. I almost expect her to interrogate me, her look is so intense, but then she tips her head to one side and smiles. "I looked up his name," she says. "Ego Arcadia. I see why your friend laughed when he was introduced." She pulls a book off the shelf but keeps it in her hands. "Are you telling me Ego Arcadia *is* George Small?"

I nod. "Unless he has a twin."

"That's seriously the *same* guy?" The repetition of the question, even if it's different words, makes it seem too intense, like maybe she already knew but for some reason doesn't want me to know she knew. Which really makes no sense.

I nod again and let a smile spread over my face.

"Well, fuck. I guess he changed his ideas about what satyrs really are."

I don't say it, but I'm not so sure he *did* change his ideas. He never says in his new book – or his first book, that I recall – whether the satyrs he refers to are just people with "strong Pan energy" or if they're goat-legged people out of myth. He *did* change his mind about what they represent though, from a cryptid like Bigfoot to the earthly vessels of the Greek god Pan.

What I do say, pulling words out of my throat with less effort than I expect, is, "Or else he found a better way to make money writing about them." I think it might be a combination of the two; I'm pretty sure Ego wants money and acclaim, but I think he might also be serious about spiritual development. In his newest book, he wrote about sacrifices to Pan to awaken your own inner deity, and then in the next section he talked about finding an existing satyr to "borrow" their Pan energy. What if he's still talking about cryptids, only those cryptids are *also* people with the kind of energy he wants to collect? Fuck, now I'm confusing myself.

But what if Ego is advocating for blood sacrifice without really saying so? Suddenly I want to be at home texting Silas to come over and keep me company.

I mean, obviously satyrs aren't real, but Silas's family *is*, and what if Ego decided to sacrifice *them*, thinking they are actual satyrs? And you'd think that would make me want to stay far away from the guy, from Ego, but it doesn't. It makes me want to find out what he's up to even more.

I realize I haven't been listening to what Celeste is saying. She's holding out the book, so I take it and look at the cover.

"That one will give you an overview of the basic state of Pan worship among contemporary neo-pagans," she says, then hands me another book. "And this one is great for the history of the revival of the cult of Pan, right back to medieval Europe."

"Oh," I say, staring at the second book. "I did have this one on my list to get."

"If you want, I can look around online and see what else is out there and order whatever you need."

"That would be great," I say, suddenly feeling overwhelmed by her kindness.

"Come on up to the counter when you're done browsing and I'll get your email, so I can send over anything that looks promising."

I nod and spend some time wandering the shelves, picking up and putting down a Greek mythology themed tarot deck and laughing quietly when I find a whole shelf, right at the back of the store, of romance novels featuring ancient deities or settings. I can't resist a very smutty sounding one about an American tourist who meets a tribe of satyrs on a seemingly uninhabited Greek island.

When I reach the counter, a couple books on general Hellenic neo-paganism added to my pile, she asks for my info and adds it to her computer, setting me up with a loyalty account at the same time. Just as I'm about to push my stack of books across the counter to pay, I see a brass statue on the shelf behind her.

"How much is that?" It's a scale replica of a Roman statue found in Pompeii, thought to be a copy of a Greek marble. Pan leans close to the shepherd Daphnis to teach him how to play the syrinx, and it's one of my favorite pieces of ancient art. It's sweet and sexy at the same time, and I love the gentle strength depicted in Pan's body posture.

Celeste turns around to see what I'm looking at, then names a price that would make a serious dent in the money my mom sent me. I have exactly the place to put it in front of one of my bedroom windows.

She lifts it from the shelf and puts it on the counter in front of me. It's almost two feet high and captures the original in perfect detail.

"I shouldn't," I say.

Just then my phone vibrates. *got urself some books?* it says, and I laugh, snap a photo of the statue, and send it back.

Celeste raises an eyebrow. "Not asking permission, I hope. I'd drop a guy who didn't let me spend my own damn money."

"Oh no," I say, trying not to sound either too annoyed or too eager to please. (How can I feel like both?) "Silas and I don't even live together."

She smirks. "Yet," she says. "I saw the way you two were practically falling off your chairs to be close together, even when you didn't want to be seen holding hands in public."

I flush hot. "It has nothing to do with not wanting to be seen," I say.

She blinks in surprise, and I realize that this time, my annoyance did come out in my voice.

"Sorry," I mutter.

"No," she says. "I was out of line. And I get it. Great Valley sucks for queer people. Pagans, too, by the way. I can't tell you how many times I've had to pay someone to clean Christian evangelical graffiti off my windows."

She puts a hand over mine when I fidget and carefully line up the books I'm buying on the counter.

"I get it," she says softly.

I don't know what to say to that, so I just nod, and pull my hand slowly away.

My phone vibrates again. *did u buy that??!!*

I laugh and text back. *Thinking about it. Shouldn't. Want to. Probably won't.* Then I tell Celeste. "I'll think about the statue."

She nods. "I can always order another one if somebody buys it."

On the bus on the way home, I have to listen to two old white guys complain about the "wokeness" of their grandkids and I just want to disappear into my seat. When they finally get off the bus at the LRT stop the guy in the seat next to mine mutters, "I'd thought they never go away," and I snort. He looks at me sidelong and grins. "I hope I never get that awful when I get old," he says.

"I plan to get *more* woke," I say, surprising myself when it spills out of my mouth easily.

He laughs. "Me, too, man." He leans across me to pull the cord for the next stop, and I gather every ounce of courage I can muster.

"Not a man, actually," I say, and he glances at me and seems to study me for a moment.

"Sorry." His tone seems genuine.

"No problem," I say, and he smiles as he gets up and exits the bus, leaving me with an aching stomach but a feeling of gladness for having spoken up.

By the time I reach my stop I'm one of the last people on the bus and it's starting to smell like cooking outside, which reminds me that I'm going to have to buy groceries soon.

I smell onions and bacon and warm dough as I walk up the block to my street and it doesn't smell like it's coming from the restaurant downstairs; they mostly do fancy salads and soups. Just as I round the corner my stomach lets out an embarrassingly loud gurgle.

I hear laughter, deep and rich, and see a figure leaning on the wall next to my door, square boxes balanced in his hands.

"I took a gamble," Silas says. "And from the sounds of it, it was a good thing."

"I did eat today," I say, pretending to be indignant, but I can't really pull it off. I'm smiling too much.

He glances at my backpack as I slip it off my shoulder to dig out my keys. "Doesn't look like there's a statue in there," he says.

"I got some books." I unlock the door, and we go in, my belly growling again as the smell of the pizza fills the narrow hall.

"Well, you don't need a statue when you have the real thing."

"What?"

He leans over to kiss my cheek. "I can be your Pan and teach you to play." He says it with a distinct leer and laughs when I smack his shoulder.

"You want to teach me to play the Pan flute?"

His smile grows and I add, "And if you make a crack about Pan's flesh flute I will hurt you."

"Please hurt me," he says and ducks away. Then he adds, "But if you want to learn how to play an *actual* flute, I'd be happy to teach you."

Chapter Fifteen

T HE PIZZA IS GOOD, and we actually use the time to go over our prof's preliminary notes on our joint project, so it feels like we've accomplished something. I really enjoy working with Silas and using my brain and by the time we've gone over every comment I wish I could think of something else we could work on.

I keep having the feeling, though, that there was something I was going to tell Silas, something important, but every time it occurs to me it slips away again.

The evening slowly turns to night outside the window, and I know we've both got class tomorrow, but I don't want him to go. I think, maybe, that he doesn't want to go either. (I hope he doesn't want to go.)

And then, when I'm in the bathroom, frowning at myself in the mirror as I wash my hands, I get a cheeky, bold idea that is so unlike me I immediately push it aside. But when I leave the washroom, I head for my bedroom instead of going back to the living room.

In the top drawer of my dresser next to my boxer briefs is a small neatly folded pile of bras. Well, bralettes, really, stretchy and trimmed with lace. I haven't got anything to fill an actual bra, but a bralette sits snug over my pecs and sometimes it feels nice to put one on, to indulge the feminine part of my nature in a way I don't really dare to do in public.

I bite my lip and take out the one on top. It's emerald green and silky, with a wide band of lace around the ribs. Before I can change my mind, I pull off my t-shirt and put on the bralette instead.

I'm breathing too fast but when I catch sight of myself in the mirror on the antique makeup table that serves as a desk I stop breathing altogether. I look… I look good. *I* think I look good.

"Fuck it," I mutter under my breath, and I make myself walk out of the room. I pop the top couple of buttons on my fly, letting a bit of my boxers show – by some fluke of luck they're green too, but a darker shade – and then I walk into the living room with my head high.

"Hey, Alder, I've re-written our intro paragraph. Tell me what you think," Silas says as I round the corner. When I don't say anything, he glances up. His mouth falls open and he drops the pen he was holding.

I make myself keep walking across the kitchen floor until I'm facing him over the coffee table where both of our laptops are open. Then I stop and wait.

"Oh, sweetheart," he says, his voice a deep rumble. "Look at you."

I don't know if his words are good or bad, but they make my heart quicken and my fingertips tingle. I should say something. I *know* I should say something, but all words have fled and it's everything I can do to keep breathing.

Silas's eyes rake over me, up and down and up again, pausing on my chest. He stands, cocking his head to one side as if to see me from a new angle. He rounds the coffee table and reaches for me, setting his hands lightly on my hips.

"Hi," I say, which is about the stupidest thing I could say, but it's all that will come out.

"Alder," he says, like a whisper that skates over my skin and gives me goosebumps. His hands slide up from my hips to my ribs until they meet the edge of lace and then they pause. "I like this," he says. "I like this very much."

"Oh," I say, like a sudden release of breath. "That's good."

"Did you do this for me?"

I shake my head. "For me," I say, "But I hoped you'd like me in it. I've never put this on when anyone else was here."

"I do like you in it." His thumbs slip under the lace, brushing my skin, and then he finds my nipples and I gasp because they've never been so sensitive. They harden to little nubs that he teases and rolls under his thumbs, and I want to collapse, to pull him down on top of me.

"Is this okay?" he says, watching my face.

All I can do is nod.

He smiles and pulls me closer to kiss me, slow and careful, tongue sliding next to mine. I twine my arms around his neck and his hands move to my back to press me against him.

"Do you want me to stay tonight?" he asks when we come up for air.

I nod again.

"Do you want me to take you to bed?"

Another nod. Fuck, I need to find words soon. "Yes," I finally force out.

"Can I use your shower?"

Confused, I just say, "Of course."

"If I'm staying, I'm probably not going to have time to go home and shower before class," he explains. "And, anyway, I'm one of those weirdos who prefers to shower before bed."

"Me, too."

"Shower with me, then?"

"Okay." My whole body is flushed and tingling, eager to be naked with him, wondering if this will be the night he finally fucks me, and then realizing I don't care as long as he touches me, and I touch him.

We make our way to the bathroom, arms around each other, kissing, stroking, and by the time we bounce off the door frame and end up next to the tub, we're both naked and hard.

When I turn to start the shower, he runs both hands down my back and settles himself against me, cock lying pressed into my ass crack. I don't want to move, but I straighten slowly, and he holds me close, hands brushing my chest again and making my nipples tingle.

"I never used to be so sensitive," I say, my voice coming out ragged.

"Maybe I have a magic touch," he growls in my ear.

It's corny, but it turns me on anyway. "Fuck, Silas."

"Mmm."

He helps me into the tub and washes my hair for me and lets me wash his, and all the while I'm trying to keep my hands from shaking. Finally, he takes the showerhead off its hook and examines it, smiles, and twists it until the water comes out in a pulsing massage setting. I didn't even know it could do that.

With me pressed close to his chest, he runs the water massage over my neck and shoulders, and I relax against him. I'm still so fucking horny I could scream, but it also feels nice to just rest against his chest while the water works out knots in my muscles I didn't even know were there.

He moves it slowly over my back, then my ass, and then I startle, almost pulling away, when the blast of water hits my asshole.

He laughs, but gently. "Can you put your foot up on the side of the tub for me, sweetheart?" he says.

I swallow. The massage water is directed at my lower back now, but I know what he wants me to do, and I think I know why.

I steady myself on his chest and lift one foot to the edge of the tub, nudging the shower curtain aside a little.

"Arms around my neck," he murmurs, so I wrap my arms around his neck and look into his eyes. "Let me know if you don't like this," he says. "Okay?"

I nod and close my eyes as his mouth finds mine and his hand presses on my back to hold me, and the pulsing water from the showerhead slips down my ass crack.

At first, the water just beats against my asshole, massaging me until I'm drooping with desire, and I understand why he wanted me to put my arms around his neck. It's almost too much to keep myself upright. And then he shifts the angle of the showerhead, and the water hits my relaxed ass and penetrates me, pounds into me in a way that feels weird at first, but then very, very good.

I drop my head back and moan. I can't help it. Holy fuck.

"Feel good?" Silas says.

I try to make words but all that comes out is a needy sound. Then I manage to assemble my faculties enough to realize what the immediate result of having water shot up my ass is going to be. The water is going to come back out.

"Si," I say, my voice a croak.

"Mmm?" He's nuzzling my neck, nibbling and licking, and it's almost as sexy as the massage on my ass. *Up* my ass.

"The water… it's…"

He chuckles into my neck. "It's going to drip out, yes." He pulls back to look at me, then moves the shower head away, twists it back to normal flow and hooks it on its holder.

I suddenly feel the need to crouch down, to shit out the water and whatever else comes with it, but there's no way I'm doing that in front of Silas.

"I'll be in your bedroom when you're done," he says, and he gets out of the tub, towels off quickly and leaves with the towel wrapped around his waist.

As soon as he's gone, I crouch and let the water run out of me, squeeze until there surely can't be any left, and then stand up and wash myself. I don't look to see what else the massage rinsed out of me; I don't need to see my own shit sliding down the drain.

I climb out, unsteady on my legs, my skin tingling and my ass aching to be penetrated again. I dry off and wrap the towel around my waist and see the emerald green bralette hanging off the doorknob. Did I put it there when Silas tugged it over my head? Did he? I pull it on and settle it over my chest.

On the one hand, I want to be completely naked with him, but on the other, I want him to see me as I see myself: as man and woman both. A blend of the two. Small cock and small breasts and all of me aching for his touch.

(Oh God, really Alder? Dramatic much?)

He's waiting in the bedroom as promised, and the covers are folded back, the towel he was wearing spread out on the bed, but he's not in it. He's standing, naked, slowly stroking his cock and watching the door.

He smiles when he sees me and holds out both hands, so I cross the room to him, bolder than I feel, take his hands, and pull him close. His mouth on mine is hot and demanding, no longer careful, and I respond with the same ferocity.

When he breaks away, he steers me towards the bed and gently tugs away my towel. The bralette he leaves, but he strokes his thumbs under the lace band again, teasing my nipples until I close my eyes.

"Get on the bed for me?" he asks, voice soft, asking, not demanding despite how commanding his mouth just was on mine.

I sit on the edge of the bed and pull him closer, digging my fingers into his hips and stroking my tongue over the underside of his cock, teasing him with the tip of my tongue.

He strokes my hair back from my face and steps slowly backwards. "Will you get on your hands and knees for me, sweetheart?" he says.

When I do, he puts a hand between my shoulder blades. "Shoulders down," he says, "Just like that."

I look at him and he looks at me, drinking in the sight of me, ass in the air. Then he sits on the bed behind me and kisses my back, right in the divot above my ass crack. I press my face against the mattress as he spreads my ass cheeks apart and then… nothing. I hear him breathing and feel his hands on my ass.

"Fuck, Alder," he finally says. "Even your asshole is perfect."

And before I can think of a suitable reply – or any reply – his tongue is tracing a burning line down my crack and circling my asshole, and I can't think at all.

He circles me, rims me, at first soft and slow, and then more insistent and then he stops, the tip of his tongue poised in the exact center of my asshole.

I know I've been making embarrassing wanting sounds the whole time he's been eating me out, but now they get louder, and I think I actually whine. (Fuck, really?)

His breath is ticklish on me as he withdraws his tongue and places a hot kiss on my asshole.

"Do you want me to stop?" he says.

"No," I manage to gasp out. "No, don't stop."

Then his mouth is on me again, his tongue spearing into my ass and my needy noises turn to outright moans. I can't stop and I don't care how embarrassing I sound. He's fucking me with his tongue. (And how fucking *long* is his tongue?)

"Please," I manage. "Silas. Make me come."

(God, I really *am* embarrassing.)

He makes a rumbling noise in his chest that vibrates through his mouth and into my ass and I swear I feel it in my cock, too. Then his hand slides around my hip to curl around my cock, to stroke while his tongue fucks me and fuck I'm moaning again and spurting onto the towel and every part of my body is tingling with the pleasure of it.

His arm wrapped across my hips keeps me steady and his face against my lower back is warm. He helps me lie down, pulls the spunk-splattered towel off the bed and kneels, looking down at me. He's still hard, erect and magnificent, his foreskin pulling back to expose his head. I want him in my mouth.

"Come here," I say, and reach out to circle him with my fingers, softly, teasing, tugging until he moves closer, until he straddles my chest. I have to let go of him to push myself up onto my elbows to reach, so he holds himself, dips his cock down until I can get his head in my mouth and then he strokes with strong sure motions as I suck, tease, and suck again.

"Fuck, Alder," he says. "Both ends of you are perfect and pink and I want to bury myself in them."

I let my lips curl upwards but keep working, teasing his foreskin with my lips, pushing my tongue against his slit until his breath gets fast.

"I'm going to come, sweetheart," he says.

I take him deeper in my mouth, and he groans.

"I want to come on your face," he says, meeting my eyes. "Can I come on your face, sweetheart? I want to see my cum dripping off your beautiful eyelashes."

I tilt my head back, letting my mouth slide off him, but keep my lips parted, and I close my eyes. "Yes," I say, and he moans, just as loud and wanting as I did, and splatters my face when he comes.

I open my eyes cautiously – there is, indeed, spunk dripping off my eyelashes – and lick my lips, pulling in the salty taste of him where he hit my mouth.

He's looking down at me again, the expression on his face one of... wonder? Then he crawls backwards until he's leaning over me, arms braced on each side of my head, and he leans down to kiss me, to poke his tongue into my mouth and taste himself there.

I feel limp, spent, and completely sated. I'm not exactly inexperienced in sex, but I've never felt so fulfilled after, especially without any actual fucking happening.

Oh God, I don't want this to end. I don't want him to lose interest, to decide I'm not who he thought I was. And why the fuck can't I just be happy with what I have instead of terrified to lose it?

"What's wrong?" he says, reaching for the tissues and carefully wiping my face. "You looked content, but then you frowned."

"Nothing," I say, then remember that pretending to be okay when I'm not is the best way for things to *stop* being okay, according to my therapist.

"I just don't want you to go," I add.

He tosses the tissues onto the nightstand and settles down next to me. "I'm not going anywhere, sweetheart," he says, tracing the band of my bralette with one finger and then meeting my eyes. "Can you try to believe that for me?"

I bite my lips and nod. "I'm sorry."

He shakes his head. "You have nothing to be sorry for. And I *like* you. Even when you're anxious. Even when your self-confidence takes a nosedive. I like you, Alder, and I'm not going anywhere."

Then he pulls the covers up over both of us and snugs his arm around me and I fall asleep thinking maybe this time I got lucky.

Chapter Sixteen

I WAKE ONCE DURING THE NIGHT, roll over, and find the solid wall of Silas's back next me. I curl into him.

"Okay, sweetheart?" he says, his voice sleepy, and I feel bad for waking him, but instead of apologizing like I might once have done, I just curl closer.

"Yeah," I murmur. "I'm good."

Morning is a repeat of other mornings he's stayed, only it's my alarm that wakes me, not the sun. I'm alone, but quiet noises in the kitchen tell me he's still here, making coffee.

Maybe I did get lucky this time.

The rest of the week is busy for both of us, with assignments and reading ramping up, and profs expecting us to be settled in and ready to work. When Friday comes, I intend to text Silas, to see if he wants to come over, but I fall asleep before I even eat dinner and don't wake until sometime late at night.

I sit up carefully on my couch and stretch to ease the kink in my neck. I grab my phone to see that it's nearly three in the morning and I have two texts from Silas.

have a good week? is the first and then, a few hours later, *did u fall asleep?*

I get up to make toast because my belly is complaining about missing dinner, and as I wait for the toaster to do its thing, I type slowly.

Busy week, I write. *You?* I hesitate before sending, because I don't want to wake him if he's asleep. But if our positions were reversed, I'd rather be woken up than not know if he was upset with me or something. But then I'm a lot more needy than he is.

The toast pops up, startling me, and my thumb hits "send" by accident. Oh well, that decides that, then.

I butter my toast, add a thick layer of peanut butter and a drizzle of honey, and contemplate my phone again.

I type, *I fell asleep as soon as I sat down. Just woke up*, and this time I don't hesitate to send it. The three little dots appear to show he's typing an answer.

had a dream about u, he says, and I blush even though there's no one to see. I didn't dream about him, but I've been thinking about him constantly, finding my skin going hot at awkward moments when I remember the feel of his mouth on my skin, or the rumble of his voice, or even just the way he looked at me when I came out of my room in the emerald green bralette.

Oh, yeah? I answer.

i woke up w a circus tent for bed covers, he says.

Oh God, now the entire surface of my skin is hot. I probably look like a patchwork of dead white and hot pink. I could power a small country with the heat I'm giving off.

I almost (almost) ask for pics, but I'm not sure I'm into sexting or nudes. Maybe, but I don't think I could bring myself to send any back. I'm not trusting enough, and that's not fair.

What did you dream? I say instead.

ill tell u next time i see u, he answers. *next time were alone.*

Tomorrow? I say.

weve got that pan thing, he says.

After that?

count on it

Then we say our goodnights, with a lot of hearts and kissy face emojis. I finish off my toast, brush my teeth, and go to bed. I'm certain I'll lie awake for the rest of the night, thinking about him, about being naked with him, but I drop off almost immediately and wake to a bright morning. A bright, *cold* morning that makes me curl up under the covers and contemplate just staying in bed all day.

Eventually, I get up and adjust the thermostat, which I had turned way down due to the warm weather and the fact that the restaurant downstairs leaks heat upwards, so I never actually need to use much electricity in the winter.

Then I settle down with coffee and my laptop, Ego's books close to hand, to wait for it to be time to go.

There's another email from Satyr Rising LLC among the spam, this time a personal message, and not just one from Ego's mailing list.

Dearest Alder, I'm looking forward to introducing you to the rest of my circle and seeing how you fit in.

I snort and take a long sip of coffee. I've pretty much never fit in anywhere in my life, except maybe rock-climbing camp, and that was before I developed social anxiety.

I hope you've had time to read through my little missive on our local cryptids. Perhaps you've even figured out why I gave it to you, though I left that name and profession behind some time ago, just as you left behind your name and gender.

Wait, is he comparing changing study topics and pen names to coming out as nonbinary? He is, isn't he? That feels weird, deep in my gut, though of course people change occupations all the time.

Speak with me alone this evening and I will enlighten you further. You have great potential. Yours in Pan, Ego.

Great potential? Really? I'm not sure what to think about that. Every time I've met Ego, he's left me feeling inadequate and confused.

Oh shit, and *that's* what I meant to tell Silas, that I kept forgetting. That Ego Arcadia thinks – or once thought – that there were actual satyrs running around in the woods of Arcadia County. That he thinks he can somehow absorb their "Pan energy" in an unspecified ritual. And that maybe he thinks a group of Pan worshippers who migrated to North America way before other white people *are* those satyrs. That maybe he thinks Silas's family are satyrs and… I don't know, might be trying to find out more about them.

Ego Arcadia said Silas has strong Pan energy, didn't he?

I shake my head and move my laptop aside, setting it on top of the books so it's not in the way of me typing on my phone. I pause to scratch the back of my right hand, just above my thumb. It's so *itchy*. I realize, as I scratch, that I have a rash there, a small patch of reddish bumps like a thumbprint that's been bugging me for a while without me really noticing.

The buzz of my doorbell startles me out of the reverie I've fallen into, and I realize it's later than I thought. I've missed lunch and it's just about time to go meet Ego and find out what his "circle" is all about.

I get up and hurry out the door and down the stairs to let Silas in. He's carrying a heavy-looking box and unsuccessfully trying to hide a grin.

In my apartment, he puts the box on my battered wooden coffee table with a thump and pulls me into a hug. The kiss we share is long and intense and makes me want to abandon plans of going out in favor of going to bed.

"I could do that every day," says Silas when we break apart.

"Yes. You could," I say, and his grin widens.

"Multiple times a day."

"Yes." That gets me another kiss, one that leaves my knees weak.

"What's in the box?" I say, when he finally lets go and steps back.

"That's for later," he says. "Assuming you want me to stay tonight."

I can't stop the happy smile that grows, but I say, "What if I don't?"

"Then you'll just have to wonder."

I stick my tongue out at him, give the box another considering look, and then say, "What do I wear to this thing?"

Silas shrugs. "You'd know better than I do about dressing for a neo-pagan ritual. I just went with business casual. I assume he'd have told us if we were meant to dress in a specific way." He unzips his jacket, a leather biker one that shows off his narrow hips, to let me see the deep green button-down he's wearing with black dress pants and the coolest pair of wingtips I've ever seen. They're chunkier than usual and two-tone black and green. I don't think I've ever felt shoe envy before. (But I am totally feeling it now.)

"Help me pick something?" I say, and he follows me into my bedroom. I don't have much that would qualify as business casual, so I pull out my one pair of dress pants – charcoal grey wool – and then stand staring into my closet.

Silas comes up behind me, puts his hands on my shoulders, and gently moves me aside. "Put the trousers on," he says. "I'll find you a shirt." He pauses. "If that's okay?"

I'm curious to see how he'd dress me if he had a choice, so I nod and strip off the ratty sweats I'm wearing to put on the dress pants. Then I sit on the bed and watch as he goes through my meagre closet, taking hangers out to examine what's on them, then putting them back. Finally, he holds up a burgundy long-sleeved tee I'd forgotten was in there. It has a deep vee neck and a cut that's much too flowy to be masculine.

He quirks his eyebrows at me, and I shrug. "Got any more of those pretty bras around?" he says, and I feel heat in the back of my neck.

I bite my lip. "Are you sure?" I say, and I don't even have to tell him why I'm worried.

"I think where we're going should be safe, and if it isn't we leave," he says. "If you can't be your whole self in a spiritual celebration, then what's the point?"

I nod uncertainly.

"And you'll be wearing a jacket over top on the way there." He holds up the top again. "But I don't want you to be uncomfortable, sweetheart. I can pick something else." He turns back to the closet, and I only hesitate a few more heartbeats. "In the top drawer," I say, and point at the dresser when he turns. He flashes me his dimples, then opens the drawer to rummage.

"Oh, perfect!" he says, and holds up a black bralette trimmed in lace, with lace straps, and… well… basically it's entirely lace.

I stand still and let him pull my hoodie and tee over my head and then I pull on the bralette when he hands it to me. I reach for the burgundy top, but he says, "Wait." I stop and meet his eyes. His face is serious, his eyes dark. "You're beautiful, Alder," he says, then takes my shoulders and turns me towards the mirror. He stands behind me, looking at my reflection over my shoulder. "Look," he says.

I've always liked my body, but I'm used to putting myself down for other people, used to feeling like I'm not enough for them. Now I try to imagine what he sees.

He kisses the side of my face. "Okay, now put on the shirt." He hands it to me and settles it on my shoulders when I've pulled it over my head.

The v-neck shows off a lot more of my chest – and the lacy bralette – than I ever would have dared, and now I remember why I hung it in the back of the closet. I'd bought it on a whim while I was shopping with Alison, and paid more than I probably should have, liking the way the bamboo jersey draped and how the deep burgundy somehow made my hair look redder and my eyes look darker and richer.

It looks almost elegant, and I look… I look like someone might glance at me and wonder whether I'm a man or a woman (because most people don't consider that there might be another option). I look androgynous, which is obviously not every nonbinary person's goal, but which has always been mine.

"Hey," Silas says gently, and I focus on his face in the mirror, and then on my own, because there's a tear trickling down my cheek. "Do you want to choose something else?" he asks.

I shake my head. "No. No this is perfect. I look…" I wipe the tear away impatiently and breathe deep. "I look like me."

The evening's ritual is to take place at a rented space downtown, not at Ego's farm in Arcadia County, which is good because that would have been an hour's drive at least and neither Silas or I have a car.

If we're deemed suitable for the group, apparently, we'll be invited to the actual equinox ritual tomorrow, which *will* be at the farm, but that's something to worry about later. Like if we decide we want to join.

Ego greets us at the door, shaking Silas's hand and then engulfing mine in both hands. His fingers are rough and at first I really don't like the way he's touching me. But then he smiles at me, a secret sort of look, and says, "I'm so glad you both made it. Do come in," and it feels nice to be welcome, to be wanted.

Silas looks at me oddly as I let Ego lead me into the room, where cushions are arranged in a circle around a bronze cauldron decorated with fruit (only some of which is seasonal) and flowers (out of season and not local anyway). We each sit on a cushion, and I look around at the other people already here. Most of them look like very ordinary people you might pass on the street or in a mall; most are probably in their thirties and forties, but a few are older and a few younger. I wonder if they're regulars or other prospective additions.

Equally spaced around the circle are seven toga-clad people, including Stefan from the coffee shop event. It takes me a moment to realize that everyone here is a man, or at least very masculine-presenting, and everyone except the toga-clad is wearing dress pants and a button-down shirt.

I'm the only one who looks a little different.

Breathing becomes harder as I feel anxiety building up, so I try to concentrate on my heartbeat and on drawing in slow, even breaths.

Silas reaches over and takes my hand. "Let me know if you need to leave, sweetheart," he says softly, so that only I will hear him.

"I'm okay," I say, and when he raises his eyebrows, I say, "I *will* be okay."

"All right," he says, squeezing my fingers. "Let me know if that changes."

I nod and there's no time to say more because the rest of the cushions have filled and Ego steps into the center of the circle and drops a handful of something into the cauldron. Smoke billows out and I realize there was charcoal burning in there, waiting for incense.

I inhale carefully and recognize cedar and juniper – a mix I used to burn myself, for cleansing, when I studied Wicca and before I moved to an apartment with an oversensitive smoke alarm that I can't pull the batteries out of. There's pine in the mix, too, and cinnamon, and it's strong enough I need to suppress my urge to sneeze.

"Welcome, everyone," Ego says. "Most of you know each other, of course, but we are here today to meet two new men I've selected to apply for membership."

I sit up straight at the word "men" and notice Silas scowl out of the corner of my eye. Someone on the other side of the circle snorts. Then Ego turns to look at me, and puts his hand to his mouth. "Oh, pardon me," he says, his elegant tones somehow making it less obvious that he's over-acting. He knows exactly what he did and, presumably, he did it for a reason. I just don't know why.

"One man and one… I believe nonbinary person is the current terminology?" I think he's expecting me to agree, but I'm wishing too hard to be swallowed up by the earth and trying too hard to breathe normally to say anything at all.

The only thing that helps, a little, is knowing that Ego had some reason for singling me out, for making it obvious to his followers that I am not like them, and I want to know what that reason is.

Ego meets my eyes and smiles, a much colder expression than the warmth he greeted me with. Then his expression suddenly turns friendly, and I stay quiet out of sheer confusion.

"Our new man here, Silas, has exceptionally strong satyr energy, as I'm sure you'll notice. Alder, on the other hand, not being a man, has something more subtle, something I expect none of you have encountered. I am curious to know what each of you thinks once we're finished here tonight."

He turns away and I try to force out words, except I have no idea what to say, except maybe if I'd known this was a space only for men I'd never have come. I'd have stuck to my email interviews and left it at that.

Stupidly, I want to cry. I want to get up and leave, because so what if this group isn't for me? I'll find another; I'll go meet Silas's family and see if *they* have a place for me. (But what if they don't either?)

I try to get to my feet, to leave before I can be disappointed even more, misgendered again, maybe, but I can't move. I can't even open my mouth to ask Silas to take me home, even though I can feel him looking at me, can feel his concern as if he's said it out loud.

Ego looks around the room, and everyone says words of welcome and claps and I try again to get up and leave, but my head feels muddled and the whole back of my hand is itchy.

Why am I so itchy? I look at my hand and the rash has spread, covering my skin with redder, itchier looking spots in the shape of fingerprints. When I look up Ego is watching me again.

"Never fear, dear Alder, I'll speak to you alone soon." I try to open my mouth, to reply, but I can't. I feel woozy.

When I look at Silas again, he smiles at me, and I think whatever concern he had is gone. Doesn't he feel what I feel? I want to tell him that I want to go home, but now he's looking away and listening to whatever Ego is saying, and somehow I can't make out of any of it.

It's English, I recognize that much, but I can't make the words make sense and I want to scream. Then the words come clear again and I realize Ego is re-telling myths of Pan, describing his possible origins and what they might mean to the men of today. He smiles and looks at me. "Or the nonbinary people of today."

I smile back because I matter to him. He's recognized me, finally, and he wants me to join his group.

Ego keeps speaking, only now he moves slowly around the circle, kneeling in front of each seated person. He puts a hand on each of their heads and speaks a few words just for them, and each man smiles and nods and looks pleased.

When he gets to me, his hand on my head is warm and comforting. "Sweet Alder," he says. "Did you read my booklet?"

I nod. "Yes," I say. "Is it real?" (Is it real? Of course it's not real.) (But surely it *is* real.)

He smiles like a saint blessing his flock. "Oh, it's real. And I think you and I together can awaken Pan using that knowledge."

I blink at him, not sure what he's saying, except that he wants *my* help. "How?" I say.

"Not yet," he says, gently, kindly. "Tomorrow I'll come for you, and then we will change the world."

Then he gets up and moves to Silas, who smiles, but it's a reserved expression, like he's being polite, but not really buying what Ego is telling him. Does Ego want Silas's help, too? He chose both of us, so surely he must. That will be nice, if Silas and I can both help Ego and connect with our inner deities. Silas already looks like a god.

When Ego returns to the center of the circle, he begins a sort of call-and-response, and I don't know the proper words, but somehow they come out anyway, and he glances at me with a smile again. It goes on and on and I always seem to know the correct answer even if I couldn't have told you what it was afterwards, and with each round I feel energy building in the circle, swirling around us with Ego at its center.

I begin to *see* the energy as a blue-green glow, like a whirlpool around us, and when Ego raises his hands, we all get to our feet and call out one final response as we also raise our arms. The magic feels good but suddenly I want to go home again because none of this makes sense and when I look at Silas, he's even more godlike and beautiful and oh fuck he has horns and please I just want to go home but I don't because I feel like I'm part of something but it's something not right.

Ego drops his arms and the magic bursts from the circle all at once. Everyone starts embracing each other and smiling and nodding, and everyone seems to want to shake Silas's hand. I stand alone, watching as Ego speaks to Silas and Silas nods. Then both Silas and Ego turn to me, and I realize from his expression that what I experienced was not what everyone else felt.

Silas's eyebrows pulls together and Ego smiles again, too friendly. I don't move; I can't move, I can't think how to explain that nothing makes any sense, that maybe I knew the words, but it wasn't really me that knew them, or maybe it was, and I'm just confused.

Silas takes a step towards me, ignoring the rest of the people who want to shake his hand. Ego looks on, amused, as Silas realizes something is wrong, that I'm not okay.

"Alder?" says Silas, pushing aside someone who wants to talk to him in order to get to me. I'm not moving, but I feel like I'm being pulled farther away. Why is he so far away? I thought he was right next to me.

"Are you okay, sweetheart?" he says, and I realize that at least he's making sense, that I can understand *him* even if everyone else's words have turned into a nonsensical wall of noise. I try to smile as everything goes grey except the beige carpet rushing up to meet me.

Chapter Seventeen

I COME TO IN MY OWN BED, my head fuzzy and my stomach threatening to turn inside out.

I sit up quickly, get tangled in the covers and almost fall to the floor, but then Silas is there, holding me.

"It's okay, sweetheart," he says. "You're okay."

"Gotta puke," I choke out, and he lets go of me, then suddenly my bedroom garbage can is in my lap, just in time to catch the vomit spewing uncontrollably from my mouth. Silas's arm is strong around me and I lean on him while my stomach heaves. When I finally stop, he presses a kiss to my temple and holds out a tissue for me to wipe my mouth.

"Water," I say and my voice sounds like my throat was scraped raw with an ice cream scoop, which is also pretty much what it feels like.

"You want me to leave the garbage can?" he says, nodding at the receptacle wedged between my knees.

"Maybe," I say.

He lets go of me slowly, like he's trying to make sure I won't fall off the bed. Then he leaves and I hear water running and clutch the edge of the garbage can like I'm drowning and it's a floatation device. I don't think I'm going to throw up again, but I sure don't feel great.

The water Silas brings me is only tepid, not ice-cold, which is probably for the best. I rinse my mouth, then sip slowly, mouthful after mouthful, until I've emptied the whole glass.

"Better?" he says.

I nod. "Yeah, thanks."

"You want me to make you some tea?"

I think about that but find it hard to make my thoughts come to order. "I… no. Maybe in a bit." I put the garbage can carefully on the floor next to the bed and realize I'm still wearing the black lacy bralette and boxers from yesterday, but my dress pants and top are hanging over the back of a chair. Silas is wearing boxers and one of my t-shirts that, even though it's too big on me, stretches across his chest to show off his pecs in full definition.

(I wish I was in good enough shape to appreciate the view more.)

"What happened?" I say, staring absently at the back of my hands.

"I was going to ask you that." He climbs onto the bed to sit beside me, and I let myself lean against him.

I scratch my hand, and he takes it in his, pushes my other hand gently away and looks closely.

"When did this start?" he asks, pushing my other hand away again when I try to scratch.

"Last… Um. I noticed it was itchy when we got back from coffee with Ego, but it might have started before that. The rash came a few days later, I think. It got worse last night. I… I think I noticed it during the ritual, but it's all kind of fuzzy."

"During the ritual?" He holds my hand lightly but firmly.

"I think so." I frown at the bumpy reddened skin and tug at my hand. He doesn't let go. He's frowning at it and brushing his thumb over the rash and that should make it itchier, but it doesn't; it almost seems to help.

"Do you have any calamine or anti-itch cream?" he asks, finally looking up at me.

"I think there's some in the bathroom drawer. Under the sink."

He gets up and goes out while I stare at the back of my hand and try not to scratch it. I have a flash of memory – at least I think it's a memory and not just a weird dream – of Ego Arcadia looking at me as I'm realizing I'm about to pass out and giving me a secret sort of smile. Then he looked at Silas, who seemed to be crawling with shadows that turned into large, curling horns sweeping back from his forehead to tangle with the dark curls of his hair.

I jump and almost scream when Silas climbs back onto the bead and takes my hand again. "What is it?" he asks, as he twists the top off a tube of ointment and spreads some on the back of my hand.

I realize I'm staring at him, half expecting him to sprout horns.

"After we sat down last night, at the ritual…" I pause, searching for the words, and make myself look away from his face to watch him spread ointment on my hand. He's so careful it's sweet. For once, I'm not struggling to make words come out of my mouth, I'm only trying to find the ones that will explain what I remember of last night.

Silas waits patiently, letting go of my hand to put the cap back on the tube and then stroke my hair so softly it's barely a touch.

"It was like everyone was suddenly speaking a different language. I mean, I knew it was English, but it didn't make any sense. I couldn't make it make sense in my brain."

His lips brush my temple. "You talked, though," he says. "You knew all the responses to Ego's words and said them perfectly clearly."

"I know," I say, my frustration leaking into my voice. "I started to understand what he was saying again, and I felt my mouth open and words came out, and they were the right words, only I don't know how I knew them and I forgot them as soon as I spoke." I sigh and lean on him again, wanting to feel his strength. "And… I thought I could see magic, like the ritual was calling magic around us and it was like a blue glow that swirled around the circle. It… it kind of *filled* us and surrounded us, and then when we all stood and raised our hands it… burst outwards and vanished. I thought I was seeing magic, only I was confused because I didn't understand any of it."

I stop to wipe away a tear that's escaped my eye, and then it's joined by more and I have to turn away from Silas to grab a tissue, so I don't drip snot down my face. (Why am I so fucking weak?)

"It's okay, sweetheart," he says, tucking me against his side when I'm done blowing my nose.

I pull in another deep breath, let it out, and concentrate on my heartbeat until it steadies.

"When we first got there, I… I didn't want Ego anywhere near me. But then he suddenly seemed nice. I…" I almost don't go on, feeling ashamed of my own sudden changes of heart, but Silas's arm around me gives me courage. What the hell, he's going to find out what a freak I am eventually. "Then I wanted him to like me. I was… I was flattered that he seemed to single me out, even when it felt like a punch to gut the way he talked about me being nonbinary."

I burrow my face into his shoulder, but then make myself look at him. "And I was jealous that he seemed to think you were something special, too, which is so dumb." I bite the inside of my cheek. "Then, right before I passed out, you… you looked like you had horns."

"And then you puked." He sounds thoughtful. And angry, but not at me. *For* me.

"I'm sorry."

"Shh," he says. "It's okay." He breathes into my hair and says, "I almost got up and walked out when he pulled that, 'I believe that's the correct terminology' bullshit."

Stupidly, that starts me crying again. "Me, too," I say. "Only I couldn't move. It was right after that when I couldn't understand what people were saying. I wanted to tell you that I wanted to go home, but I couldn't say anything."

"Oh, sweetheart," he says. "I'm so sorry. I should have noticed. I should have realized."

I shake my head. "Am I going crazy?"

"I think you were drugged."

I sit up straighter so I can see his face. "What? How? I didn't eat or drink anything."

"The same way you were drugged at the coffee shop." He reaches for my hand and brushes his thumb over the rash.

"Through my skin? What kind of drug does that? And why didn't it affect Ego, or you when he shook your hand?"

"I don't know, sweetheart. I just know that twice now, Ego Arcadia has touched you when you didn't want to be touched and then you suddenly wanted to be his best friend."

"And then I hallucinated."

"Something like that."

"But why?" It comes out pathetic, like a child protesting unfair treatment.

"I don't know. Maybe he wants to use you, and drugging you is a way to make sure you cooperate. Maybe he wants to set us against each other. He seems awfully eager for me to join his group."

"He… I think he said something about us, about me and him, accomplishing something together."

"He didn't say what?"

"No. He seemed to think I should already know, but I have no idea." I want to just ask "why" again, but I don't, because something is tugging at my thoughts, something I'm supposed to remember. Is it to do with Ego? It won't resolve into anything tangible.

And then I yawn, which makes Silas yawn.

"How about we try to figure this out in the morning?" he says. "I know where I can borrow a car, if you feel like going for a drive out of the city somewhere."

"Like where?" My eyelids are feeling heavy and it's still dark. My body is determined to get more sleep, even if I want to stay awake and puzzle over recent events.

"Wherever you want."

"Will you take me to your sheep farm?"

He pulls away to look at me, as if startled by my request. "It's a long drive, there and back, but yeah, I'll take you there if you want. If you're ready to meet my parents."

"Okay." Unbearable sleepiness is creeping over me faster now. I have no idea what time it is, or even where my phone is, and I find myself unable to care very much.

"Do you think you can sleep now?"

I nod, so he tucks me in and nestles in next to me. I drift off quickly, to dreams of my mother warning me of danger, and of the forest at night, and fear that somehow becomes joy, because I'm being chased through the trees, only it's Silas chasing me and when he catches me, he's going to tumble me into a bed of moss and pleasure me until the sun rises.

I wake once, early in the morning as the room turns from black to grey. The other half of the bed is empty, but I hear movement in the kitchen, so I roll over and go back to sleep, back into dreams of the forest and my satyr lover and his improbably long tongue.

When I wake again, it's much later, enough later that the sun has passed across my bedroom window and is almost out of range. I sit up and blink. My eyes are crusty and my stomach hurts but rumbles with hunger, so I must be improving.

I pull the bag out of the garbage can and tie the top shut, so I don't have to smell the puke in it, and carry it with me to the bathroom. I might as well empty all my garbages while I'm at it. I take my time brushing my teeth and washing my face, checking the mirror to see how awful I look.

There are dark circles under my eyes, almost green, that stand out on my pinkish skin, and my eyes are bloodshot. I look like shit, but there isn't much I can do about it. I pull off my bralette and boxers and toss them into the basket by the door. The hot water of the shower feels so good on my skin that I linger and only get out when I remember that Silas will have made coffee, and he promised to take me for a long drive.

Back in my bedroom I pull on fresh boxers and my favorite jeans, then feeling daring, I put on a pain grey sports bra and decide on the same t-shirt that I wore on my first day of grad school, obscene satyr and all.

Then I remember I'm going to meet Silas's family today, so I pull a deep green hoodie on over it.

When I go to the kitchen, I'm expecting Silas to be waiting, sipping coffee and looking at his phone. The room is empty, and there's no sign of coffee. The French press is still disassembled and upside-down in the dish rack next to the sink.

I look around. Except for the box on the coffee table, and my too-big t-shirt draped over the back of the couch, there's no sign that he was here at all.

Maybe he went to borrow the car?

I check my jacket pocket for my phone, pulling it off its hook by the door, but it's not there. My wallet and keys are in their usual pockets, but no phone. I remember that my dress pants were hanging off a chair in my bedroom, to I check them next. Nothing.

I look around slowly and spot my laptop, so I start it up and set it on the counter while I fill the kettle and measure coffee into the press. I feel like I'm thinking through mud. Hopefully caffeine will help.

With that taken care of, I sit in front of my computer. My email holds only the usual spam, plus a few school-related things I'll look at later. And one message from Ego. Nothing from Silas.

I open Ego's mail, just the thought of the weirdness of last night making my chest tight.

Thank you for your presence last evening. Your friend Silas proved to be a most welcome source of satyr energy, and I am eager to pursue its use more fully with you. See you soon, dear Alder. Yours in Pan, Ego.

What the fuck am I supposed to make of that? He writes as if I know what he's talking about, but I don't; his words only make me feel uneasy. I close my mail program and start up the app that locates all my devices. It shows my phone somewhere very close by, so at least I didn't leave it at Ego's rented space last night. It must be here somewhere.

It's only after I've scoured my apartment twice, even going so far as to pull the cushions off the couch and chair, that I think to open the door and check the hall. I mean, why would I leave it there? But I was pretty out of it last night – to the point that I don't remember anything after passing out, let alone what I might or might not have done after getting here.

I find it halfway down the stairs. And then I notice that the street door is open. I sit on the stairs a moment, contemplating the open door. I can understand it being unlocked. Silas doesn't have keys, so he wouldn't have been able to lock it after he left.

Silas left.

I make myself get up, walk the rest of the way down the stairs, and close the door. Then I make myself go back to my apartment, plug in my phone, pour my coffee, add honey and cream, stir, and take a sip.

Finally, I tap the screen of my phone and put in my passcode.

There's nothing new in my messages. Nothing from Silas since yesterday, from before we went to Ego's thing. I push aside the unpleasant feeling that's building in my gut.

Silas left.

I drink more coffee and try to decide what sort of message I should send, or if I should send one at all.

One part of my brain is telling me Silas finally realized I'm not what he wants, that my unhinged behavior last night – passing out and puking and being weirdly confused – was the last straw and he left without waking me to avoid a scene. (I wouldn't have made a scene.) (Not until he was gone, and it was only me to witness my pathetic neediness and my tears.)

The other part of my brain is stuck on how he held me last night, how he stroked my hair while I threw up, how he offered to make me tea, and how he still called me "sweetheart" in his deep rumbly voice.

Finally, I just type, *Good morning*, and send it.

He doesn't reply right away, but he might be driving if he's borrowed a car, and he doesn't always answer quickly anyway, so that means nothing, despite what that one part of my brain is shrieking at me.

I sit at the kitchen counter, drinking coffee after coffee, not moving except to get up and pee. I don't eat, afraid I won't keep anything down, even though I don't feel too awful, considering.

I pretend to work on an essay, then I pretend to read an article, and finally I look at my phone again.

And I type. *I'm sorry I'm such a fucking mess. I understand if you don't want to see me anymore.* I send it without thinking too carefully. (If I thought about it, I wouldn't have sent it.)

(I probably shouldn't have sent it.)

Then, after a couple of hours, I collapse into a miserable ball on the couch. I want to cry – I feel like crying – but no tears come, so I just lie there feeling sorry for myself, staring at the cardboard box on the coffee table.

Finally, completely sick of myself, I get up and get a knife from the kitchen and cut the tape on the box, fold open the flaps, and look inside.

And then tears do come, in such a flood I can barely see. I reach into the box, hands shaking, and pull out a two-foot-tall brass replica of a Pompeiian Roman copy of a Greek marble of Pan teaching the shepherd Daphnis to play the syrinx. I put it carefully in the middle of the table.

And I grab the empty box and fling it as hard as I can across the room.

It hits the door with a surprisingly loud bang and I'm about to follow it with an agonized scream.

Silas left.

Silas isn't answering my texts.

Silas doesn't want me anymore.

The door opens and my heart leaps. I rub at my face hastily, telling myself how stupid I was to jump to conclusions, drawing in a breath to say his name.

"Si –"

It's not him.

Ego Arcadia, dressed in a toga that's far too brief for the autumn weather, especially now that it's finally turned cold, steps through the door as if it's his own apartment he's entering. Behind him, Stefan scowls at me. He's wearing a toga, too, though he's smart enough to have sweatpants under it and a coat over top.

"Did I come at a bad time?" Ego says, as if he's dropped in for tea.

"Get the fuck out of my apartment," I say, filling my voice with a strength I don't really have. The part of my brain that told me Silas was gone for good is happy that Ego is here; that part of me wants to invite him in, to offer him coffee, to fawn over him until he likes me.

The other part of my brain is the part that managed words. That part wants him far away. That part wonders if he's the reason Silas is gone.

"Oh, come now, dear Alder. Why so angry?" He looks around. "I do like your art." He spots the statue. "Especially that one." He looks back at me.

I'm frozen in rage, and not a little fear. If he drugged me, he could do it again. He could get me to do whatever he wants. The most frightening thing is that there's part of me that would welcome it.

"Leave me alone," I choke out. I can't seem to make myself move.

"Now, now, that's not what you really want, is it? You came to me with questions about Pan, and at first, I thought were just another unworthy seeker." He smiles a not very comforting smile. "I thought your friend Silas much more worth my time." He taps his chin, like he's being thoughtful. "But you, it turns out, have a remarkable talent, and that talent will make many things possible. Now, come with me and I'll share with you the deepest secrets of my path, the things I didn't dare put in any book for the public to see."

"Where's Silas?" I ask.

"Running around naked in the woods of Arcadia County, I should think," he says. "Today is the equinox, and tonight his kind will be rutting and fucking and getting disgustingly drunk to celebrate."

"What?" I feel very very off, like Ego's drugs are affecting me again, even though he hasn't touched me.

"Didn't he tell you?" His voice is light, polite curiosity that I know must be fake. "And surely you saw him during the ritual? I so hoped it would help you see what sort of creature you'll allowing to taint you."

"What?" Why is that the only word I can say?

"He's a satyr, sweet Alder, strong in Pan energy but unable to use it for true enlightenment. His kind are good only to bring spiritual harmony to people like you and me." Now his look turns cruel. "Only you aren't meant to achieve it by bending over for him."

"Get out," I say, but it only comes as a whisper.

"Ah, I so hoped you had seen the truth and beauty of my path," he says, turning his features into showcase of patient disappointment.

I shake my head. "You're not making any sense."

"Don't you want, with all your heart, to find a spiritual path that honors Pan? One that appreciates you for who you are and doesn't try to fit you into a pre-conceived idea of who and what you should be?"

I stare at him. I want to hate him, but he might as well have spoken aloud my deepest desire. (My deepest desire, save one.) "Yes," I whisper.

"And I mean to give that to you. Will you come with me?" He holds out a hand and I almost take it, but then I remember what happened last night.

"No," I say. "I... want those things, but not like this."

"Not like what? I haven't told you about the ritual yet."

"But Silas —"

"Silas has left you, Alder. Don't you see? You are meant to do this with me."

Stefan shifts in place next to him and turns his scowl equally on Ego and me.

"Go away," I say.

Silas has left me.

Ego sighs. "Very well." He turns towards the door. "Stefan…"

Stefan grins then, and there's nothing friendly in it. He crosses the floor, and I try to dodge away. He grabs my hand, and I use my other hand to hit him. I'm no good at fighting, but I know enough that I've escaped getting beat up more than once by inflicting just enough pain to get away and run like hell.

"Oh, really," says Ego.

I try to move away as he approaches, taking something out of a fold of his toga as he comes. A small jar, I think. I can't escape him and keep out of Stefan's reach at the same time, not with Stefan's hand around my left wrist like a shackle.

"Hold still," Ego says, and reaches for me, I duck but he manages to smear something across my cheekbone that itches and burns, and suddenly I feel weak.

"Bring him," he says, turning away again.

"I'm not a him," I say, not sure why it feels so important that I say it. Like, staying on my feet should probably be more important. Getting away should be more important. "I'm a they."

Stefan and Ego both ignore me as my vision starts to go soft. I try one more time to get away, to run, but Stefan's grip is strong, and I trip and suddenly I'm looking at the hardwood floor of my apartment from over Stefan's shoulder. Why was I trying to get away? Ego is my friend.

But Stefan is not. I try to kick him, to pound his back with my fists, to *not* suddenly start liking these people this time.

Oh God, Silas left me, and I'm alone with this freak who thinks he can use magic to gain everything he wants. Who thinks I'll help him.

"No," I say, and suddenly Ego's feet are on the floor under me, pale and sandal clad. He needs to cut his toenails, which is a really stupid thing to notice.

"Sleep," he says, taking my right hand and smearing more of whatever it was in that jar on my skin. "It will be easier that way." And I sleep.

Chapter Eighteen

I WAKE WITH A SORE BACK and a sick feeling in my gut, and I'm really fucking tired of passing out.

I try to sit up and I can't, and that's when I realize I'm tied down on a hard surface. And it's dark, with only flickering uncertain light around me. All around me in a circle. I breathe slowly and try to make sense of where I am.

I smell damp and suck it in through my nose, close my eyes to try to sense it better. A faint dripping sound from somewhere nearby suggests a cave. It reminds me of the time I went cave climbing, the year before I broke up with my ex, and he started a fight because I was so excited when I got home. I never went again.

I open my eyes and wonder why I'm not terrified. I feel calm, a little angry, but not afraid. (I should be afraid, shouldn't I?) My mom used to say I was good in a bad situation. Calm and reliable.

This seems a little far past "bad situation." But once again my mom's premonitions turned out to be right. I almost laugh out loud, but I don't know if I'm alone or not.

Smooth but irregular stone walls confirm "cave" and I think I even see some kind of paintings, ancient rock art, but the light is too uncertain to be sure. I almost dislocate my shoulders trying to look around me, and I definitely pull something in my neck, but I don't see anyone else or hear another person nearby.

My arms are tied over my head, a bit more than shoulder width apart, and my ankles are similarly tied below me. I wiggle to see if there's any give in the knots, any room to slip out, but whoever tied them knew what they were doing.

How the fuck did I end up here?

Oh, right. Ego Arcadia. I guess refusing to go with him means being kidnapped and tied up in a cave, but for what? He wasn't happy when I told him I wouldn't help him. (I did tell him I wouldn't help him, didn't I?) And he wasn't happy that I didn't even understand what it was he wanted me to help him with. Okay, fine. But what does he plan to *do* with me?

Dread settles in my gut when my brain finally connects the clues. Ego thinks Silas is a satyr. That's what he meant by "his kind" celebrating the equinox in the forest, isn't it? Ego wants me to help him use Silas's satyr energy in some kind of ritual, and it's something he can't publish in a book.

Ego wants me to help him sacrifice Silas.

My breathing speeds up until I'm hyperventilating, and I have to force myself to take slow, deep breaths so I don't pass out again.

Ego wants me to help sacrifice Silas.

Silas left me.

But wait, then why am *I* trussed up in a cave? I crane my head again, trying to see the surface I'm tied down on. Is it an altar? Oh God, is Ego going to sacrifice *me* because Silas isn't here?

(Breathe, Alder. Just breathe.)

Silas left me to be kidnapped by Ego. To be *sacrificed* by Ego.

No. Fuck, no. I'm not even going to think about that. If I start crying now, I won't be able to stop, and crying isn't going to get me anywhere. I need to escape.

Then something else connects in my brain. I'm not the sacrifice. *I'm bait.* I feel a truly awful feeling of relief. Ego isn't going to sacrifice *me*, he's going to keep me tied up until Silas comes for me, and then he's going to catch Silas, and sacrifice *him*.

I need to figure out how to warn Silas.

But Silas isn't going to come. Silas was already gone before Ego arrived, with no note left and no word since.

Silas left me.

The spot on my cheek burns and itches where Ego spread his drugged ointment, and my hand is so itchy it's almost enough to distract me. I hear a high-pitched whine, and it takes a stupid long time for me to realize it's coming from me. I force myself to breathe slowly again and push thoughts of Silas aside. I almost manage a laugh when I think about how I can write up this whole experience and use it in my thesis, once I get out of here.

There's a rattle of stone from somewhere, echoing quietly, and then an electrical whine, like a small motor under strain. It stops and I hear the familiar snap of carabiners and the rustle of harness and rope. It's not far off, maybe down the dim passage I can just make out in the wall past my feet.

My feet are bare and dirty and dead white against the dark. They look pathetic, just like me. (Fuck off, Alder. Now is not the time for self-pity.)

Another motor whine and more rope sounds, and now I hear voices, low enough I can't make out words. Then they get louder.

"I need you ready, Stefan," says Ego, his voice coming closer.

"But I can help with the ritual. You said if I did those things for you, I'd become your second."

"And so you will."

"You let me help last time."

Last time? They've done this before? Did they sacrifice someone?

Ego sounds like he's getting irritated at a child for asking too many questions. "After I ascend tonight, you will take my place as Master of Ritual."

Fuck, he really *does* have an ego, doesn't he?

"Fine," mutters Stefan. "But good luck getting that freak to help you."

"Alder is… different, I agree, but it's a difference that will work to my advantage. I have an idea for a new component to the ritual, one that will make it more effective." He pauses. "And he *will* cooperate. I've given him enough drugs he'll suck my cock if I ask him to."

Both the "he" and what he says he can make me do almost make me throw up, and I'm really not lying in a good position for that.

I don't catch what Stefan says in response, but Ego laughs. "We all know how you feel about men fucking men, but it was not something the Greeks shied from. And I don't intend to have him pleasure me, I intend to pleasure myself." He pauses again, as if amused at Stefan. "And since Celeste has suddenly decided she doesn't wish to be my nymph any longer, I'm going to need release. Why not make it part of the ritual? Why not use it to channel even more magic. Did you *feel* how Alder could call magic?"

"Yeah, he was… pretty good."

"He was remarkable."

"But you don't have to fuck him."

"Would you rather I fucked you?" Ego laughs. "Oh, not so anti-achillean after all, are you? You *do* want me to fuck you."

"Only to improve the ritual." Stefan's voice is sullen.

I'm even more confused now, trying to sort thought what I'm hearing. Is the Celeste he's referring to the same one who works at the Spiral Gate? Did she know him all along? Was she his lover? I feel betrayed, even though I didn't really know her. I *liked* her. I wanted to be her friend.

Then the next part of what he said sinks in as I hear the electric motor whine start up and recede. He intends to make fucking me part of his ritual, and he sounded like he thinks I'll be willing.

My breath gets fast again, and I have to fight not to beg for my freedom when Ego walks into the cave. I also have to fight to hold back tears because I won't show him any weakness. I won't. (Please don't let me show weakness.)

"Ah," says Ego. "You're awake, good. I hope you're a little more reasonable now." I hear his footsteps approach and then I see him, past my feet. He walks around the stone slab until he's next to me, and then he leans over me. "You do want to help me, don't you?"

His voice is so soothing, so reasonable. Of course I want to help him. I shake my head, trying to find that anger I felt when I first woke here, or even fear. But all I feel is muddled, and warm. So warm I might fall asleep.

"Now, now, be a good boy and stay awake." Ego pats my face, and I realize I've let my eyes fall closed. I open them and look up at him. He's smiling and it feels good. He's smiling at *me*.

"I'm not a boy," I say. I think I'm supposed to be angry about that, but

I can't remember why. Does it matter if he thinks I'm a boy? (It *does* matter. It matters enough that I almost find that anger.)

"Of course, my apologies. But I need you now, dear Alder."

"Need me for what?"

"I need you to call your satyr friend."

"Silas isn't a satyr."

"Oh, but he is. You saw his horns for yourself."

"That wasn't real. I was drugged." That wasn't real, was it? I thought I only fantasized about Silas with horns because I like satyrs, and I like Silas.

Silas has left me.

"It *was* real. My drugs bring clarity, not hallucinations."

Of course it was real. Ego knows these things.

"I need you to call Silas, Alder."

"How? I'm tied up and I don't even know where my phone is."

"Well, I can't untie you yet, my dear. Soon, but not yet. And you don't need a phone to call him." He moves around by my head and puts his fingers on each of my temples. I try to flinch away, but then I remember that Ego won't hurt me. He likes me.

I shake my head hard to clear it and graze my itchy cheekbone against the stone and the pain helps me think a little better.

"I won't call him," I say. "I'm sorry, but I won't." And I *am* sorry. I want to help Ego, but even if Silas left me, I won't betray him.

"Do you think he loves you?" says Ego.

"I don't know," I reply, feeling misery wash over me.

"He can't love you, Alder. His nature doesn't allow it."

I try to make sense of that, but it's hard to think past the effect of the drug so I say, "Why did you drug me?" and it comes out like a child's whine.

"You didn't want to help me, my dear. But you want to help now, don't you?"

"Will you drug Silas?"

"Perhaps. I don't think I'll need to, though. I think he will take your place willingly."

"But you said he doesn't love me."

"He *wants* you, though."

Silas wants me.

"And if I must drug him, I will. Surely you know it's a time-honored tradition to drug a sacrifice. The Incas did it, and the Celts. It helps the chosen face their destiny head-on, without any embarrassing fear." He leans over to look at me upside-down. "You don't want your friend to piss himself when he meets He Who Brings Fear in Quiet Places, do you?"

I don't think anything would make Silas piss himself in fear, *especially* not meeting the ancient god of his people.

"Fuck you," I say, startling myself. Wait, I *like* Ego. Don't I? But he wants to sacrifice Silas.

"Later, sweet Alder. That's for later, and it's *I* who will fuck *you*, to honor our god and celebrate my ascension." He smiles and straightens up. "You should be flattered. It used to be Celeste who made herself available to me after a ritual. You know Celeste? Lovely dark skin, big brown eyes, long hair you can hold on to?"

"I hate you," I say.

"Well, apparently so does she, now." He laughs. "She doesn't approve of me working with you. She thinks you're pure and innocent, as if someone who fucks a satyr can be pure. But no matter. Once the sacrifice is complete, you'll be falling all over yourself to offer *me* your ass." His fingers stroke the hair back from my temples. "And anyway, you don't hate me."

"No. I don't hate you." (Yes, I do, dammit.)

"Now you're going to call Silas for me."

"I don't know where he is."

"That doesn't matter." His voice sounds calm and reasonable. Why was I so angry?

"I don't have my phone."

"You don't need your phone." He touches my temples with his fingers. "You have magic, just enough to be useful. And your lover is a satyr, so he'll hear you."

Silas is my lover. I smile, but not at Ego. I smile at the memory of Silas kissing me.

"I don't know how to call him," I say.

The blow is so sudden there's no way I could have anticipated it. It's only an open-palmed slap, from one side, but it's quick and well-placed, and the whole side of my face stings. My teeth have cut into my cheek and my ears ring.

"Now, see what you made me do?" He strokes where he hit me, gently.

I blink away tears and try to fight back panic. My ex used to say that, when he got so angry at me that he threw something, or punched something. But at least he never hit *me*.

"You know how," Ego says. "You knew how to see your lover's satyr nature without anyone telling you what to see."

How does Ego know what I saw? Did I tell him? I don't remember telling him, but there's a lot I don't remember, like why he wants me to call Silas.

"You don't make any sense."

He smacks me again, from the other side. This blow has more force, and I hear something crack in my neck. The muscle I strained earlier twinges, and more tears come to my eyes, no matter how I try to fight them back.

Ego puts a hand on either side of my face, and I wince, but his touch is gentle now and the sting of his blows fades.

"You stubborn, stubborn creature," he says, his voice all reason again. "Just concentrate on him and call him in your mind. He will hear, and he will come. And when he does, he will take your place on the altar, and you will take your place beside me."

I want to tell him to go fuck himself, but a warmth is drifting through my body, and it feels nice.

"Go on, now," he says, and I smile at the gentleness in his tone and close my eyes. My head spins, but I let it, and it eases off, turning to gentle sort of rocking in my thoughts.

Silas, I think. Then, *no*. "He won't come," I say, aloud, softly. Ego has moved away, and I hear him doing something behind me where I thought I glimpsed a table while craning my neck to see where I was. There's a crackle and the cave fills with the scent of burning cedar and juniper, pine resin and fir needles, a touch of cinnamon.

He chuckles and turns back to me to smooth my hair off my face and run a sticky finger over my lower lip. It itches and burns and somewhere in my brain, I realize he's given me another dose of his drug. "He will come," he says. "Your Silas can't resist you, my sweet Alder, because you have a spark of magic no satyr can resist."

"I what?"

"It's why I chose you. It's why he's drawn to you. But you mustn't think it's love."

No, of course not. Silas doesn't love me. He hasn't known me long enough. And even if he had… My memory chooses that moment to bring up all the degrading things my ex said to me, and I feel a tear slide down my cheek, the salt stinging where I scraped my cheekbone on the stone.

"Of course," I agree. "I'm… I'm not worth loving."

"Ah, now, I don't think I'd go that far. I'm sure *somebody* could love you. But not a satyr. They're barely more than animals, Alder. Monsters in their true form."

I shiver, remembering the glimpse of Silas with horns, Silas with strange eyes that flared green, Silas with furry legs that bent the wrong way and ended in cloven hoofs.

"I called him," I say, not sure if I really did, part of me hoping I didn't. Even if Silas doesn't love me, can't love me, he doesn't deserve to be killed.

"Good for you. With his help, with his blood, we'll call our god to us. I will become his one true priest on this Earth, and you will be my acolyte, my second."

"I thought Stefan was your second?" I blink up at him and smile dreamily.

"Not if you do your job," he says, stroking my hair again. I remember, vaguely, that I don't like him touching me, but I don't remember why. It's nice. "Now I want you to call him again, to make sure. Will you do that for me?"

Something about his phrasing makes my stomach lurch, makes me want… I don't know what. When I close my eyes and think, *Silas*, it's with real longing. Oh God, Silas. "No," I say softly.

"Call him." Ego's voice is steel.

"I did." I'm crying again and I don't even know why. If I get out of this, I'm going to make it my mission to never pass out again, and never cry again.

"Good boy. Sorry, not a boy. But you did good."

Did I? Silas left me; he won't come when I call. And if he does come… It doesn't feel like I've done good, but I'm confused, and nothing is making sense. Even my own memories.

"Alder," Ego says softly. "When he comes, you must not be afraid."

"Afraid of Silas?" Why would I be afraid of Silas? Silas likes me. No, Silas left without even leaving a note because I passed out and puked and cried all over him.

"You have had a glimpse of his true form, but when he comes, when he steps into this sacred circle, you will see him wearing his monstrous shape in the flesh. It can be… disconcerting."

"Oh." Now I just want to sleep. If only this bed wasn't so hard.

"I will protect you, Alder, so you needn't fear."

"Okay."

"Picture him and call one more time."

I call Silas to mind, trying to remember what he looked like with horns, but what comes to me is him standing naked in the middle of my bedroom, stroking himself as he waits for me to get out of the shower. I remember how his mouth dropped open, just a little, when I came into the room and he looked at me like I mattered, like even if he wanted my ass, he also wanted *me*. All of me.

And then he left.

"Stop crying, Alder. Silas will come for you, but you must be strong and resist him when he gets here."

I swallow with difficulty. "Promise?" I say, feeling like a little kid. My dad was hard to get a promise from, but if he gave one, he'd keep it. I try to be like him that way. When I fell from the glacial boulder in our back yard and broke both wrists and fractured my tailbone, he had said he'd sign me up for rock-climbing camp that summer if I stopped trying to climb that boulder.

"Promise?" I'd said, and he had promised, and that summer, after my bones healed, I got to spent two glorious months learning to climb properly. I didn't even try to get up that boulder again until I knew how, and my dad had grinned at me, and told me he was proud of me. My dad used to be proud of me.

"I promise." But it's not my dad, it's Ego.

"Okay," I say, and I try to picture Silas again. This time, I remember him stopping to tell me my shirt is cool, and I looked up to see a man who looked like a Greek god smiling at me. I had met his warm brown eyes, and I started to fall. *Silas. It's a trap.*

Maybe he won't come now. Oh God, I still want him to come. I want him to rescue me. I want him to not be the monster Ego says he is.

But I'm afraid Ego is right.

"What if he doesn't come?" I say.

His hands pause from stroking my hair, then resume. "He'll come. I've attracted his kind before, and I'll do it again in future."

"Before when?" I look up at him, at his calm, sure face. I want him to be proud of me. (Don't I?)

"Never mind, sweet Alder. Just know that the ritual works very well, and if you do your part, I will share some of the power I raise with you. You can have anything you want."

Then he steps away from me and raises his arms, and begins speaking in Greek, circling the cave, and sprinkling water from a bowl with a pine branch. I recognize the actions as a rite of purification, but I can't concentrate well enough to understand the words. I'm better with ancient Greek, anyway, written down, with a dictionary close to hand.

He circles the cave several times, but I lose track of how many. My head is spinning again, and I can see the thin barrier he's raised where the candles make a circle around the floor of the cave. The whole place seems to glow faintly blue.

I don't feel anything now except empty. Even my sadness, even my anxiety have been drained until I'm just a husk, waiting to be filled with something else. My back aches and one of my thighs is cramping and my right shoulder has developed a shooting pain that spears right up my neck, but even that doesn't feel like anything.

Ego leans over me again. "You wanted to know what will happen if your Silas doesn't come?"

I try to focus on his face. "What happens?" I say, but I'm not even curious anymore.

He lifts a knife into my field of vision. "You take his place." He puts his hand under my jaw and forces my head back and I don't even care that he's going to kill me. I just stare at the knife as he brings it down toward my throat.

Chapter Nineteen

"You really don't want to do that." The voice is deep and resonant and rumbly, and I want him to sing lullabies to me so I can sleep, but I also want to scream because that voice is everything I fear and everything I love.

I smile, though, even as I remember there's a knife aiming for my throat, fingers wrapped tight around it. I probably *should* scream, but my head is held back at a painful angle and I'm having trouble even breathing. Then the hands move away, the one holding my jaw and the one holding the knife. I can breathe, but my head still spins, and everything shifts around me, and glows.

"Pan comes," says another voice. "Can you feel him?"

Fear clutches my belly, and then the deep voice says, "No, only a little pan, and you're lucky for that."

"Ah, it's you," says the second voice. "You're right, satyr." Ego, that voice is Ego. "I *don't* want to cut this boy's throat. I want you to take his place."

"Still not a boy," I say, lifting my head to try to see between my feet, to see the owner of the deep voice. I know that voice, don't I? (I know that voice from a dream of being chased through the forest at night.) "Won't ever be a boy, no matter how many times you call me one, Dad."

Then I laugh, because that's not right. Ego isn't my dad. And that makes me remember I should be afraid, only I'm not. The panic is gone and I'm empty.

Silas left me.

Silas.

I lift my head again and he steps out of the dim passage into the flickering uncertain candlelight. And then I very nearly *do* scream because the blue glow and the incense smoke and the candles make Silas look monstrous. Two curls of hair look like horns and his eyes are wrong. They glow green and the pupils are too big and the wrong shape. The shadows paint his legs with fur and his feet end in hoofs.

I pull in a ragged breath and blink, and then he's just Silas, naked and magnificent and… Naked? Should he be naked? I can't keep my head up any longer, so I rest it on the stone again. It must be part of the hallucinations that he looks naked. Is he even really here? I raise my head again, and he does seem to be here.

"Are you okay, sweetheart?" he says.

"Are you really here?" I say, and let my neck relax again. It hurts.

"I'm here, sweetheart. I'm going to get you out of here."

"You left me."

"I'm here." He says it so gently I want to cry again, but no, I swore off crying. No more tears for Alder.

"You're here to take his place, satyr," says Ego, moving to stand next to me.

"Their place," I say, but everyone seems very far away.

Silas moves closer, right to the edge of the circle of candles. "The fuck I will," he says.

"It's a trap," I say, finally managing to get more than one braincell to fire at the same time.

"I know it is, sweetheart. But I'm not alone." He shifts his weight.

Ego laughs softly. "Who else did you bring with you? The rest of your degenerate clan?"

"My family is in the woods, making sure no more of your lot are lurking around. You haven't got one of us trapped alone, this time."

This time? Was there another time? Ego said something about another time, too.

"Perhaps not, but you know how this must go. You know what your obligations are." Ego sounds perfectly reasonable, and I'd believe him if I understood anything he was saying.

I look up at Ego, studying what I can see of his face from the extreme angle I'm viewing him from. His chin is raised, and he looks at Silas with disdain. If he needs Silas so badly, why is he being so awful?

"The ritual has begun, the sacrifice offered," says Ego. "You know what happens if an offering is not provided. None of us wants that."

"You don't know what you're messing with," says Silas, shifting his weight again.

I pull on the ropes binding my wrists and try to reach the knots with my fingertips. It doesn't do any more good than it did last time.

"I know exactly what I'm doing."

Silas snorts air out of his nose, like an angry bull. "If you wake him with a blood sacrifice," he says, anger evident in his voice, but carefully controlled, "You wake the god who panicked the Persians at the battle of Marathon, who slaughtered thousands to save his Athenian friends. You wake not only the god who brings fear, but the god who hunts, the god who takes what he wants, and the god who kills the civilized to protect the wild."

Silas's voice is fierce, and even though his anger isn't directed at me, it frightens me. Ego said he would protect me, but what if he was lying?

"Our god is all these things, of course. But he is also lust and joy and passion. He is gentleness and music and protection of the innocent."

"He won't be if he wakes from dreams of blood."

"Whatever he will be, he will give me all that I desire. I nearly succeeded last time. This time I am better prepared."

"He will give you all you want, and then destroy everyone around you."

I can't follow what they're saying, all this talk of blood and desire and power. Why can't we just be nice to each other and let everyone live?

"Alder is a pacifist," says Ego, and I realize I said that bit aloud. I didn't mean to say it aloud.

"Let them go," says Silas.

"I'll happily let him – *them* – go when you take their place. A sacrifice is required, a suitable offering. You know this." He places a hand on my forehead, and I can't remember if I should flinch away or enjoy it, so I don't move at all. "Alder will join me as my acolyte and together we will harvest your satyr energy to call our god Pan back to the waking world."

"You're so full of shit I found you by following the stench," Silas says, but I think I hear something uncertain in his voice. I try to see him better, but I can't tell much in the flickering light.

"Hm," says Ego. He turns back to me and puts his hand under my chin to pull my head back again.

"You promised," I say, and this time I manage to thrash against the ropes, to try to pull away from his touch, but all I manage to do is hurt myself. The knife in his other hand is bright and sharp.

"What did he promise you, sweetheart?" Silas asks, but I can't talk with my throat stretched out. Then he says, "Wait," and Ego lets go of me and steps back.

"Yes?" says Ego.

Silas ignores him. "Close your eyes for me, will you sweetheart?" he says and when I look at him, his eyes are sad. I try to focus on his face, but everything is blurry. "You don't need to see this," he says, his voice gentle and kind. "Please, sweetheart?"

I let my eyes drift closed. Maybe Ego is right, and Silas will never love me, but he calls me "sweetheart" like he really means it. Then Ego grabs a handful of my hair and yanks and my eyes snap open again.

"Oh, I think our dear Alder really should see this."

Silas growls under his breath and steps over the circle of candles. Shadows gather around him, and I blink quickly, trying to focus. A trickle of fear begins to fill the empty spaces in the hollow that my emotions have become. It fills my empty belly, too.

I'm not seeing this. It's Ego's drugs. Am I seeing this? (Oh God, I'm seeing this.)

His eyes change first, flaring green like a cat's in the light of the candle flame, only unlike a cat's his pupils are rectangular and horizontal. I've seen eyes like that, on a goat.

Then his ears draw out to points tipped in fur, and two long horns, dark with pale tips, push out of his forehead and curl back over his head.

His posture changes as his legs bend wrong, sprout fur and hoofs. He takes a step closer to me and I feel a scream building and clamp my teeth together so hard they grind, trying to keep it in.

"I'm sorry, sweetheart," he says, and I see the flash of his teeth, not like a goat's at all, but a predator's, big and sharp and made for tearing flesh. "This isn't how I wanted you to find out."

"You're –" I snap my teeth together again, because the scream is still there, still trying to tear out of my throat.

"I'm a satyr," he says, as if that's just something a person can be. A cop, a professor, an artist, a satyr. And it hurts that Ego was right, because somewhere deep inside I needed to believe that Ego was lying, that Silas was just a man who could love me.

"You're a monster," I say, and the words catch, and choke me, but at least they keep me from screaming.

He flinches, like I've slapped him, and Ego laughs.

"While I hate to be the type to say, 'I told you so,' I did tell you. Your lover is a beast and will act as beasts do."

"Alder knows exactly who I am." Silas's words hiss out in a dangerous tone and Ego takes a step back.

But I didn't know who he was, did I? He didn't tell me any of this.

"Let them go, or the sacrifice that wakes Pan will be you."

Ego smirks. "Did I mention, Alder, that we're here tonight to wake a sleeping god who was once rumored to be dead?"

"You said you would become his priest," I say, like I'm reciting a lesson at school. I don't know where the words come from and it reminds me of the ritual last night, only this time at least I understand what I'm saying.

"So I will," he says. Then to Silas, "I'll let *them* go as soon as you assure me you'll take *their* place."

I should be insulted by his emphasis, but all I can do is stare at Silas and try to keep from pissing myself.

"Find another offering," says Silas.

"It's too late."

Silas's nostrils flare like a beast's and I look away. "Fine."

Ego waves his hand and takes a step back and I squeeze my eyes shut as Silas sits on the stone next to me.

"I'm sorry, sweetheart," he says. I keep my eyes shut tight.

His hand is warm on my face, soothing the sting where Ego hit me and where I scraped my cheek on the stone. "Get away from here," he says, softly. "Get out of this cave and get far away. Go home and get your degree. Live a good life, sweetheart."

I'm too afraid to look at him. Maybe I feel too guilty. (I *am* guilty.) But I manage to say, "What about you?"

"I'll be around. I don't intend to let this asshole slit my throat."

So, he *is* leaving me. Or am I leaving him? I called him a monster. (He *is* a monster.)

He leans over and I feel his breath on my face an instant before his lips touch mine, press gently, and open. His tongue strokes over my lower lip and then inside my mouth, and there's a reason that's bad but I can't think what it is, so I just jerk my head sideways and away. He sighs.

"I'm sorry," he whispers, and I feel the ropes fall away from my wrists. I'm vaguely aware of Ego cutting them, then moving around me to cut the ones at my ankles. I'm free.

For a moment I don't move and neither does Silas. Why isn't he trying to stop Ego? Then, very slowly, Silas topples sideways, and Ego catches him.

"Help me with him, please, Alder."

Something hurts in my belly, but I don't know what it is. I get up on shaky legs and back away from Ego, knocking a candle out of place. "Is he dead?" I say, and it makes me want to cry. Why do I want to cry? (I swore off crying.)

"Only sleeping. Now help me get him onto the altar."

I don't know what to do, so I stand and look at Silas, see how wrong he is, how bestial. That's what Ego wanted me to see, isn't it? He doesn't want me to see how peaceful Silas looks asleep, how beautiful his long black eyelashes are against his cheeks, how... No, I won't think of anything. If I think, I'll drive myself around the bend.

The fear is creeping into my empty emotional spaces again and I can't breathe. I don't know what to do.

Ego looks up at me. "Do you want to take your place at my side, Alder? Then begin by helping me with this creature."

"I can't," I say, backing away until I hit the wall. My groping hand finds the emptiness of the passage. "I'm sorry, I can't do this." I don't even know if I'm talking to Ego or Silas, but I know I need to get away. I turn and bolt into the passage. My legs are clumsy from being tied up, my feet asleep, and I almost fall right out of the cave entrance when I trip over an uneven spot on the passage floor.

There's rope hanging past the opening, and I grab it. I know what to do with ropes. I don't have a harness or anything, not even shoes, but one summer at climbing camp we learned how to rappel with only a rope, by wrapping it a certain way around our bodies and holding it just so. It was meant to be used only for emergencies, but I practiced over and over until I could do it easily.

And I do it now, letting my focus on climbing overtake me, hold the fear at bay, and clear my head as much as it *can* be cleared. Slowly, I make my way down the cliff face to the steep slope at the base of it, then clamber down to night-damp grass, stiff and dead and soon to be flattened by the autumn rain and later by snow.

When my feet touch the grass and I see the forest looming ahead, the fear returns, even stronger, building and building into panic until I'm running headlong into the trees. There's a narrow path, dirt and stone and tree roots, and terror chases me down and steals my breath and still I run.

I run until my foot catches on a root, and I'm flung face first into the dirt, wind knocked out of me, *terror* knocked out of me. I lay for a while on the damp ground, trying to remember why I was so afraid.

I push myself up to my hands and knees – one knee hurts where I bashed it, and my jeans are torn. I try to stand, but my ankle won't hold me, and I fall again, fingers clutching at roots and moss and all at once that scream I held at bay when my lover turned out to be a monster rips out of my throat.

Except it's no longer a scream of fear. It's anger and frustration and disgust.

Not at Silas. Not even at Ego.

At myself.

I'm a coward. I've always been a coward. Because isn't that what anxiety is, at its root? Fear? Cowardice? (My therapist said otherwise, but she didn't even *have* anxiety, did she?)

I scream until my throat is raw and then I sob until I hiccup. (So much for swearing off crying.) Then I kneel there in the dirt until I start to really feel the cold and I shiver so hard I can't even stay kneeling.

The moss at the side of the path is cold but soft and it reminds me of something, but my teeth are chattering so hard I can't remember. I turn my face into it and breathe in its damp scent. I dreamed of this. No, not this, but of Silas, chasing me through the forest. I fled him like I'm fleeing him now. Except it *wasn't* like that. I fled, but I *wanted* him to catch me.

I wanted him to catch me.

And he did, laughing, tumbling me into the moss and kissing me and tracing every part of me with his tongue until I cried out for him to take me, to take all of me. I dreamed that he pushed my knees up to my shoulders and fucked me, gently, then fiercely, until I'd spurted hot spunk over both of us and he had moaned my name as he emptied into my ass.

And it had been perfect.

I make myself open my eyes, breathe deep, and let the shivers come. Let the emotions come, creeping back in to fill the emptiness. They can't drive out the fear, but they can make it less terrible, more bearable. Slowly, I get back onto my hands and knees and borrow a small tree to pull myself up to stand. My ankle doesn't want to take my weight, but it's going to have to, because I won't make it out of here alive if I don't move. It's fall and getting very cold, and I'm only dressed in jeans and a tee, with a hoodie over top.

Another breath, another look around. I'm on a path. A path must lead somewhere. I'll get out of here, and I'll find a cop, and…

That doesn't make sense. I wipe my face with one hand and find it smeared with dirt and snot, so I pull up the hem of my hoodie to clean my face as best I can. And when I do, I see the flash of white from the design on my black tee.

I forgot I'm wearing the lewd satyr shirt, red "censored" letters hardly covering his enormous cock. He holds his erection in both hands and stares at it as though surprised at his own prodigious size. I had laughed when I saw it online and had to buy it.

And that's why Silas had stopped to talk to me, the first day.

Silas.

How can I leave him to be sacrificed just because he turned out to be a beast out of myth and legend? I mean, it's not like I haven't jerked off to pictures of x-rated Greek art since I'd first fallen in love with stories of Pan. Fuck, my first wet dream had featured the version of Pan from the copy of *The Wind in the Willows* my grandparents gave me for Christmas one year.

Silas told me to go. He told me he'd find a way to escape, that his family was in the woods nearby. He told me he'd be around, but that I should live a happy life. Without him. He planned to live, but not have a life with me in it.

Because I'm afraid.

He didn't leave me, but I sure left him.

I am a coward, after all.

And Silas was unconscious because Ego had smeared his drug on my lip. Ego knew Silas would kiss me. Ego knew.

How had I let him turn me away from the one person who was always on my side?

Silas kissed me.

He didn't leave me, he came to save me. And I abandoned him.

I look back down the path, clenching my teeth to keep them from chattering. I'm cold and hurt and afraid, and the man who looks at me like I mean something is about to be killed by an egotistical, delusional follower of an ancient god who is apparently asleep deep beneath the forest of Arcadia County.

Just as I take a careful step along the path, the forest goes very quiet, noises I hadn't realized were all around me suddenly obvious by their absence.

The owl perched in a nearby tree stops hooting to its mate several trees over, crickets stop chirping, and even the last few frogs still awake in some not-too-distant pond stop croaking.

The forest feels utterly still. Expectant. And then, fear, so intense the panic I felt earlier seems trivial in comparison. It's a terror so overwhelming I feel it coming, like a wave washing over the trees, and it hits, and I can't move, can't think, and even my shivering stops. And before it's even really sunk in that it's *there,* the fear ebbs away, slipping past deeper into the forest, heading the direction I came from.

And slowly, the night starts up again. The owl offers a mournful, long "hoo-hoooo hoo hoo hoo," and its mate responds. The crickets resume all at once and a frog croaks tentatively, followed by another, until there's so much noise I can hardly believe it ever seemed quiet. Wind whistles between branches, leaves rustle on trees and rattle as they fall to the forest floor, and very far away a wolf howls.

"Oh, God," I say, and then I realize how exactly right that is. One of Pan's epithets was – or I guess is, since he still has followers – The God Who Brings Fear in Quiet Places, just like Ego was fond of saying. Pan gave his name to panic, but what I just felt, what the whole forest felt, was something much deeper than mere panic as we normally think of it.

That was what the Victorians called "the sublime," what the original meaning of "awesome" was. That was *him*. Pan.

Oh fuck, I hope that doesn't mean he's awake. I hope that doesn't mean that Ego has sacrificed Silas and achieved his goals.

If Silas is dead, that's on *me*. If he's dead, I've killed him. And I can't stand that thought. Not that I'm responsible, but that he might be gone.

He can't be. I can't bear it.

I love him.

I turn back the way I came and start to walk. My ankle protests but I ignore it, and it holds.

Oh, God.

I start to run.

Chapter Twenty

IT'S TAKING TOO LONG to get back to the cliff. My ankle won't let me run very far at a time and I need to keep slowing to a walk to let it recover.

But I keep going. I feel stupid and weak, but I keep going. I have to try to stop Ego, to free Silas, to prevent whatever that was I just felt from manifesting.

From awakening.

Now that I'm in the cold and moving, my head has cleared, and I feel unbelievably stupid for believing anything Ego told me. Okay, maybe he was right about satyrs existing, but he was wrong about Silas. Silas came back for me.

(Silas came back for me.)

It's dark, only a thin sliver of moon casting any light at all, and I find my way as much by feeling the dirt path between the trees with my bare feet as by seeing the faint gap in the forest.

Silas didn't leave me. I still don't know why he left with no note or text, but it hardly matters. He came for me. He came to *rescue* me.

And he took my place on the sacrificial altar.

I force my thoughts off that circular, useless path before I start whining at myself for being a coward and just try to focus on breathing, on my heartbeat, on feeling for the dirt path. When a straight stretch opens up and I can almost see, I run. And slowly, eventually, I make it back to the meadow.

The faint moonlight picks out the uneven surface of the cliff and there, a little more than halfway up, I see the cave entrance. I almost think I can see the very faint flicker of candlelight in the black opening, but maybe that's just wishful thinking.

It looks very high up, and I have nothing but a damp rope dangling down. How did Ego and Stefan manage to climb it? How did Silas?

How am *I* going to climb it?

One handhold at a time, that's how. I force myself to clamber up the steep slope of rocks and debris at the base of the cliff to where the rope hangs, swaying slightly in the breeze that's starting to pick up.

I shiver again, as I have been off and on since I stopped running away, but I take hold of the rope and look up. I'm exhausted, and even fresh it would be hard – if not impossible – to climb hand-over-hand all the way up. But I know how to tie a rope to catch me if I fall, and I know how to make a knot that's adjustable with one hand so I can shorten it as I climb.

I wrap the rope around myself and tie the knot carefully, testing it twice to make sure it's right. And then I climb. The rock face is truly shit for climbing. Too much of the exposed stone is weathered and crumbly, and there are too many pockets of dirt where twisted trees have taken root, further destabilizing the cliff.

But I have no choice. I move slowly, brushing away loose fragments with my fingers and finding the best holds I can, wiggling my toes into cracks and chinks until I'm sure they're bleeding. It's probably for the best that my feet are so cold I can barely feel them. Except that also means I can barely feel my footholds.

Every few feet, I pause and adjust the rope, shorten it, check that it's secure, so if I fall it will only be a short distance. It will hurt like hell, but I won't die.

Somewhere that I think might be about halfway up I feel the forest go still and silent again, and I clamp my mouth shut against a scream, press my face into the stone, and squeeze my eyes shut. I cling to the rock as panic fear washes over me and builds in my throat until I choke trying to hold back the shriek building there. If I scream, I might fall, and I need to keep climbing.

Above me, I think I hear something high-pitched. Was that a sound of terror? Oh God, is Silas screaming?

As soon as I can make my limbs move, I keep climbing. Hand hold, foot hold, adjust rope, and continue. Until the damp rope refuses to loosen. I can't shorten it, can't even untie it. I cling to the side of the cliff and try to see how much farther I have to go, but I can't lean far enough away from the cliff face, can't risk shifting my weight outwards. I'm barely hanging on as it is. I try one more time to loosen the knot, without success.

The wind is still picking up and it catches at my hoodie. I suppress another shiver. I need to get inside, to the relative warmth of the cave, before I'm hypothermic. I need to move.

Hand hold, foot hold, move the dangling rope out of the way. Hand hold, foot hold, and I swear it goes on forever and my fingers and toes are numb. I can't feel the rock properly and one hand slips and I nearly fall. I barely bite back a scream and fumble for a new hand hold and one of my fingernails tears. If my hands weren't so numb, it would probably hurt a lot more.

I don't fall, somehow, and it turns out I'm nearly there. Just to my left I can see the dark cave opening, and I only need to move sideways a few feet. Except that few feet of lateral motion prove to be more difficult than it should be, and I have to climb up past the entrance before I can move to my left and then slowly, painstakingly down until my feet find empty air and I realize there's a metal hook embedded in the stone several feet above the entrance where the rope is attached. Only the rope is caught, blown by the wind, on a projection of rock, which is why I ended up so far to the right.

I just climbed hundreds of feet up a cliff on a rope caught on a spur of a crumbling rock face. And now I'm stuck.

I wedge my hands and feet as securely as I can and then let go with my right hand and grasp the rope. There's blood dripping down my wrist from my damaged fingernail, and I can't even feel it. I take a deep breath in and flip the rope sideways and up.

It stays caught.

I let out the breath, breathe in, and try again. On the third try it slips free and I grab for my handhold as the length of rope above me falls and tugs at me where it's tied.

Then I let go carefully and grab the rope where it dangles past me. I don't have enough energy to pull it up one-handed and wrap it properly, so I wind my arm into it and carefully let go of the cliff with my left hand and free my feet, until I'm dangling high above the ground.

Slowly, carefully, I lower myself. Once, my hand slips, burning my palm, but my other hand holds firm and as soon as the lurching in my belly stops, I keep going.

By the time I swing myself through the cave entrance, I have no strength left and no idea how I'm going to rescue Silas, assuming he's still alive.

(He *has* to be alive.)

I crouch in the passage, fighting with the damp rope to get it off me, trying to catch my breath, and put my hand down on something metal. I move so my shadow isn't covering whatever it is – not that there's enough light to even cast much shadow – and stare at the object for way too long. Wheels like a pulley, but motor driven, and attached to a harness. Then I remember the electric motor whine I heard as Ego and Stefan arrived at the cave.

It's a motorized climbing device. Clamp it to the rope and the wheels run you up or down. It doesn't seem very safe, but I suppose it's easier than coming up the way I did.

Once my breathing is mostly normal again – as if I can breathe normally when I'm this afraid – I stand up and feel my way along the wall. I really hope there's only one passage. It would be just my luck to make it all the way back to the cliff and all the way up, only to die lost and wandering in the cave.

But soon enough, I see flickering light and hear chanting in Greek. And then, slurred and weak, but still deep and beautiful, Silas's voice.

"He's not going to anoint you his earthly representative, you know." He sounds so tired.

Ego continues chanting.

"If you've studied as much as you claim to, you'd know Pan is a very physical sort of god. When – *if* – he wakes, he'll be his own representative.

He'll frolic in the forest, call nymphs out of the trees and mountains, and anyone who hears him will be his priests.

"You won't be a chosen one, Ego. You'll have awakened a god from dreams of blood, and you'll not only have to face his spiritual attention, you'll have to face him in the flesh."

Ego finishes his chant and says, mildly, "I believe you told me he was going to awaken bloodthirsty, not lusty."

"He'll be both, and each made worse for the other. My point is, you're not getting what you want by doing this. He won't grant you the magic to fuck anyone you want. He won't give you money and fame. If by some fluke he decides to favor you with anything, it'll be fertile flocks and the ability to call birds with music."

"I've had a taste of the gifts of Pan. How do you think I achieved what I already have?"

"You wrote a couple of decent books, that's how. Murdering my cousin only gave you the ability to see us more clearly."

Murdering his cousin? Is that what Ego meant when he said he'd done this ritual before? Oh god, did Silas already *know*?

(He couldn't have known. He wouldn't have let me get involved with Ego in the first place if he'd known.) (Unless I was bait for Silas to catch Ego, too.)

I crouch low and peer around the edge of the passage, but I can't see anything except the altar and a curve of the circle of candles. Knowing I'm going to be extremely visible, I slowly stand up.

Silas is looking right at me.

My heart feels like it stops and all I feel is terror. Then it eases and I feel relief. He looks unhurt. Beyond him, Ego has his back to me, doing something at a table set at the rear of the cavern, just inside the ring of candles.

Silas jerks his head slightly to one side and relaxes it back onto the stone of the altar. I move back around the edge of the passage, pressing myself against the wall, just as Ego turns around, knife in hand.

And then the world goes quiet again and I feel the fear creeping closer.

"Hey," Silas says. I edge forward again. Ego is focused on Silas and doesn't see me. I can just meet Silas's eyes despite the angle of his head. He nods very slightly. I don't know what he's trying to tell me, but I know I want to look into his deep, understanding gaze. I don't deserve the soft emotion I see there, but I want it so badly I have no words.

He fucking terrifies me, even as his presence comforts me.

"What?" says Ego, lifting the knife so the candlelight gleams along its edge.

"Do you feel it?" Silas says. "He's coming."

"I felt it last time, and yet he isn't here."

"The panic spells will get closer and closer, more and more intense. When the fear stays and doesn't go away, when you completely lose your ability to think, then he'll be here and it will be too late."

I think Silas is talking to me, explaining what's happening, as much as he's talking to Ego.

"Then let it come."

"Last time, you screamed so loud I thought you'd puncture my eardrums, and the time before that you ran face-first into the wall."

Ego ignores him, and Silas grins, a grim and not at all comforting look. The fear approaches and I keep my eyes on his and somehow... somehow, I can feel the fear, the panic, but I don't tremble, I don't scream, I don't even curl into a ball on the floor of the cave like I want to.

I just look into Silas's strange, monstrous eyes and know I'm protected.

Ego goes very still, then whirls, sees me, and shrieks. "No, you're dead!" He screams, and I'm pretty sure it's not me he's seeing at all. He shoves past me, and I don't know why, but I tear my eyes from Silas's, turn as Ego goes by, and make a grab for his knife.

I drop it as soon as I have it and fall to the floor, curling into that ball after all. I shake as panic washes over me, but I don't run.

This time, the fear goes on and on for a long while and I think it must be the end, like Silas said, that Pan is awake and any second he'll be here, angry and looking for blood. But at last it eases, and I become aware of the world around me again. I'm sweating, which makes me colder, but I'm still alive.

The wind whistles past the mouth of the cave, and I think I can hear Ego out there. Or maybe he's gone. Charcoal crackles from across the cave, and I can hear Silas breathing.

Silas.

"Sweetheart," he says. "You should have run."

I stay where I am, clutching the wall of the passage, staring at him. He's tied the way I was, muscular arms over his head, stretched out towards the corners of the altar stone, and his ankles nearer to me. His legs are hairy, furry, and his feet are cloven hoofs, and looking at him makes me afraid all over again.

"I did run," I finally say, my voice coming out small and hoarse, trembling with weakness and fear. I won't be afraid. Not of Silas.

(I am *so* afraid of Silas.)

"But you came back." He watches me, keeping his face carefully still, like he doesn't dare let any emotions show.

"You didn't leave me." There's no time for this. I *know* there's no time for this, but I can't help it.

"I got called away," he says. "Sweetheart, can we talk about this later? Ego's ritual to wake Pan has set things in motion that I don't know how to stop without completing what he started."

"But you're still alive."

"And so is he." He nods towards the dark space behind me, where I can hear faint noises.

"What do I do?" I ask, and I can tell from Silas's face that he doesn't know, but what little he does know isn't good.

Ego's knife is there on the floor, so I pick it up and force myself to walk into the cave, to step over the edge of the circle of candles. Several of them have gone out, knocked aside by Ego's sudden flight.

"You must finish this, Alder," says Ego from behind me. I don't turn, I just look at Silas.

"He's not wrong, sweetheart. One way or the other, we need to end this ritual."

Now I do turn. Ego is standing just inside the passage, smiling at me.

"You returned as I knew you would," he says. "Now take your place beside me as Pan's chosen."

I look away from him, at the ring of candles, then I slowly bend and replace the ones knocked aside, relight them, and look back at Ego.

"Good boy," he says.

"Still not a boy," I reply, but my voice is calm and even. I have no idea what I'm doing, but I know I have to do something. I walk around the altar stone to stand at Silas's head. He looks up at me.

"Of course," says Ego. "My apologies. Carry on. Finish the ritual and join me." He comes closer, stepping over the circle of candles and smiling.

I ignore him and look down at Silas. He waits to see what I'll do.

"You're a monster," I say.

"Yes," he replies, "but I'm *your* monster."

"Are you?"

He smiles, and even on his monstrous face, that grin is the Silas I know, the *human* Silas, dimples and all. "Always."

I look up at Ego, who is beaming. "Wake him," he says. "Wake Pan with the blood of the satyr and you and I will ascend."

I want a lot of things in life. I want to be loved, and I want a career that means something. I want financial security, and I want to not be made to feel like a freak every day I don't look like people think I should look.

I don't want whatever Ego is offering.

"If I kill him," I say. "*I'll* be the monster."

"You will be the one with all the power. The monster-*slayer*." Ego takes another step closer, almost close enough to take the knife from my hand.

"Let *me* be the monster, sweetheart," Silas says, "I already am, anyway." And then I know what to do. I bring the knife down quickly, once and then again, and Ego's face turns ecstatic. Until Silas sits up and lunges for him.

I move quickly around the altar to cut Silas's ankles free and almost cut his leg open when Ego shoves past me again and flees down the tunnel. Silas is after him so fast I sit on the altar stone to catch my breath.

I hear his hoofs, and then a scuffle and a scream. Footsteps come slowly back down the passage.

I make myself stand, move to the middle of the circle, and hold the knife ready. Like I know what I'm doing with a knife.

A shadow appears in the passage, too bulky to be Ego. Silas steps into the light, human again. My breath catches and I don't know if it's fear or wonder.

"Sweetheart," he says, but I can't relax. I keep the knife between us.

"Did you…?" I can't finish the sentence.

"I didn't have to," he says. "He tripped on an uneven spot on the floor and went out the cave entrance head-first." He tips his head to one side. "I don't think he suffered."

"Does that count as an offering? Does it end the ritual?"

"It will be enough to wake Pan, yes."

"So we're in trouble."

His shoulders slump. "We will be very soon."

"What if…" I fumble for words, trying to find a shape for an idea forming in my head, remembering how Ego had intended to "improve" the ritual. "What if we give another offering?"

"More blood will only make things worse, sweetheart."

"Not blood," I say. My arm is shaking with the effort of holding up the knife. I'm so tired, but there are things left unsettled that I must do before I rest, things that would still be there to deal with even if we weren't about to get a visit from an angry god.

I bite my lip and look into his eyes and somehow, I don't even have trouble getting out the word I need to say. "Love."

He tips his head the other way and his eyebrows draw together. Then he seems to realize what I'm saying, and he steps across the candles. I don't even flinch as his eyes turn strange and his horns sprout, and I let him take the knife from my hand and put it on the altar.

"I can do that," he says, so quietly I barely hear. Then his mouth quirks up on one side. "I already love you."

Chapter Twenty-One

He stops in front of me, so close I feel the heat off his skin, but he doesn't touch me.

"When were you going to tell me?" I ask. Even I'm not sure if I'm asking about him being a satyr or him loving me.

"I wanted to tell you, sweetheart, believe me."

I look away from his eyes, at the altar, the flickering candles, the faint images on the walls that might depict people with goat legs and horns.

"I suppose I wouldn't have believed you." I still don't know which option I'm talking about.

"You're hurt," he says and this time he does touch me, his fingertips just brushing my cheek where I scraped it on the rock, where Ego hit me.

I shake my head. "We don't have time to tend my wounds," I say. I swear I can already feel the forest going quiet again, far off, but moving closer.

He says nothing; he just looks at me, as if *I'm* the one with the answers. Then he says, almost tentatively, "In my family, our priests are those who are… between. Some of our priests have been unable to take fully human shape. And some of them have been trans."

Now I look into his eyes, search them to try to figure out what he's saying. "You told me."

"Our current priest-in-training is nonbinary," he says.

"Is that why you liked me?" I tip my chin up, trying to make myself feel more courageous by acting defiant.

He shakes his head. "I liked you before I knew. Remember? I kissed you before you told me your name and pronouns." He leans his head forward so his forehead touches mine, and I feel the brush of the bases of his horns. "And we already talked about this."

"I remember," I say.

"I think that's when I started to fall in love with you. When you gathered your courage to tell me your name was not… what I thought it was. I could see you were afraid, but you did it anyway."

"Say that again," I say, trying to keep my breathing even and not succeeding very well.

"Which part? That I fell in love with you?"

I press my lips together, not trusting myself with words, and nod.

"I love you, Alder," he says. "And I am so fucking *in* love with you."

I stare into his eyes a moment longer, and then I say, "Please kiss me."

His mouth on mine is soft, like he's making sure I really want this. He terrifies me, I can't deny it. I've always had a thing for satyrs in myth and art, but face-to-face with the real thing, I'm so afraid I'd piss myself if I'd actually had anything to drink in the past day. I'm pretty sure I'm too dehydrated now.

He pulls away after a moment. "I can't take human form inside this circle," he says. "I'm sorry." Then he gives me a lopsided smile that only shows one dimple. "But I'm still me."

And that feels like a punch to the solar plexus. "I'm still me." I said that to my dad when I came out to him, and he wanted to know why I decided to change. I hadn't decided anything, I explained, and I hadn't changed. I had only found a better label. And I had said, "I'm still me."

His hand touches my shoulder. "Alder?"

I meet his eyes again.

"What do we do?"

He's looking to *me* for answers. How am I supposed to know how to lull a bloodthirsty god back to sleep? But I think I *do* know.

"We offer him love," I say. "We offer him *our* love."

"How?"

"The same way they did in the temples with… with temple prostitutes."

His other hand comes up to cup my cheek. "I don't think temple prostitutes were offering love," he says.

"No, they were offering pleasure. But I think the principle is the same." I bite my lip again. What if this doesn't work? What if it *does?* "We… we make love, here in his sacred cave, on his altar, and fill his dreams with… with intimacy. With caring."

He kisses my forehead, and I can smell his skin, his sweat. It's wild and bestial, but not unpleasant. Musky, but like a thick cologne and not like B.O. I hope I smell half as good. I probably stink of fear and exertion.

"Can you do that?" he says, softly.

"Can I let you make love to me? I think I can manage."

He laughs, just a little huff that stirs my hair. "Can you love me, sweetheart? I can smell your fear."

Fuck. I *do* stink like fear.

"I…" I can't keep looking into his eyes, because they're full of raw emotion, the desperation to know my answer, and the fear that it won't be what he wants.

I put both hands on his chest. His hair is thicker in his satyr form, curlier, but still soft. I bury my fingers in it, and he draws in a sharp breath.

"I am afraid of you," I say, and see his throat bob as he swallows. "But that's only because this is new, and sudden." I slide my hands from his chest to his shoulders, then back again. "But you've had my heart since you told me I was beautiful."

His breath comes out in a rush. "Alder."

"You're still my Silas," I say. "Whatever kind of legs you have."

"I am yours," he answers.

I nod and step back, letting my hands fall away from him, and turn to face the table where Ego kept his tools. A small bronze bowl holds charcoal, more than half turned to ash, but with some red glow still present. There's a paper baggie labelled "Pan blend" next to it, so I dump some of the contents onto the charcoal and it begins to put out a fragrant smoke.

I take a deep breath and pull off my hoodie, tee, and sports bra in one motion, then yank open my fly and let my jeans and boxers slide down my legs.

"You can still get away," Silas says, but his voice is shaky, and I think I can hear his desire in it.

Silas *wants* me.

He struggles to keep his inhales and exhales even, and I can almost feel him watching me. I turn around, slowly. His lips are slightly parted, showing the white flash of his teeth, and his nostrils flare.

"Sorry," I say. "I probably don't smell very good."

"Sweetheart," he says, his voice barely more than a whisper.

I turn back to the table and grab the only other item on it: a fancy bottle of olive oil. I don't want to think about what Ego intended to use it for. I wish I didn't know what he was going to use it for. I pull the top off and spill some oil into my hand, set the bottle on the altar, and step close to Silas again. He still hasn't moved, like he's afraid he'll scare me.

I press against him, chest-to-chest, and his hands come up to grasp my arms. I kiss him, slowly, deliberately, and as I slide my tongue into his mouth, I slip my oily hand between his legs to find his cock, hidden in his thick fur. He groans into my mouth as I find him, and squeeze, and slide my fingers over him.

I feel the terror slide closer, outside the cave, but nearly here. I move my mouth away but keep stroking him, and his hands slide across my skin, caressing my back, my ribs, my hips.

"I want you to fuck me, Silas," I say. "I *need* you to."

He shakes his head slightly. "I can make love to you without fucking you, sweetheart. We don't have any condoms."

"I know," I say. "I know how good you are. But *this* time, we need to… to offer everything we have." I know fucking isn't like the ultimate expression of love or anything; there are so many ways to be intimate. But in this case, the symbolism of it, of me offering myself and Silas taking me, all done in love and caring, is important. I think. (I hope.)

I move one hand up his belly and back to his chest, marveling at how amazing his chest hair feels under my palm. "I've been tested. Every time I… Well, I've been tested a lot, and I'm clear."

He breathes carefully. "Me, too," he says. "It's been a while, but I was tested after my last attempt to fall in love."

That almost makes me pull away, but Silas's past doesn't matter, and neither does mine. Only right now matters.

Then a cold breeze finds the cave entrance, perhaps in advance of the panic, and I shiver.

"You're cold," Silas says, and moves past me to the table. With a sudden yank, he pulls free the heavy red velvet tablecloth. The packet of incense tumbles to the floor, but the brass dish only shifts a little. He wraps the tablecloth around me, pressing me close to him. "Let me warm you."

I smile and wrap my arms around him, pull him back towards the altar until I'm sitting on it. He leans over me, and I slide my oily hand over his cock again until he kisses me and presses me down into the stone and climbs on after me. I let him lean over me, kiss me, touch me, and I run my hands over him, from the long, soft hair on his hips and groin – like an angora goat's – to the curly crisp locks on his belly and chest. And I tighten my arms around his neck to pull him closer, to get my tongue deeper into his mouth.

The fear arrives, and I wonder if I should look into his eyes. But his mouth has found the sensitive part of my neck, under my ear and behind the angle of my jaw, so I just close my eyes tight and let the fear fill me until the fire he's awakening in my skin flares up and combines with it and I feel it in my cock, making me hard.

I want to tell him how I feel, more than just, "You have my heart," but there are no words. It's not even anxiety keeping me silent; there is no trace of my nemesis. I'm too full of fear and lust and longing. And I just don't know *how* to say what I feel. There's too much.

The panic seems to pause now, like it's a sentient thing that's noticed us and I know if I'm going to speak, it should be now. I arch my body under Silas, wrap a leg around him, and say, "Si?"

He lifts his head to look at me, and I see the desire burning in his eyes. Desire for *me*. "What is it?"

"I do love you," I say. The panic settles in, but it… changes, somehow.

He kisses me instead of answering me and reaches for the bottle of oil. "Are you sure?" he says.

"I'm sure." I touch his cheekbone with one finger and trace it to his ear. I shiver as the panic ebbs and flows in my very bones, but I ignore it. "I love you, and I want you inside me."

His eyes keep searching mine. "You're still afraid."

"Not of you. Not anymore."

"Are you sure?"

"Are you?" I say it with a note of challenge in my voice and he blinks, startled, then smiles.

"I've always been sure of you, Alder." He shifts awkwardly to tip some oil into his hand. He licks his lips. "So, let's share some love and send this god back to sleep with sweet dreams."

He slips his hand between my legs, slippery fingers tracing my cock, fingering my balls, and then dipping farther back to pause, just before touching my asshole.

"Does he have to sleep?" I say, closing my eyes and feeling the shapes of his shoulder muscles under my palms.

"I don't think the world is ready for him," he says, fingers drawing circles around my asshole until I arch towards him. "And I don't think he'd much like the world as it is now. It's better he sleeps."

He pushes two fingers into me, and I let my head fall back, let the sound of my pleasure spill out of my throat and the panic shifts and changes again. It eases. "Silas." I just need to say his name, and it comes out half moan.

"Alder," he replies, and that turns to a moan, too, as my hand finds his cock again, and I stroke and tease.

I open my eyes to look down at my small, pink member next to his bigger, darker one. I shift my grip so we're sliding together and in response, Silas buries his fingers deeper in my ass. I look tiny next to him and for a fleeting moment I get that old feeling of shame, but then it's gone. I love how different we are.

He glances down to see what I'm looking at, and smiles. "You're so beautiful," he says, and his breathing is ragged as he pushes his hips against my hand, making his cock slide along mine. I let my head drop back again, let my moan of pleasure out again, and it gets suddenly louder as he slips his fingers out of me, and back in, only three this time, pushing me wide open and making me want everything he'll give me.

"I love you, sweetheart," he says.

This time, when I open my eyes, there's no fear left in me at all. His eyes glow green in the candlelight and maybe he looks monstrous, but it's also a kind of beauty.

"Fuck me," I say and let go of our cocks to grab my knees instead and pull them up towards my chest. "Please, Silas."

"Tell me you love me first," he says, removing his fingers and bracing himself over me.

"Make me," I tease.

He raises his eyebrows and shifts his weight to one arm so he can take his own cock in his hand. Then he uses it to caress me, circling my asshole with its tip and pressing me open, just a little, but not plunging in.

"Oh, God," I say. "I give in. I love you."

He leans closer, kisses my neck and says, "Say it again, sweetheart, please? Make me believe it's true."

I push his face away, so he has to look into my eyes. "It *is* true, Silas. I don't care if I've only known you three weeks, I want to spend the rest of my life with you." It bursts out in a flood of emotion, and he tilts his head to look at me, a gesture so familiar now that even the horns and the beard can't make him look any less than himself.

"Oh, sweetheart," he says.

"I love you," I say, and pull his face back down to me. "Fuck, Silas, I do love you."

And then I tighten my legs across his back, pull his hips towards me, and feel my asshole gape to let him in. I moan into his mouth, clinging desperately to him with arms and legs both, trying to make him penetrate me faster than he's willing to.

He enters me slowly, a little at a time, and I realize I've got tears streaming down my face, so I keep kissing him, hard, so he won't notice.

I forget the fear even exists.

He pulls away then, brushes tears from my face with his thumb on one side, and with his lips on the other. "Am I hurting you, sweetheart?"

I shake my head. "You feel so fucking good."

"Are you sure?" He keeps pressing forward slowly, too slowly, until I feel the curls of his pubic hair against my ass. My cock and balls are trapped between us, the pressure of his belly bringing me close to coming before I really want to.

"Fuck me," I say. "Oh God, please. Fuck me and make me come."

He starts slow, sliding a little way out, then back in, but then he's as caught up by the pleasure as I am and his thrusts get shorter, harder, and faster.

"Tell me if I hurt you, sweetheart. Can you do that for me?"

"You're not hurting me, Silas. Oh fuck, I want to come."

The panic isn't in my guts anymore, but I still feel it, lurking. And then I feel *him* approaching. Not just the panic he sends, but the god himself. Pan. A stray stone rattles across the floor of the passage, and I hear the slow tap tap of hoofs. The smell of musk and forest wafts into the cave with the autumn breeze.

"Sweetheart." Silas clears his throat, and I can tell he's still holding himself back. "Alder, fucking in the presence of a god can be… intense. Okay? It'll feel so fucking good, but it might feel like it's too much."

Shadows shift at the edges of my vision. Tap tap tap of hoofs on stone. Heavy breathing and musk.

"Silas, he's here."

"I know, sweetheart. Just look at me."

The only response I can give is a long, loud moan. I'm going to come just from the feel of his belly muscles on my cock. Oh God, I'm going to come *right now*. And I do, and it lasts way longer than any orgasm I've ever had, spunk pumping out of me and my back arching until I feel like it might snap. I cling to him and lose myself completely until I hear him moan, too, and I swear I can feel his jism filling my ass.

"Silas," I gasp, when I can relax my muscles again. "Oh fuck, I felt you come."

"I'm not done, sweetheart, I'm sorry." He shifts away from me enough to slide a hand between us, to curl his fingers around my cock and I can't believe I want him to keep touching me after the orgasm I just had, but I do. Then he bends to take one of my nipples between his lips and the stab of sensation that hits me is like nothing I've ever felt.

He keeps fucking me, and each thrust pushes my cock through his fist until I yell, and he's suddenly pulling out of me, spilling an impossible flood of semen across my belly and I'm screaming but it's not fear and I come again, so hard my vision would go gray if I had my eyes open.

And then, finally, we both relax. Silas braces himself on both elbows over me, and I let my limbs sprawl across the stone. The tablecloth is tangled over one shoulder, but I'm not cold anymore. The musky forest scent intensifies until it's all I can smell and for a moment, I think I might come again, just from that.

Then it fades and is gone, and it's just the two of us in the cave.

"You said it would be intense," I say, when I can breathe properly again. "Have you done this before?" I can't help the tiny bit of jealousy in my voice, though I aim for teasing.

But he shakes his head. "I've heard stories," he says. "But you're the first and only."

"Good," I say, and he laughs.

His spunk seeps out of my ass, and I revel in the feeling. I look at my belly, pools and strings of translucent white across my muscles from both of us.

"I didn't even know I *could* come twice," I say. I dip two fingers into the mess on my skin and swirl it around. When I lift my hand to examine it, Silas dips his head and wraps his lips around my fingers to suck and lick until they're clean.

He grins. "Now that's my kind of sacrament," he says. I look at him a moment longer, then dip my fingers again and bring them to my own mouth to taste us. Together, we taste like no semen I've ever ingested, and I've swallowed enough to have a representative sample. We taste tingly, like music; salty, but also sharp like spruce needle tea. And yeah, I'm aware that makes no sense. (But if you could taste it, it would make perfect sense.)

"Is he asleep now?" I ask, and Silas strokes my hair back from my face and it feels so different from the way Ego touched me it might as well not even be the same gesture.

"He is, and I think we've given him a few nice things to dream about."

I smile at that. "I think I have a few nice things to dream about, too."

"Only you don't have to dream about them, sweetheart," Silas rumbles in my ear. "You just tell me, and I'll make them all come true."

Chapter Twenty-Two

As much as we want to linger on the altar, to curl up together and rest, it *is* cold, and stone does not make a comfortable bed. Finally, we both sit up and Silas takes a corner of the tablecloth to wipe my belly off.

"I can do that," I say.

"I like taking care of you," he says, and keeps wiping.

I blush, and watch his hands, strong and careful, like he always is with me. "I like being taken care of," I admit. "I always… My ex always made me feel selfish for it."

He kisses my cheek. "Don't," he says. "Don't ever feel selfish for enjoying something I like giving you." He turns my face gently towards him. "And I'm not your ex."

"I know."

"And I meant it when I said I love you."

"I meant it, too," I say, though now that the urgency is over, I can't quite bring myself to say it again. "I just… I'm scared."

"Of me?'

I shake my head and get up to get my clothes. "Not of you." I pull on my jeans and then my shirt and sit next to him again. I lean on his shoulder.

"I'm not your ex," he says again. "And I'm not any of the guys you fucked after you broke up with your ex."

"I know that, too. I just… It's hard for me to trust people." Fuck, why do I sound so pathetic?

"People terrify you." He says it so simply, so matter-of-factly that it seems perfectly normal. Reasonable, even.

"Social anxiety fucking sucks. But that's not why I'm afraid." I turn my head to bury it against his shoulder.

"Then tell me. If I can do anything to help, let me know. Because, sweetheart, I am very, very serious about you. I want… Fuck, I know it's too soon, but I imagine spending the rest of my life with you. Sharing my family's traditions, our religion, our food." He laughs softly. "I'll have you loving olives yet."

I laugh, too, and didn't I say something not so different to him, in the heat of passion? That I wanted to spend my life with him? I let out a deep sigh that feels like it releases a lot more than air. "It's me," I say. "I've always had a thing for Greek myth, for satyrs, for Pan. But then I meet them, and I run." I lean away from him, but he puts his arm around me. "Silas, I'm a coward."

He pulls me against him again. "No, you're not. You ran because the actual god of panic *made* you run. No human can resist that. And you came back. Alder, you *did* resist in the end, you fought through it, and you came back. Being afraid doesn't make you a coward. Being afraid and acting anyway makes you courageous."

"You helped with the panic."

"Only once you got here. You must have got through two or three waves of it before that, all alone. That was you, Alder. *You* did that."

I consider that. Maybe… maybe he's not wrong. "I couldn't let him kill you," I say. "I realized my life was better with you in it." I pick at a thread on the torn knee of my jeans. "Which is a pretty selfish reason to save your life."

He snorts. "I *am* pretty good in bed."

I smack his chest gently with an open palm and he catches my hand and presses it against his skin. "Not that, you cocky monster."

"Monster, am I?" His voice is teasing but there's an undertone of worry.

"*My* monster," I say, and it's almost a repeat of the things we said while Ego tried to get me to sacrifice him, but somehow, they mean something different now. Or, not different, *deeper*.

He kisses me, just a soft brush of his lips on mine.

"I meant that you challenge me," I say. "You make me want to be a better scholar, a better thinker, a better person. You make me want to be creative, to find joy in everyday things." I lean forward to lean my elbows on my knees, and his hand is warm on my back. "You make me feel like it's okay to be myself, no matter how weird I am."

"It *is* okay to be yourself," he says. "And I will fight anyone who tries to tell you otherwise."

"My hero," I say, teasing, except I mean it.

"No, you're *my* hero, sweetheart."

We sit a little longer and then I say, "Why did you leave last night?"

He stretches. "I was stupid. I got a message that looked like it was from my parents and sounded like something bad was happening. And since Ego was so fucking weird at his ritual, I was already on edge."

"Oh, shit," I say, sitting up straight. "I forgot to tell you. Ego used to be one of those cryptozoology guys, and he thought satyrs were real and in Arcadia County and –" I look at him. "I guess he wasn't wrong."

"He wasn't wrong."

"I meant to tell you. He gave me a book about it, only I kept forgetting." I shake my head. "I don't know why I kept forgetting."

"Ego's drugs, probably. Your lower lip is all red and cracked."

I touch my lip and feel the flaking skin. "Fucker," I say.

"Yeah." He slumps over and leans on his knees. "So, I got this message, and instead of phoning my parents like I should have, I borrowed my dorm mate's car and drove straight to the farm. Of course, everything was fine, but it turns out my parents and the other families have known about Ego's commune and have been keeping an eye on them. They were very confused when I suddenly showed up in the middle of the night, though."

"Shit."

"I should have left a note, or texted, but once I got there, they kept me busy with questions and with telling me what they knew, because it turns out we each had different parts of the puzzle, and by the time we put all the pieces together, he'd have already grabbed you." He looks up at me, and I reach out to brush aside a curl that has fallen over his eyes.

"I heard you call me," he says. "We didn't know he'd found the cave, until then."

"There's a picture of it in the book he gave me."

"Fuck. Can you give it to me so I can pass it on to my parents? They'll need to figure out what to do."

"Of course. I meant to all along, only I could never remember when we were actually together." I put my hand on his and squeeze. "It was a trap. I bet Ego sent you that message to get you here. Maybe he hoped to catch more of your family."

"I know it was a trap, sweetheart."

"He killed your cousin."

"Last summer, but we didn't realize the connection until tonight."

"You let him take you."

"Yes."

"For me."

"Yes."

I look at him again, really *look* at him, and see a man who looks like a Greek god who looks at *me* like I'm the most amazing person in the world. And I'm still afraid, but I won't let that stop me. Not anymore. So when he says, "Do you want to meet my family?" I answer, "Of course I do."

Only I didn't realize he meant did I want to meet his family *right now*.

When we get to the cave entrance and look down, dawn is starting to turn the sky pale, and I suddenly feel all my weariness at once. Silas insists on lowering me down the rope, which is probably for the best, because my arms are trembling, and I doubt I'd even make it halfway on my own.

I don't watch him climb, because I'm too worried he'll fall, but he joins me quickly where I'm sitting on a rock at the bottom of the debris slope.

Right below the cave entrance, there's a splotch of dark red with too much texture to be just blood, but there's no body.

"My family's taking care of it," Silas says. "There are procedures.

They'll come and clean up the cave, too." He doesn't say any more and I don't think I should ask. Maybe one day, when his family accepts me and knows I'm trustworthy.

I do ask about the rest of Ego's followers, presumably waiting at his rented farm, and just get the same answer. "There are procedures."

I don't push. To be honest, I'm not sure I really want to know.

We're only sitting at the bottom of the slope a short time when people appear out of the trees. They don't say anything and I'm too tired to say much, either. One man who looks a lot like Silas hands him some clothes, which he puts on, and then we follow his family into the trees. I can't help limping, no matter how I try to keep my steps normal; even without the twisted ankle and the bruised knee, my feet are torn up from running through the woods and climbing a cliff barefoot.

Silas notices and stops me, and bends for me to climb onto his back. I'm about to argue – I know he's had a long night, too – but then I realize I'm just too fucking tired.

When we come out of the path onto a dirt road and cross it to a farm with white rail fences and two white houses on opposite sides of a long driveway, I realize that I had nearly made it to safety last night, before I decided to turn back. If I'd carried on only a little bit longer, I'd have ended up here and Silas's family would probably have helped me.

And maybe they'd have saved Silas, but Pan would have awakened instead of being lulled back into a pleasant sleep.

We go to the larger of the two houses, lit up with friendly-seeming light, and Silas puts me down and takes my hand and leads me into a kitchen with a huge wooden table dominating it. We sit, and before anyone says anything, an older dark-haired woman with the same gentle brown eyes as Silas passes around white ceramic cups and fills them with strong coffee.

The room erupts into a babble of voices in English and Greek and I can't seem to focus on any of it. Someone presses a coffee cup into my hands, and I sip and it helps a little. The room seems crowded with people, quite a few of whom bear a strong resemblance to Silas. The two older men who stand leaning against the counter I guess must be his father and maybe an uncle. The older woman with the same eyes must be his mother. She stands behind his chair, a protective hand on his shoulder, and every once in a while she looks at me and smiles.

The faces all start to become a blur, a crowd of almost-Silases. Except one, a person of indeterminate gender about my age who only looks a little like Silas and watches me curiously. I wonder if they're the priest-in-training he mentioned. Not all nonbinary people are androgynous, of course, but very few cis people try to look that way on purpose.

I smile tentatively at them, and they smile back, a cautious expression at first, until I guess they decide I'm genuine and then the smile opens up.

"All right," Silas's mother finally says, loud enough that everyone else falls silent and looks at her. "We have a lot to discuss," she says. "But we also have two young people here who have had a very long night." She looks at me and smiles. "They need food and a bath, medical attention, and sleep. More or less in that order."

She looks at Silas and then back at me and I feel warm inside that she said, "young people" and not "young men" even though it may be a coincidence. "Will you introduce our guest, Silas?"

"This is Alder," Silas says. He smiles when he looks at me and I smile back. "They're…" he pauses, and I nod and his smile grows. "They're my partner, and they saved my life tonight."

I blush hot, but I keep my eyes on his so I can get words out by pretending I'm only talking to him. "After you saved mine," I say. I wish I could disappear, but for Silas, I'll be brave.

"Now," says Silas's mother, after a chorus of "hello" and "thank you" and a list of names I'll never remember and have probably already forgotten because I can hardly even remember my own name right now. She shoos people out until only she and one of the older men remain. Then she starts putting plates of food on the table and I'm almost asleep in my chair, but famished, so I eat whatever she puts in front of me until I'm full. Halfway through a piece of spanakopita I realize that not a single dish had olives in it. And now I'm *really* about to fall off my chair.

When I look up, Silas's parents are gone, and I flush at the thought that I didn't thank them properly.

"Come on sweetheart, let's get a shower and bandage you up."

I nod, because I don't have the energy to say I'd really rather just sleep, and I let him lead — and then carry — me up some stairs to a big white bathroom where he helps me undress and helps me shower and helps me dry off. And I sit on the edge of the tub while he cleans and bandages my feet, my knee, and my finger, and swears quietly over my swollen ankle.

Then he carries me up another staircase to an attic bedroom and puts me in a deliciously soft bed and just before I fall asleep, I say, "I have class tomorrow."

I don't even dream, and I wake up with bright sun through sheer curtains and the heat of Silas in bed next to me. I look around for my phone before I realize it must still be at my apartment.

Silas stirs and sits up and yawns.

"What time is it?" he says.

"I don't know, but I have class today."

He climbs out of bed and stretches, treating me to a very nice view of the entirety of his naked body. "I texted both our profs last night to say we had a family emergency." His eyebrows crowd together. "I hope that's okay."

"I really do feel like shit," I say.

"You look great," he replies, then disappears out the door. I hear his footsteps descend the stair and then water running. He comes back a few minutes later.

"My mouth tastes like ass," I say.

"There's a toothbrush for you in the bathroom downstairs. You can use my old bathrobe." He points to a terrycloth robe hanging on the back of the door.

"How come you're okay walking around naked?"

"Because I happen to know my parents are out doing chores most of the day, so the likelihood of running into them is very, very small."

"Oh." I go to the bathroom, pee, brush my teeth, and wash my face. I still look exhausted, faint stubble shadows my jaw, my lip is still dry and cracked, and my cheek is scraped, but I look a lot better than I felt last night.

When I return to Silas's childhood bedroom, he's sitting on the bed holding his phone to his ear. "Yes, sir," he says. "Alder's just come back from the bathroom. Yes, sir." He holds it out to me, and I take it and mouth, "Who is it?"

He mouths back, "Your dad."

My dad? How? I steel myself for whatever comes next. "Hello?" I say as I sit on the edge of the bed.

"Alden." I wince, and Silas tugs the edge of the robe down to kiss my shoulder.

"Dad," I say. "I don't –"

"Shit, right. You want to be called Alder. Alison told me that." The fact that he swore, when my dad almost never swears, keeps me from retorting, "*I* told you that."

"How did you get Silas's number?" I try to make the question sound neutral, to not show any emotion at all until I know why he's calling. It's hard, because he's already stunned me by calling me Alder.

"Your mother was worried. Had one of her dreadful feelings, real bad. Anyway, you didn't answer your phone, so I called the University. Got lucky that someone happened to be there on a Sunday, though they didn't want to give me your friend's number. I guess I sounded like a panicked parent, though, because they finally gave it to me, and it's taken this long for anyone to answer."

I digest that a moment, before I finally say, "I left my phone at home, sorry."

"Tell that to your mother," he says. "Listen, Alden, Alder, sorry."

"It's okay," I say, even though really, it's not. It *hurts*. He's trying, I have to give him that, but he could have started trying two years ago.

"No," he says. "Your mother was so worried I couldn't help think about… well, about if something really did happen to you, and I couldn't stand the thought that your last memory of me was of… was of me being an asshole because I couldn't be bothered to understand you."

"Dad." Tears are running down my face, and Silas's arms are tight around me, his face pressed into my back.

"Let me finish. No, first, tell me you're okay so your mother will stop worrying."

"I'm okay. Mom was right. Something bad did happen, but I'm okay."

"Good, good. Hear that? He's… they're okay." I hear my mother's sigh of relief in the background.

"Tell Mum I love her."

"She heard you. Now let me finish."

"Okay, Dad."

"You're my s–" He stops himself and I hear the click of his teeth coming together. "You're my kid, and I love you, no matter what. But I'm an old bugger. It's going to take me a while to get used to calling you a different name and different... different pronouns."

"I know. It's okay." I don't know what to say. The real shit thing about social anxiety it that it can affect you even with people you've known all your life, people you should be comfortable with, especially if your relationship has been strained since you hit adulthood.

"I know this is important to you. Alder. So it should be important to me."

"Thanks, Dad."

"Your mother tells me you met someone."

"Yeah. You were just talking to him." I put my free hand on Silas's arm where it crosses my chest. "I like him a lot."

"Him, right." He sighs.

"I still like guys, Dad. That hasn't changed since I hit puberty."

"No, I suppose not." I hear him sip something and set down a cup on the table. He must be in the kitchen. "I want to meet him."

"I'd like you to meet him."

There's a brief moment of silence. My dad doesn't talk a lot, and I've always wondered if he has social anxiety, too, and he somehow fought his way through it to be able to function around other people.

"Is he good to you?" he says, voice blunt, almost belligerent, and I smile. Of course that's what would matter to my dad. Not what Silas looks like, or even what he does for a living, but how he treats me.

"Yeah, he is," I say.

"Not like that last guy. I didn't like him."

My dad doesn't know about all the guys there have been since, one- and two-night affairs, and one that lasted most of a month.

"Not like him at all. Silas is... he's amazing." I feel a flush creep up my neck and look at Silas as he unwraps himself from me to lounge on the bed. I smile and he grins back.

"Good. You'll bring him next time you come home?"

"I will."

And that's all we say. I talk to my mom for a few minutes and then hang up.

I look at Silas and he looks at me, and for moment I don't notice his hand creeping up under the hem of the robe I'm wearing. Then his hand slides over my thigh and he says, "Let me be good to you sweetheart."

I smile more and shift so I can pull the robe slowly off my shoulders. And stop when I see him staring.

"What?"

He sits up and climbs off the bed then takes my hand and pulls me over to the bedroom door. Behind where the robe was hanging is a long mirror. He stands me in front of it, and slowly pulls the robe away, revealing my naked body.

"Look at yourself, sweetheart."

At first, all I see is me, not very tall, lean and decently toned, too pale, too freckled, small dick.

Silas's hands rest on my hips, slide around my belly and move slowly upwards. I watch them as they curve over my ribs and cup my chest.

"Holy fuck," I say, as his hands cup my tiny, perfect breasts. "Did you do that?"

I meet his eyes in the mirror, and he says, "I would have if I was capable, but all I can do is make your hurts hurt less and your pleasure a little more intense."

"You have magic?" I ask. I shake my head and look at myself in the mirror again, step closer to study myself, put my hands on my chest to touch myself. I wonder if I should feel afraid or weirded out, but all I feel is more like myself. "How?"

"If I had to guess, I'd say Pan was saying thank you for the pleasant dreams."

"Holy fuck."

His hands cover mine and his fingers find my nipples. "Can I be good to you now, sweetheart?" he says.

"Fuck yes," I say, and he is.

(So good.)

About the Author

NICO SILVER LIVES like a hermit on the edge of the woods, but haunts used bookstores like a wraith. They fully expected to be found someday as a mummified old corpse crushed under a toppled to-be-read pile, but the rise of e-books has made that somewhat less likely, though the books will always outnumber even the dustbunnies. Nico will read just about anything, including the instructions on the back of medicine bottles, but has a particular fondness for good stories with a hint of magic. They write dark, sexy urban fantasy, and sometimes dream in black and white.